BALLING THE JACK

A NOVEL

FRANK BALDWIN

SIMON & SCHUSTER

SIMON & SCHUSTER
Rockefeller Center
1230 Avenue of the Americas
New York, NY 10020

Simon & Schuster and colophon are registered trademarks
of Simon & Schuster Inc.

Designed by Jeanette Olender
Manufactured in the United States of America

10   9   8   7   6   5   4   3   2   1

Library of Congress Cataloging-in-Publication Data
Baldwin, Frank, date
Balling the jack: a novel/Frank Baldwin.
p. cm.
I. Title.
PS3552.A4485B35   1997
813'.54—dc21   97-6124   CIP
ISBN 0-684-83360-3

FOR LORA

THANKS TO MOM AND DAD.

THANKS TO JILLIAN MANUS.

THANKS TO BOB MECOY.

THANKS TO THE READING GROUP—
CYRIL, JACOB, KAY, AND MERRILL.

SPECIAL THANKS TO DONNA LEVIN.

*I did not care what it was all about. All I
wanted to know was how to live in it. Maybe
if you found out how to live in it you learned
from that what it was all about.*
—Ernest Hemingway, *The Sun Also Rises*

**Balling the Jack (slang)—To risk everything
on one attempt or effort.**

LET ME tell you about the bets.

I work as a paralegal in a Wall Street firm. Every Friday morning they pay me $447 and every Friday night I bet four hundred of it on a ball game. If I lose, I go the next week on the rims. But if I win—and I win a lot—I take on the town.

Here's the system: All week I mull over the matchups, and by Friday one or two start feeling like winners. Friday after work I buy a Foster's Oil Can at the deli across the street and start the long walk up the East Side to Adam's Curse, my home bar, where my bookie Toadie waits on his stool. I go over the games, weigh the angles. Nothing too scientific in my method. I'm partial to hot pitchers, even on the road, and I steer clear of the big favorites. Pick them and you have to give away two or three runs to Toadie, runs that always seem to come back in the late innings and bite you in the ass.

Just last month I had the Braves giving three against San Diego. They coasted into the ninth up 8–2. I had the money counted already and was spending it in my head on the blonde at the jukebox. Had the restaurant picked out, the wine, was holding the cab door for her, telling the driver my address, thinking I'd give my roommates a little treat, maybe even put them in the mood.

Then, bam! The rookie that Cox trotted out to pitch the ninth walked the bases loaded, Joyner unloaded them with a shot into the upper deck, and just like that the bet, the date, a week of fun down the toilet, and Toadie clapping me on the back, saying, "Tough one, kid." That's one of two phrases he knows. When I win he says, "You were born lucky, kid."

Tonight I'm going with the Phillies on the road over the Cards. Schilling starts for the Phils and he's on a big-time roll. It's an even game, too, so I don't have to spot Toadie any runs. Just the usual four bills once I'm in the door. Most bookies don't need the cash up front, but Toadie works the low end of the betting public, and he won't issue a stub without the dough in his pocket. He's not much to look at, Toadie. The same combat pants every day, a sweatshirt over his gut, and a brown rug on his bowling-ball head. Coke-bottle glasses that make his eyes bug and lips stretching out of his face like—you guessed it—a toad. A money belt around his waist for the stash.

I don't think I've ever been in Adam's Curse when he wasn't drinking bourbon and taking bets. He's worked some deal with the owner, Stella, who's in tight with the cops. He can afford to slip her ten percent or so, I'm sure, because Toadie takes down the regulars pretty good. In a year of betting, though, he hasn't made anything off me.

Tonight he's in his usual spot and grunts in greeting as I walk in.

"I'll take the Phils," I tell him, counting out four hundreds into his palm.

I take a seat at the long oak bar and let out a breath. The sweet release I get handing over the money is the best part of the week. Five days to earn the bread, to agonize over the pick, and ten seconds to put it all on the line. Now my work is over and I'm like a priest who quits praying and leaves the rest to the man upstairs. It's out of my hands.

Betting all you have cleans the system. Spend enough time in the office I work in and you start to think the point of life is to stay on an even keel all the time. Just today, our receptionist Kay passed around a sign-up sheet for a stress-reduction program the partners are touting. That's a big theme around that place—avoiding stress.

Me, I think they have it all wrong. I think we *need* to jack up the old ticker sometimes, like a car needs to get onto the highway and go full out once in a while. It's good for us.

Don't get me wrong. I'm all for computers and cash machines. But let's face it: a lot of modern life isn't exactly out there on the edge. How many times do you feel your heart in your chest these days? Your first night with a girl, maybe, sprinting from a mugger, I guess, or if the Knicks make it to the finals. But that's about it. Work? I've been there a year now and I don't think my pulse has topped forty yet. That's why I bet. I mean, it's for the bucks too, sure, but not only. Betting it all reminds me I'm alive.

I guess I should have been around twenty thousand years ago. Back then, nobody had to go out chasing thrills. They had all the excitement they could handle just staying alive. Look at the caveman. He could pretty much count on jacking up his heart rate a few times a day. If he wanted to eat he had to kill some beast with two-foot fangs. That'll get your blood moving. Then there were invasions to repel, the harsh elements to battle, and one wild animal or another set to pick him off if he dropped his guard. Sex, too. It must have been tough enough charming some Jane back to the cave with grunts and hand signals, but if he did win her over, there was always some brute with a club on him ready to knock our boy out of the picture.

Now we've gone all the way the other way. We move paper around the desk all day, order in from a deli, and rent a movie with our squeeze at night. If we have a squeeze. But that's another story.

I just shake my head at these tea hounds who live on the safe side all the time. I can't imagine never gambling on anything. Never risking the last dollar; the hangover, the slap in the face. Risk and reward, baby. Risk and reward.

These few minutes before game time all the crap in my life drains away. Stella asks who we're rooting for this week, pours me an Absolut on the rocks, and I feel myself go empty. At peace for the first time all week. My calm holds through the starting lineups and the national anthem.

With the first pitch comes the rush and I'm off. Living in the purity of the big bet. Feeling the surge one minute, the clutch of panic the next. I take in everything: the ump's low strike zone, sure to hurt their starter; the wind blowing out to left, ready to give my sluggers a boost; the first sign of fatigue in my pitcher. I feel every pitch in the gut and come up out of my chair for a rally. I talk to the managers.

"Don't sacrifice. Not here. Show some balls—play for the big inning. No—don't walk him—they'll pinch-hit. That's it, send the runner. That's it!"

I rock back and forth, swear at the screen. I'm happy. At stake is the good life. Lose and I'm a drone again, kissing ass at the firm, stuck in the pad all week eating instant noodles, just enough money to live on till next Friday. A schmuck like everyone else. But win and I'm the man. Eight hundred bucks in my pocket and six nights to spend it. The first winning Friday of each month covers the rent. The rest of them I eat well, drink well, spoil my date, if I can get one. What more could a guy want?

Tonight the Phillies do me solid. Down 1–0 early, Dykstra, ex-Met and a bit of a gambler himself, doubles in two in the fifth and seals it with a poke in the ninth. Schilling does the rest. Goes all the way on a six-hitter, striking out the side to end it.

"You were born lucky, kid," says Toadie, handing over the money with a scowl. I count it out onto the bar. I give Stella a high five and settle my tab, throwing in a bourbon for Toadie and a round for the alkies at the end of the bar.

Man, I wish all you christers who rail against gambling could feel the rush of victory just once. You'd come around. As I leave, Stella calls after me.

"You ready for Tuesday night, Tom?"

"You bet."

CHAPTER TWO

MY ROOMMATE is the nicest guy in the world. Fill his hat with piss and he'll apologize for not owning a bigger one. If the meek ever inherit this place, he'll be at the head table, wanting a spritzer to wash down his paté—if it's not too much trouble, of course. As I walk in tonight he and his girl are on the couch, watching the second of two rented Italian films. They started them early, I'm sure, to leave plenty of time for discussion.

If you guessed I don't like him too much, you're right. Mike seemed okay when I answered the ad, but that was a year ago and I wasn't too picky. I was just out of school, staying with my aunt and her brood in Queens. One more night at that dinner table and I would have done myself in. Mike wasn't queer, I could move in right away, and you can't beat the East Village. Three stops on the subway to Wall Street and stumbling distance to my favorite bars.

Back then Mike was a regular guy. He'd take in a ball game, get drunk now and then, even chase a little tail, in his own fashion. For him that meant answering the lonely-girl ads in the personals. Three months ago his pen pal Molly moved in and Mike's been sliding down the manhood tree ever since.

He's about hit the bottom branch. Won't touch a drop, can't waste his time on sports anymore, and forget about dragging him out to see a band. Hell, he won't put a piece of food in his mouth without clearing it with her first. Hey, if he wants to cut his balls off, that's his business, but he's started in on the lectures and between the two of them there's no relief. On drinking: "Well, of course I stopped. Molly's in AA. I'm showing my solidarity." On football: "How can you call it a sport when grown men deliberately try to hurt each other?" On late-night skin shows: "It's not just the women you degrade, Tom. It's yourself as well."

It'd be one thing if they gave me a little show once in a while, since I'm not getting much myself these days. Our rooms are wall-to-wall and there isn't a concert hall in the city with better sound. Lord knows I've treated them to a few duets. Either they don't fuck at all, though, or they've figured out how to do it without a sound. Knowing Molly, she finds the whole business too messy.

What kills me about her is she could be a real babe if she gave a hoot. Her face is out of a soap commercial, country-fresh, and she's built okay, too. A little wide in the seat, maybe, but nothing a few laps in the park wouldn't cure.

She's not interested in a few laps in the park, though, or a few rounds in the sack, for that matter. Molly is one of those girls . . . well, you know the type. Baggy sweaters, big skirts all the time, combs her hair straight down. Keeps away from a razor, if you know what I mean. Just makes no effort at all. One of these days I'll have to surprise her in the shower to make sure she's got the goods down there.

She's no charmer in the personality department either. Just after she moved in I made the mistake of telling her that with a makeover and some new clothes she could be a real hot number. She's been one long sermon ever since.

Molly by herself I could handle, but she got the ring in Mike's nose early and the way she leads him around now is sad to see. First it was music appreciation, then pottery workshop. Now it's cooking class, and after the last one he's making noises about going veggie. Next thing you know I'll have a juicer on my hands.

I tried to clue Mike into my feelings, in my subtle way. Last week was his birthday and I bought him a dress. I think that got to him. He's been real quiet ever since.

Tonight, though, they're not my problem. If I'd lost the bet and were stuck in for the weekend we'd probably have it out. But I'm flush, and even the two of them can't kill my mood.

"Hi, guys. How are the flicks?"

"Nonpareil," says Molly. "Both of them beyond reproach."

One of these days she'll learn to speak plain English.

"From your demeanor I assume you won your bet. This would mean you're not in for the evening."

"I did, and I'm not. Meeting Dave at Finn's to check out the new band. How about it? Can I interest you two in some rock 'n' roll?"

"Hardly. We've got quite the day ahead tomorrow. Though I shouldn't speak for Mike."

"What do you say, guy? I'll have you back by dawn."

"No thanks."

He doesn't look at me. Must still be sore about the dress. Oh well. If I thought they'd come along I wouldn't have offered. I shower, change into my shorts and Mets T-shirt, and head out the door.

FRIDAY NIGHTS in this city are for the young. They shouldn't let anyone over thirty out of their apartment. Walking up Second Avenue, an Oil Can in my hand and eight hundred bucks in my pocket, the evening spreads before me like a feast. On the menu tonight is everything you get out of bed for: friends, women, music, drink. From a block away I can see the sign for Finn's: a neon leprechaun sitting on a shamrock, drinking from a frosty mug. I kill my beer and arc it into a trash basket on the corner. Look out tonight, Manhattan. You've met your match.

Liam Kennedy, the manager of Finn O'Shea's, takes off his shades as I enter and looks hard at me.

"Well, Tom? Are ya carryin'?"

"Thanks to the Phillies."

He breaks into a grin and grabs my hand. "That's it, lad! Man after me heart. I'll tell the waitresses—they'll keep the pints coming."

"Thanks."

These are good days for Liam Kennedy. A year ago, Finn O'Shea's was just a solid Irish bar like a hundred others in town. A few dartboards, a jukebox, a couple of brogues from the old country pouring drinks. One of five in the O'Shea chain, kept in business by the soaks and the rough Irish illegals, who roll in after work or before work or because they can't find work. When the recession hit, all the bars felt the pinch, and Papa O'Shea laid down the word: The one with the lowest receipts in six months was out of business. Leave it to an Irish boss to pit his own against each other.

Kennedy knew he was in trouble. Two of the O'Shea bars are on the Upper East Side, milking the yuppies. One is in the Village, milking everybody, and the other is in Hell's Kitchen, pulling in the Garden crowd and the Jersey high school kids through the tunnel. Finn's, though, is stuck here at Twenty-first and Second. It's not uptown, it's not downtown, and it's not midtown. Liam was getting his ass kicked.

He tried going to the other managers to see if they could put up a united front. Pool their receipts, maybe. All for one and one for all. They told him to get lost. Said we don't make the rules, Kennedy.

Up against it, he hit on the idea of pulling one of the dartboards on the weekends and sticking in a band. He booked some real morgue acts at first, old geezers strumming guitars, singing "Danny Boy" and "Kathleen," barely keeping themselves awake. Even the alkies couldn't listen to them. Liam needed a new sound, and as luck would have it, it walked right in his door.

One day, four scruffy guys showed up at the bar clutching a demo. They called themselves the Coffin Ships, after the boats that brought so many Irish to the New World. Looking at the tiny stage, the bums slumped over their drinks, they must have started to wonder why they came. As for Kennedy, he wasn't sure he liked the looks of them.

Neither party had a lot to lose, though. The Coffin Ships had been chased out of all the local bars in the Bronx for *not* singing "Danny Boy" and "Kathleen." For them it was a chance to play inside, in Manhattan; hell, they might even let women in the bar. It beat the pants off a street corner on Fordham Road. As for Liam, what the hell. They had to be better than the last act, and they were cheap. He promised them all they could drink and twenty percent of beer sales above the average take. They promised to make a lot of noise.

By chance I caught them on their first night. Stopped in to confirm a dart match, saw them tuning up, and figured I'd give them a few songs. I didn't leave until they locked the door on me. There were only thirty of us, half of them friends of the band, but once they took the stage they didn't care.

The singer sang and played electric guitar. They had a guy on the uilleann pipes, a smooth sax, bongos, and a drum machine. They did great covers, and their own stuff was even better. Killer songs about drinking in the new country and missing the old. About fallen heroes, about workers uniting, about chasing tail. Songs funny and sad that kept you moving. I was swept along, into the second set, downing one pint after another. Jigging to the jigs, reeling to the reels, having a blast.

Late in the night they played the first strains of a song that sounded familiar but no, it couldn't be, not here, not by a bunch of drunken micks. But it was! Bob Marley, "Get Up, Stand Up," and damned if they didn't hit it just right. At 3 A.M. they sent us out the door to "Anarchy in the UK" and we spilled into the street exhausted, excited, drunk, promising ourselves we'd be back.

Nothing beats finding a new band. One day they don't exist and the next they explode into your head and are part of you. I bought the T-shirts and homemade tapes, learned all the words to their songs. Told my friends about them, passed out fliers, called the college radio stations. "What do you mean, you never heard of them? Don't you guys do your homework?"

Each week built to Saturday night. We would stake out a spot by the bar and send drinks to the stage between songs. We plotted to get them into *Rolling Stone*. Word spread. Thirty people turned to fifty, to a hundred, to a line down the block, another set on Wednesdays, a doorman, a cover, and some real faces in the crowd. Record men, dealmakers. This band was the real thing, and we were a part of it.

21

Rock 'n' roll is a language and those who speak it a tribe. A good band, when you take them to heart, gives you more than songs. They give you nights, mad nights outside yourself when you feel your youth so strong it breaks through your skin. We would all be packed together, swaying, roaring the chorus to "Free Us Now," our insides hollowed out, our fever rising with the music. At the peak we could barely stand it. We were no longer citizens. Our jobs, careers, parents belonged on another planet. We wanted only this world, right here, and so long as this song didn't end we had it. Then the last chord crashed and we stood dazed, famished, like lovers stopped before the finish.

We looked at each other, really looked, on the verge of something, all of us. Some shared truth inside us the next song promised to reveal, if we could just hang on. And in the instant before it started a line from a college teacher I hated would come back to me. "You kids think the answer's in a rock song, or between a woman's legs." Well, some nights it is, Teach, and as they broke into "Irish Freedom" I started rubbing up the girl next to me, and when she rubbed back I pulled her through the crowd, out the door, into a cab and gave it to her right there in the back seat, my face in her shirt as we took off, covered in sweat, the words of the last song still ringing in my head.

No wonder they stand up in Congress and plot the death of rock 'n' roll. This stuff *is* dangerous.

The Coffin Ships hit the big time, as you might have guessed. Signed on the dotted line for one of the giants, and a month later here came the MTV truck, right into Finn's to film the video! You'll see our gang in the back if we survive the edit. These days the band keeps pretty fast company. The singer drinks with movie stars of Irish blood who pop in after a shoot, and you can often see the sax player on Page Six in the *Post*. Even the drummer, who hasn't been sober since the first gig and was a little short of hat size to start with, never leaves without a girl on his arm.

Finn's is a star now too. When the band's first album took off, so did the bar's rep as a launching pad. Writers started coming around. First the underground press, then *The Voice*, and finally, yes, *Rolling Stone*. Liam sits them all at the bar, pours pints and tells again how the new home of Irish music in New York began as just a dream in his head. He's always careful to imply he's a bit of a musician himself, though as a businessman there's not the time for it.

When the Coffin Ships's album hit the Top 10, the majors declared roots Irish music the next rage, and suddenly anybody with a cousin in Ireland and an amp had a shot at a contract. They all wanted to play Finn's because that's where the scouts were. Told Liam they'd play for nothing for a shot at the big time, so that's what Liam pays them. Books the best for Friday night, the others for Monday and Thursday, throws in an open mike on Sunday and now he fills the place every night, at ten bucks a head. Takes in three times the other O'Shea bars combined. Liam still stops in on them from time to time. "Just for a pint, y'know, and to see how they're getting on. We Irish stick together."

A few weeks ago I saw the Coffin Ships for the last time. Headed over Saturday night, as usual, drinking an Oil Can, getting psyched, but when I saw the line down the block I slowed, and at the door I couldn't bring myself to go in. I watched through the window awhile. Saw them set up, dive into the first set, the crowd going nuts. I thought back to the first night, just a few of us there, the magic feeling you get at the start of things. Was it really a year ago? I remembered the first time I heard them on the radio, turning from the deli register with a beer and stopping dead as the singer's voice came through the speakers, singing "New County Down." I thought of all that and then I tipped my beer to them, through the glass, and walked home.

When you're with a band from the start and they make it big, there comes a time they don't need you anymore. They belong to everyone now and not to you. Letting go is like ending an affair. The last few Saturdays were rough.

Dave says the buzz on tonight's band is good, though. Some outfit called Aisling Chara—you tell me how to pronounce it. The singer is supposed to have a real set of pipes, they got some little guy plays hell out of the electric cello, whatever that is, and according to Liam, if Neil Young ever hears their cover of "Cinnamon Girl," he'll go back into the studio and get it right this time. Maybe I'm back in business.

Dave waves from a choice spot between two groups of girls. When I reach him he's trying to explain the concept of a body shot to a pretty German. He claps me on the neck.

"How 'bout those Phillies!" he says. "I talked to Stella. Guess you're buying tonight, huh?"

"All weekend. Pint?"

"Sure, and one for Angila if you can. And shots of Jägermeister. Maybe my German will come back to me."

Looking at Dave you'd never guess I spent half my nights freshman year sleeping in the lounge. A shade under six feet, a bit on the heavy side, dark hair, dark eyes, a small mouth. Not GQ material by a long shot, but Dave gets laid more than anyone I know. It isn't even close.

He's off to a slow start tonight. As the drinks come, I turn just in time to see Angila land a good slap on his kisser and storm away.

I laugh. "You always said you could take a punch, Dave. What happened?"

"I don't know." He works his jaw in his hands. "I thought

24

I told her she has nice eyes, but my German's a little rusty. We should have gone to a better school."

"I'll drink to that. Next ten bucks I give goes to the language department. Cheers." We do our shots. "Say, who's the new waitress?"

"Something else, huh?"

She really is. Slender, with a strange, graceful walk, as if she were on her tiptoes. Blond hair all down her back and a shy smile when I overtip. I wave her back for another round.

"Hi, we'll take two more. I'm Tom Reasons, by the way. This is my friend Dave."

"I know. Liam told us about you. Says I should bring them as you finish. Says you're loaded."

"Well, I am tonight anyway. What time are you off?"

"About three."

"Ever go for a bite after work?"

"Not with a customer." She smiles, only not so shy this time, and glides into the crowd.

"Jesus, Dave. How 'bout that accent? She could tell me to go fuck myself and it would sound like a come-on."

"I think she just did. Anyway, you don't want to be messing with her. She's Kennedy's cousin. Trust me, the ring would have to go on before the shirt came off. She's Catholic."

I'm convinced if I picked a girl off the street Dave could tell me her name and the chances of landing her.

"What's wrong with Catholic? We're Catholic."

"Nothing, if you want to get hitched. But if you don't . . ." Dave shudders. "Tom, I swore off Catholic girls this morning, and this time I mean it."

I laugh.

"I'm serious, Tom. From now on it's the first question I ask." Dave shakes his head, looks pensive. "You know, it's al-

25

ways the same story. You knock yourself out for them, take them to a great place, and they're a lot of fun. They love to drink, to dance, and the way they dance you can't wait to get 'em in the sack. Everything's perfect until you shoot the dead bolt, and then it all falls apart. The kissing's fine, but you reach for the shirt and the wrestling match starts." Dave takes a swig of his pint. "Even when they want it they manage to ruin it, Tom. They can never admit they're actually going through with it, so foreplay is out. Right up until you get it in they're telling themselves they're just fooling around, that nothing's really happening. Once it's in, they warm to it, of course, and you get your ten good minutes, but then the party's over. Next morning the beer's worn off and you can tell straight away there won't be any encore. She's clammed up, grabbing her clothes, won't hardly look at you. You leave feeling like you shot the Pope."

Dave's made this speech before, and every time he winds up back here at Finn's with ten pints in him, standing in a sea of Irish girls. Something has to give, and it's usually Dave.

The band's done tuning up and we turn our attention to the stage. I love the moment just before a band plays the first note. Anything is possible. I'm on my toes, leaning forward.

"One last thing, Tom. Are we going to kick some Irish ass Tuesday night, or what?"

"Damn straight."

The singer steps to the mike. "A one-two-three-four."

The songs begin.

CHAPTER THREE

ANYONE contemplating law school should have to work as a paralegal and file motions at the State Supreme Court on Center Street. These guys make Kafka's bureaucrats look like a dance troupe. They have one clerk working the counter here, who I get every time. A real giant, with so much hair on him you can't see his arms or neck. Ask him to stamp the motion and he grunts. Ask him a question and he glares. You could swap him for a gorilla at the Bronx Zoo and it would be a week before either place knew the difference.

I'm in line here Monday morning, filing another motion for my boss, Carter McGrath. Boy, do I feel like hell. Just once I should try starting the week without a hangover. Carter is an associate at Farrell, Hawthorne, and Donaldson, the firm I work for. Or Fatigue, Heartworm, and Dysentery, as we paralegals call it, which about captures the spirit of the place. The firm's one of the old guard. Been on the corner of Wall and Water for fifty years. Small by New York standards—six partners, thirty associates—but a real money-maker.

I don't believe it. Five clerks working the desk and guess who gets Magilla.

"Hi, I'd like to file—"

Wham! I jump back as the stamp comes down like an anvil, barely missing my dart hand.

"Hey. Watch—"

"Next!"

He stares at me with such pure hatred I hurry out the door.

Out on the sidewalk I shake my head. I must have seen too many movies as a kid. Somewhere I got the notion this legal stuff would be a lot of fun. At seventeen, just as it was hitting me that I wasn't going to play centerfield for the Mets, an alum with his own practice came in and talked to our senior class. He explained the legal process to us. Spoke about discovery, a little on the rules of evidence. Told us how the whole system was designed for the sole aim of arriving at the truth. It sounded beautiful.

Well, I'm twenty-three now and the jig is about up. Fun? Forget it. Serving papers, tracking down cites, summarizing depositions. In a year the only fun I've had at the firm was balling one of the secretaries in the conference room. That was a whopper, I'll grant you, but it was after the Christmas party, and she's made it clear it won't happen again.

As I walk back to work from court, the boys in my skull start up the jackhammer again. The better the weekend, the tougher the Monday, they say. I'll need a lot of coffee to get through this one. I stop in at a bodega for some aspirin. Back outside, I find that by squinting my eyes almost shut I can narrow my vision to a few yards in front of me, and as my feet drag me toward the office I go back in my head to the weekend.

Aisling Chara turned out to be as good as the hype. I still can't pronounce it, but by the time they slid into a cover of "Deacon Blues" at three in the morning, I was a believer. I'm not ready to call them another Coffin Ships just yet, but I'll be back next Friday.

From Finn's, Dave and I hit an after-hours' joint on Tenth Street that I couldn't find again if I had to. The last thing I remember is Dave trying to clear my head with a shot of Absolut, sounding urgent.

"Okay, Tom, sit up. This is important. See the babe at the bar?"

I saw two babes, dressed exactly alike. The same hairstyles even, and moving in perfect unison, like synchronized swimmers. Leave it to Dave.

"Which one's yours?"

"Tom, there's only one. Now listen. Dinner at her place tomorrow, and *Basic Instinct* on cable, *if* I can recite the words to 'Mandy.'"

" 'Mandy'?"

"Yeah, start to finish. She gave me five minutes. Here, I got a napkin and pen. Let's go."

" 'Mandy'? Dave, you should decline on principle."

"Tom, look at her."

The twins crossed their legs, smiled and waved. I hit the floor.

On his own Dave couldn't even come up with the chorus, which at least left him free to throw me into a cab. After eight hours' sleep we met up again in box seats at Shea. Then it was to The Palm for the best T-bone in Manhattan, a few darts at Adam's Curse, a tequila tour of the Upper East Side, some more sleep, back to Shea, poker with the guys at

Jimmy's, and finally a nightcap at the Polo Grounds for *SportsCenter*. I'm down to a hundred bucks, but I had me a weekend.

Now I'm looking at five days before the next furlough. At the steps of the office I take a good breath, shake my head hard and straighten up. Walking through the oak doors the weekend slips away and the lights inside me dim. I'm a suit again.

CARTER CALLS ME into his office straight away to prep me on a new case. This part of the job isn't so bad. Every case sounds good the first time you hear it, and I can tell by looking at him that he likes this one.

"How was your weekend, Reasons? Did you get laid?"

"No, sir."

I call all the lawyers sir or ma'am. They like it, think it's my military upbringing. Actually it just gives me a kick.

"Young guy like you, good build, what's the problem?"

"I don't know, sir. Maybe once I'm a lawyer they'll come around."

Carter starts to laugh, stops and squints hard. "Reasons, I can never tell when you're dicking with me. This wouldn't be one of those times, would it?"

"No, sir."

Carter's not a bad guy. It's just that he was born with a stick up his ass and nothing's happened in thirty years to dislodge it. His one goal in life is to make partner, and he thinks the way to do it is to spend a hundred hours a week in the office. He's probably right. Every case for Carter is a war of attrition—whoever files the most motions wins. That means a lot of shit work for his staff, so he's not too popular among the paralegals. I get farmed out to him a lot because he doesn't like working with the girls. He says he likes to

30

swear too much and was raised better than to do it around them. The real reason is he's afraid he'll try to fuck one of them. Nobody who wants to make partner in this firm starts down that path. All in all, he's not so bad. He'll order in beer if it's going to be a late night, and wrapping up a big case can mean a long lunch at a titty bar.

"Reasons, we pulled a good one. What does the name Garrett mean to you?"

"Garrett. Wayne. Played third base for the Mets in the seventies. Had a high of sixteen homers in seventy-three."

"Not quite. Try Garrett, Winston. CEO of Pyramid Publishing. On the board at the Met. Net worth of about twenty million."

"Wow. Who's he suing?"

"He's not suing anybody. His wife is."

"His wife, sir?"

"Regina Garrett. Big socialite. Always popping up in the paper. A month ago she threw a cocktail party to honor some French designer. Small party, but top-shelf. Real A-list crowd. Had the thing catered by Prego's, a little Italian outfit. They do appetizers, cheese and crackers, that kind of thing. Well, an hour into the party, six people come down with food poisoning. Not serious, no one kicked the bucket, but apparently a real mess. People losing it out both ends, some not making it to the bathroom. You get the picture."

"Yes, sir. What caused the poisoning?"

"They traced it to the bean dip. It seems the caterer mixed together two seasonings, cilantro and pegrini. They're okay by themselves, but combine 'em and the effect on the human digestive system is explosive. Vomiting, diarrhea, the works. Now you and me, maybe we get steamed, demand our money back, that's the end of it. But to these society types, this kind of thing is the *Hindenburg*. Their good

31

name, social standing, all that on the line. And I take it this Regina Garrett is no lamb to start with. She wants a hundred thousand dollars to cover her anguish and the damage to her reputation, and a letter of apology sent to each of the guests. What do you think?"

"I don't know, sir. It sounds a little lightweight to me."

"That's because, Reasons, you don't see the larger picture. This isn't just about some bad bean dip. Mr. Garrett's company, Pyramid, is the third-largest publishing house in the city. They probably do five million dollars in legal fees a year. We shine on this one, he's indicated he'll steer some of that our way. Now what do you think?"

I think it's crossed over from lightweight to bullshit.

"I think it sounds like a winner, sir."

"Good. We depose Prego in half an hour. Mrs. Garrett we do at noon. I want you to sit in on both of them."

"Yes, sir."

GIUSEPPE PREGO WALKS into the conference room looking like a man with two weeks to live. The moment I see him I know we're working the wrong side of this case. He keeps turning his hat in his hands, patting his head with a kerchief. He looks at both lawyers with worry but with deep trust, his whole manner suggesting that some huge mistake has occurred, but he, Giuseppe Prego, is now here to talk to the good people involved and set the matter straight. I like him off the bat. In a deep accent he tells his side of the story.

His American dream started when he opened a twenty-four-hour deli in Gramercy Park in 1970. He and his wife worked round the clock, every day but Christmas. In the eighties they began catering small parties for friends and built a solid reputation for gourmet appetizers. They impressed a few upscale clients with their distinctive hors d'oeuvres and found a profitable niche working just the kind of intimate affair thrown by Regina Garrett. The way Prego tells it he made the bean dip for the party, all right, but not with pegrini.

"You must understand. I work with food twenty-five years. Anybody who work with food know you can't mix cilantro and pegrini. Never.

"That night, I deliver the hors d'oeuvres myself. I show them all to Mrs. Garrett in the kitchen. She say fine, fine, except the bean dip. She say it not look 'friendly' enough. I want to say, 'Friendly'? What is 'friendly'? This is cilantro bean dip. People will not talk to it, they will eat it. I want to say this but I don't, of course. I say, 'Mrs. Garrett, you want it to look friendly, you put some parsley on top, just a little, the green on the black look nice—you know, friendly.' I ask her you want me to do it but she say no, she will do it. So I leave, go back to my store. Then later she call up yelling about people sick and about pegrini. I say, 'Pegrini, what pegrini?' She hang up and then two days later a lawyer come into my store with papers. Twenty-five years in the same store and I never get papers from a lawyer."

He says his niece Rosa will back him up. She stayed to work the party and saw Mrs. Garrett dumping a green seasoning into the bean dip before sending her out with the tray.

When he finishes, Prego stands and shakes the hand of everyone in the room. His lawyer, the stenographer, even me and Carter. He looks hugely relieved, dabbing at his face again as he leaves. I'd bet two weeks' salary the man hasn't told a lie in his life.

REGINA GARRETT STROLLS in at twelve-fifteen for her noon deposition. One look at her and it's clear why her hubby kicked all that ass in the business world. If she waited at home for me, I'd stay in the office too. For old Winston's sake I hope he has something going on the side.

She shows up for the session in a fur, perches her ninety-five pounds on a chair and looks all of us up and down. If her features were a little softer she'd look just like the Grinch. The tanning rooms have left her a light orange and her last lift pulled the skin over her cheeks and eyes tighter than a drum. She smokes one filtered cigarette after another. I keep waiting for a poodle to jump in her lap.

To me she seems exactly the kind of woman who would destroy anyone before she'd slip one rung on the social ladder. As she speaks, her eyes slide around the room.

Mrs. Garrett says she served everything as she received it. Prego delivered the hors d'oeuvres about 5 P.M. and stayed to put the final touches on the bean dip. He sprinkled a seasoning over the top of it and she asked what it was. He said it was pegrini.

"The name jogged something in my memory, some cautionary note about its safety, the way it reacted with other spices, something. I raised the question with Mr. Prego but he waved it off. 'Nonsense,' he said. 'You can never have enough pegrini. It goes with everything.' Well, not being a chef myself, of course, I took his word for it. He came well recommended, after all. I felt a little uneasy, but I put the dip on Rose's tray and sent it out into the crowd. And then . . . oh, it hurts even to think of it, but you know the rest. As soon as people were taken ill I knew my suspicions were right. I called Mr. Prego immediately and confronted him and he—why, the man denied everything. Denied he had added any pegrini at all. And the names he called me! My word. I know I'm under oath, but I'd just as soon not repeat them. Anyway, that's just how it happened."

And I'm a Choctaw Indian.

CHAPTER FOUR

THE FIRST DRINK of the day is the best. Cools the head and marks the formal start of the evening. I could use one. I just came from the pad, where I walked in on this exchange:

"Come now, Mike, remember what we talked about. You don't want to say the Mets got killed. How about they were defeated? Or better yet, outscored?"

Mike gets a puppy-dog smile on his face and says, "Right. They were outscored."

I left without a word. What is there to say?

"Hi, Mason. Draw me the coldest one you got."

"Coming up."

Mason bartends here at Adam's Curse on dart night. He's the only real person I know who rolls up his T-shirts and keeps a pack of cigarettes in the sleeve. He slides me a pint, pops a toothpick in his mouth, and leans forward on his hands on the long wooden bar.

"I'll say it once. Ready?"

I nod.

"But in the town it was well known when they got home at night their fat, psychopathic wives would thrash them within inches of their lives."

"Pink Floyd. *The Wall*. 'Another Brick in the Wall, Part I.'"

He shrugs. "That was a gimme. I know you got a big match tonight. Next time you'll earn your suds."

I don't doubt it. Every week Mason gives me one line of rock 'n' roll. If I name the band, song and album, our team gets a round on the house. Tonight he went easy on me. When he wants to be a ballbuster he'll drop something from Hüsker Dü, or PiL. I'll run it by the whole team and still strike out.

The match he mentioned is the reason I'm here. Tonight our team, the Drinkers, takes on the Hellions for the Manhattan Tuesday Night Darts Championship. The Hellions beat us out for the league title and this is our chance to even the score.

It won't be easy. They don't make dart teams any tougher than this crew. They play out of County Hell Pub, a blue-collar Irish joint in Hell's Kitchen. One of Papa O'Shea's bars, and if you've seen it you know why they got into darts. If I drank in that neighborhood I'd carry a weapon too.

The Hellions have walked off with the last three titles, and their captain, Joe Duggan, is a piece of work. As mean a mick as ever washed onto our shores. I get spooked just looking at him. Thin and strong and pale, with yellow eyes and a bad complexion. More on him in a minute.

First, a little background on darts. To me, it's the best bar game there is. Full of skill and strategy, and best of all, you get better the more you drink. Up to a point, anyway. I learned to play from Dad, who grew up throwing for drinks in neighborhood bars in south Jersey. In college I kept a board on the back of my door and played for shots with the fellas.

One night after graduation, Dave and I challenged a couple drunks to a game in a West Side dive. Loser buys. We beat 'em four straight with their darts. After the last game they showed us empty wallets and the bigger one steadied himself with a hand on my shoulder.

"So you see, gents, we kenna pay. But a debt is a debt, so I give you this."

He handed me a business card with "Adam's Curse" printed on it.

"Go there and see Stella. Tell her Jerry sent you. She'll put you on a team and you can stop beating up on the likes of us." They rolled out the door.

The next day we looked up Adam's Curse and met Stella, the seventy-five-year old matron of the place. "So you beat Jerry, did you?" she asked.

"Four straight, ma'am."

"Don't let it go to your head. Every time he sends me a new team I let him drink on the house for half an hour. I run eight squads out of here on two nights and Jerry sent half of them to me. Now—you'll need six players to field a team. Can you do that?"

"Yes, ma'am."

"Good. I'll put you in C division—the rookie league. You can pick up your schedule Saturday night."

Dave and I signed up our whole gang from college— Jimmy, Bobby, Tank and Claire. At first, we saw the team as a drinking club. A chance to meet once a week, check out different bars, get trashed, and throw a few arrows besides. As time went on, though, a funny thing happened: we got good.

Stella gave us old boards we put up at home and practiced on a little each day. Sunday nights we entered her five-dollar luck-of-the-draw tournaments. Once we got the hang of the league matches, we found we all had the right makeup for darts—we love to drink and we hate to lose. Especially to some of the cows in C division. Every team carried at least one porker, and the lesser teams two or three. Guys who couldn't make the bar softball team but didn't want to go home to the wife, with bad breath and bellies that could stop a truck. Beat 'em and they retreated to the bar, but lose and you were in for it. They'd take you aside, give you a few pointers, tell you their whole darting history, if you let them, from the day they first picked one up. Facing guys like that week after week was a powerful incentive to get good in a hurry.

That first season we sneaked into the playoffs as the fourth-place team and pulled a couple upsets before losing in the semis. We've moved up and gone farther each season since and now, in our first crack at A division, we're in the finals.

I'm the captain and the third-best shooter on the team. No one can touch Jimmy, our ace, and Tank's more consistent, but I'm streaky and when I get on a roll, look out. I've come on strong this season since resolving not to worry about my form. Used to be I'd spend a lot of time on technique, breaking down the dart throw to its component parts—the proper grip, the angle of the elbow, the release point. I'd work on keeping my head still and minimizing arm motion. In the end I gave all that up. You can't have a hundred things running through your head when you step to the line. Now I make sure I have enough liquor in me come game time, see the target and throw. Not exactly what they tell you in the videos, but it works for me.

As captain, my main task is to set the lineups. I decide the order in singles and the partners in doubles. We carry the minimum six players, so I'm spared the worst part of a captain's job: deciding who sits out. We really should carry another body, because as it stands, if one of us didn't show we'd have to play five on six. We're pretty hard-core, though. We'd all miss a work day before we'd miss a dart night, and in three seasons we've never played short.

The chief game we play in the league is 501. Each player starts with 501 points and the first to get down to zero wins. Sounds easy, right? The catch comes at the finish. To win the game you must go out on an exact double. In darts, the double section is the strip of two-inch-by-one-half-inch rectangles ringing the outside of the board. If a player has 40 left, he can only win by hitting the double 20. If he has 20 left, he must hit the double 10, and so on. Doubling out separates the good shooters from the rest, and turns plenty of the latter into alcoholics. A lot of guys can score, but nothing sends you to the bar quicker than pissing away a big lead and losing because you can't hit that double.

To have any chance at all tonight, we'll have to hit our doubles, or "take our outs," as they say. The Hellions are loaded with shooters, and you can't give them any extra throws.

They have one guy, name of Sean Killigan, who I would pay to see. Best player in the league, except maybe our Jimmy. Only the Irish teams come up with guys like Killigan. He's tiny, maybe 130 pounds soaking wet, but he throws the sweetest dart I've ever seen. Comes out of his hand in a gentle arc and hits dead straight every time, whether he's shooting the top of the board or the bottom. A robot couldn't land it any cleaner. When he's on, nobody beats him.

Killigan has a little problem, though. It comes in a bottle.

He's a first-rate alkie, and when he drinks, his dart game goes out the window. He won't hit one 20 in three. He has a pattern to him. He'll stay off the sauce for a few months and kick ass in the league. Then one day he'll take a few nips on the job, tell off the boss, get canned, fall hard off the wagon and drop out of sight. Just when you've forgotten him you walk into County Hell and he's back, drinking seltzer and nailing 20s.

I saw him play for the first time about a year back. Right here at Adam's Curse. Our A-division team at the time, the Dudes, was taking on this same Hellion crew for the trophy we'll be playing them for tonight. I came to root on the home team, but also to get a look at this Killigan fellow, to see if he was as good as the hype. From all the stories I'd heard, the guy never missed.

Killigan had been off the sauce all season at the time and was torching the league. First in wins, first in all-star points. Nobody could touch him. Well, he comes through the door that night and I can see he's loaded. He orders a beer but Joe Duggan comes over, knocks it away and says something low and mean to him in close. His teammates take him aside, pour coffee down him, water, anything to sober him up, but no dice. The match starts and he's useless. Gets routed in singles 501, and then again in cricket, the other game we play in the league. Duggan pulled him before doubles 501, but the damage was done. The Dudes won going away.

When it was over, Duggan put his arm around Killigan's shoulder and walked him to the bar. He ordered him a beer, then pulled back and smashed his forehead into Killigan's face, splitting his nose right open and knocking him to the floor. Happened right in front of me. Sean is lying there holding his face and Duggan empties his beer on him, says, "Have that on me, you fuckin' drunk," and walks out. On the way by me he cuts me a stare and says, "Careful who you root for, college boy." That was my introduction to Joe Duggan.

Three months later we joined A division and started facing the Hellions ourselves.

As for Killigan, by the next season he was back on the wagon and back on the team, as if nothing happened. By midseason, though, he was out again, sacked from his job, kicked right into the street by Duggan, who tracked him down in some rum hole when Sean didn't show for a match. And so on.

Unfortunately for us, Killigan seems to have turned his life around. He's been off the stuff three months now. I heard he got himself a job as an elevator man in Times Square. Rumor is he even has a girl. His arm has never been better, that's for sure. We'll have our hands full with him tonight.

I flag down Mason for another pint. It's a little more than an hour before the match and the rest of the team is due here any minute. I asked them all to come early so we could get fired up.

We'll need to be. On paper we don't stack up against these guys. Top to bottom they come at you with someone good. That's why you play the match, though. Call me a dreamer, but I think we can take them, if it all breaks right. They beat us only 10–8 last time, at their place, and I saw a few chinks in their armor.

For starters, they bring nine guys to every match. You want to play for Duggan, you better win. Lose in singles and he'll sit you the rest of the night, and spit in your drink besides. We took an early doubles match from them last time and the two losers stood at the board cursing each other, ready to duke it out. That's their weakness. One big family so long as they're winning, but get them down a little and they turn on each other. If we can get ahead early tonight, we'll have a shot.

Christ, beating Duggan would be sweet. I don't know what it is about him, but from the first I hated him. Maybe it's the way he hit Killigan when he wasn't looking. Maybe it's the eyes, or because he calls me college boy. Maybe everyone's born into this world with one enemy and he's mine. Who knows. Anyway, I don't want him coming into our place and walking out with this trophy. I want to beat him at the boards, fair and square, and turn that mean grin of his around. Then maybe rub it in a little. Put some Irish music on the jukebox, hold the post-match handshake an extra second and ask him if the losers want a round on the house. Then walk the whole pack of them to the door and call out after them, "Next time, gentlemen, bring your darts."

Jimmy's voice breaks into my reverie.

"Snap out of it, Tommy. You look like you're getting laid."

I'm back at the bar.

"Hi, Jimmy. Almost as good. I was thrashing Duggan."

"The devil himself. What do you say we end his reign tonight? Mason! A couple pints for the good guys."

Jimmy is our big gun. If we win tonight, he'll have a lot to do with it. He was the only A division player to finish the regular season undefeated in singles—12–0. Even beat Killigan once. Watching Jimmy throw is always a treat. His concentration is total. Once he locks in on the target, Cindy Crawford could blow in his ear and he wouldn't notice. Sometimes after a match, if I have enough in me, I'll make a V with my fingers against the board. Jimmy splits them every time. Good thing, too, because he really fires that dart.

Before he got hitched we used to hustle a little on the weekends. I'd drop a few friendly games to some guy, get him thinking he's an ace, then ask if he wants to grab a partner and play for a little dough. Five dollars, ten dollars, whatever he wants. He would call his buddy over, I'd call Jimmy, and if we milked them just right, winning each game by a little, we could take four or five before they realized what was up.

I keep telling Jimmy he should turn pro. Hit the dart circuit with me as his trusty manager. I'd take a modest thirty percent and any women he couldn't handle. His eyes light up at that kind of talk, but of course that's all it is. Since the marriage he's lucky to make it out on dart night. Don't get me started on that.

Jimmy is tall, about my height, with brown hair he parts in the middle and a smile that goes on and off like a light switch. He carries his weight well, like an athlete, though each time I see him he seems to have a little more to carry.

"Hi, guys."

We turn around. The first sight of Claire each week is a tonic. Scrubbed features, light freckles, milk in her eye. A heartland princess in the teeth of the big city. She gives us a kiss.

"You look great, Claire. Feel hot tonight?"

"Like always."

Don't let her fool you. She may look sweet, but put a dart in her hands and Claire is a killer. She'll be key tonight. You should see these Irish guys when they go up against a good-looking girl. Boy, do they lock up. We might be in McDougal's, or O'Flannery's, and all Claire has to do is shake her opponent's hand and he starts to sweat. If the guy is getting any action at all, it clearly isn't in her league. When she steps to the line to warm up he can't keep his eyes off her ass. He's a mess before the game even starts.

In darts it doesn't take a lot to knock you off-stride. An

eighth of an inch turns a triple 20 into a triple 1. The guy gets behind early, still out of it, and then the ribbing starts up from his teammates.

"Can't beat a girl, lad?"

"What'll you have from the bar, Wally? A wine cooler?"

Brutal. So then he starts to press, swearing between throws, his dart arm full of tension. Claire hits a big round and now the pressure is really on, and the peanut gallery turns it up a notch.

"Whyn't you tell us it was ladies' night, Wally?" All of a sudden this A league darter can barely hit the board. Claire finishes him off and the guy slinks back to the bar, ruined for the rest of the evening. We've seen it a dozen times.

Dave walks in humming the Notre Dame fight song. He puts his arms around the three of us, bringing our heads together.

"Gentlemen. Claire. We WILL win it all. You know what I did last night?"

No one offers a guess.

"Think of the great fighters, before a fight."

"You slept alone," says Jimmy.

"I slept alone."

"You're a martyr, Dave," I say.

"I am that. Though I'll confess that since I swore off Catholic girls, the rotation's been a little weak." He turns to Claire. "I may be able to slip you in there."

She laughs. "I'll pass."

"Okay. But that does mean Debbie's going to have to go again on two days' rest."

Claire shakes her head. "Tell me, Dave, where do you find these women?"

"Claire, Claire." Dave takes a long taste of his pint and winks at us. "They find me."

44

Tank and Bobby walk in together and join us at the bar. Tank kisses Claire and scowls at the rest of us.

"I been thinking about this all day," he says. "Didn't get a lick of work done."

Tank was my roommate junior year. The fullback on the football team until he tore up his knee, then keg captain of his frat. He's the only guy in New York who knows more about the Mets than I do. His perfect Friday night is a case of beer and a video of the '86 Series. A solid dart player and a no-bullshit guy. Likes a head butt before every match, and as captain I oblige.

Bobby would fit nicely under Tank's arm. He's five feet three and looks fourteen years old. Nearly cost us a playoff match a few months back by forgetting his license. We paid off the bouncer to get him in but no dice getting him a drink, and sober his game deserted him. We were lucky to squeak by. Bobby is a freak of nature. He can't weigh more than 140 pounds but he goes beer for beer with any of us, and the damnedest thing is he never has to piss. We can't figure out where it all goes. He jumps onto a barstool.

"Okay, guys. Ante up."

Bobby is also the songmaster. He gets two bucks from each of us to load up the jukebox before a match. Dave held the job at the start of the season but lost our trust. He was liable to spring Madonna on us, or Loverboy. He played them back to back at midseason and we booted him. I speak up.

"Before you go, Bobby. Everyone in close. Mason, a round of tequilas, please."

"Pep talk," says Bobby.

"Who do I kill, captain?" says Tank.

"Give us the word, skip," says Jimmy.

"Put me in the mood," says Claire.

Mason pours them out.

"Okay, guys," I say, "I'll keep it simple." I look at each in turn.

"Tonight we're the '69 Mets." We raise our shots. "Bottoms up."

We toss them back, turn our glasses over on the bar and walk to the boards. We're ready.

CHAPTER FIVE

ALL A CAPTAIN can ask is to have his ace on the line with a shot to win it. Come on, Jimmy—put the stake in these guys.

An hour ago it didn't look so good. The Hellions jumped on us early, winning four of six singles. We fought back in cricket to even the score, split the first two doubles 501 games and here we are—all tied up. Our big guns against theirs in one game for the Manhattan championship. A hell of a game it's been, too. Jimmy and Tank have torn up the board but Killigan and Duggan have matched them dart for dart. Now, at the finish, all that stands between us and one hell of a party is the double 16 Jimmy is stepping up there to hit. He has no margin for error, because if he misses, Killigan gets his own chance to win it, and Sean Killigan hasn't missed all night.

I'm scoring the match. Chalking, we call it. From my spot next to the board I face the shooters and the two teams spread around the table behind them. The Drinkers stand to the left, Bobby and Claire on their chairs for a better view. Claire watches through her fingers and Bobby looks away, then back, then away again. Dave has his fist in the air, ready to yell. Tank, Jimmy's partner, gives him a nod of encouragement and takes a big draw from his pint.

Off to the right the Hellions stand together, silent. Even with a loss staring at him, Duggan's face is a sneer. He looks at me, and when he sees that I see he flicks his eyes at Jimmy, shakes his head, and draws a finger across his throat. I look back at the board. I could sure use a drink, but chalkers aren't allowed one. Christ. Playing a tough game is bad enough. Watching it is murder.

Jimmy steps to the mark. Most guys take a little extra time with the game on the line. Rub their shoulders, take some deep breaths. Jimmy is all business, though, and as he locks in on the target, my gut tightens with joy. He has that look to him, the one he gets when he's really on. Staring so hard at the board I know he can't see anything else. He pulls his arm back to throw and the rush hits me and it's all I can do not to smile. Because I know, sure as gold, that Jimmy's going to bury it. And when he does I'm the only one in the bar who doesn't see it because I'm not looking at the board but at Duggan. His face and the roar of the gang tell me it's in and I throw the chalk in the air and hell breaks loose.

I rush to Jimmy but still I'm looking past him at Duggan, who slams his darts to the floor. Bobby, Claire and Dave come over the table and all of us meet at Jimmy. Over their heads I see Duggan shake off Killigan and the other Hellions and then his eyes snap up to mine, and better even than the trophy we'll get for tonight is the sight of him. The blood wants through his face but there's nowhere for it to go, and the hate coming at me from those yellow eyes is sweet to see. Tank joins the hug, we sway for a second, the six of us, and start to collapse, and just before we go down in a pile and Claire with her sweet smell drops in my lap, I give Joe Duggan a big horse wink.

ALL HELLIONS HAVE LEFT the grounds now and the celebration is on. Stella saw the finish from behind the bar and comes round to hug us all. Stella wouldn't spot the Pope a beer but she springs for a round and sits down with us. Says of all her teams she likes us the best. Likes the way we were friends first, the way we pull for one another, the way we started at the bottom and stuck together. Of course, the fortune we spend in here doesn't hurt. If our team ever went on the wagon she'd hear from her accountant in a week.

I like to think of Stella Walker as the last of the old New York buildings. The facing has eroded a bit, the plumbing isn't what it used to be, but she's still a grand structure. And built to last. Her husband left her this place when he died ten years ago and she's run it on her own ever since. She lives just across the street and walks over every morning to open up for the faithful crew of soaks who wait outside. You should see that crowd. One time as a lark Tank and I stopped in for a beer before work. Sitting at the bar at 8 A.M., drinking breakfast, were the same regulars we see every dart night. First time in my life I ever felt like a health nut.

Stella herself doesn't knock them back much anymore, except on Saint Paddy's, but she's still a sport. She might be seventy-five, but I'd rather spend an hour with her than with a lot of guys I know. She holds Jets season tickets and slips them to Tank and me when the weather turns too cold for her. Likes to gamble a little, too. Plays the ponies through Toadie and rides the casino bus to Atlantic City twice a month. Keeps a cribbage board behind the bar and deals a mean game. A quarter a point, and if you miscount your hand she takes the points herself.

Stella likes darts best of all, though, and nothing makes her happier than watching her teams win. She'll talk about tonight's match for a month. She means it about our team, too. About liking us best, I mean. She's fielded teams with better shooters, but none with our spirit and none with our loyalty. A lot of her squads change from season to season, put together not out of friendship but to win titles. If they fall short, the aces switch teams or even bars, lured to the White Horse by promises of free beer or to Sting's to join a powerhouse, or just walking out in a huff after a row with teammates. Only we Drinkers have kept the same six from the start.

Not that we haven't been tempted. Jimmy has turned down a dozen offers to jump ship, and the Kettle, down in the Village, keeps promising the whole team five-dollar pitchers all season to come over. Through it all we buy Stella's three-dollar Buds and stay put. Adam's Curse is home, and you don't leave home because the place down the street has better rates. Not to mention that as captain I'd have to break the news to Stella. I'd rather tell Dad I'm a fruit.

Tonight we line up a round of prairie fires. Claire passes on hers, so we slide it down to Toadie, who damn near chokes on it. A prairie fire is tequila and Tabasco together in a shot glass. Hell going down and worse the next morning, but it gives you a charge. After we toss them back, Tank climbs onto the bar and leads the alkies through the Mets theme song. Then all us guys take off our shirts, draw the box score from the match on them, and give them to Stella, who signs each one with a flourish and promises they'll be on the ceiling by the weekend. Stella shakes her finger at

Dave when he offers Claire a hundred dollars to add her shirt to the pile.

"None of that. This young lady is the best thing that ever happened to you boys. Be gentlemen."

To prove our manners we form a human ricksha and carry Claire around the bar to scope a good spot on the wall for our plaque. A little later, when she's ready to leave, we see her to the street and serenade her into a cab with a chorus of "Duggan Takes It Up the Ass," to the tune of "Camptown Races." Back inside, the rest of us make a pact to defend our title and seal it with a second prairie fire.

By midnight Stella is done in, and over her protests I walk her across the street to her place. I'm still shirtless but wearing my tie now. She feels heavy on my arm. I wonder about her sometimes. She seems to leave earlier and earlier these days, and is it me or is she losing the spring in her step? In the streetlight I glance at her face and for the first time she looks like an old woman. I ask how she feels and she waves a hand.

"I'm all right, Tom. All the excitement just wears on me a little. Not that I would miss it . . ." She pats her chest. "It does the heart good." She stops at her door. "Now you go on back, Tom. People will talk."

I turn but she touches my arm, her eyes sparkling.

"I play canasta every month with Papa O'Shea, Tom—the owner of County Hell. For two years I've had to listen to how good his boys are. Thanks to you kids, *I* have bragging rights now."

Crossing back to Adam's Curse I shake my head for ever worrying about her. That woman will give the toast at my wake.

Back in the bar, Bobby waves me to our table in the corner.

"Before I go, guys," he says, "what do you say? One movie opening?"

We all groan.

"C'mon. It's a good one, I promise."

Bobby may write ad copy for a living, but his passion is dreaming up opening scenes for movies. They just come to him, he says, and whenever one does we have to gather round while he recites it and then give it a rating. Thumbs-up or thumbs-down. Bobby knows enough to catch us when we're in our cups. Loaded, they almost all sound good, though the next morning you can't make any sense of them. We give him the green light.

"Okay. Close your eyes."

We do.

"A night scene. A farmer driving his pickup on a country road. No one and nothing around. He's got a real beat-up face, depression-era, a tractor cap on his head. Probably illiterate, you're thinking as you watch. He stares straight ahead, no expression. The only sound is a commercial on the truck radio, turned low. The farmer punches the 'seek' button and Pink Floyd's 'Have a Cigar' is just starting. It plays most all the way through and still the farmer stares ahead, no change of expression. Suddenly, perfectly in sync, he joins in: 'It could be made into a monster if we all pull together as a team.' "

Everyone is quiet. Bobby looks around.

"And?" says Jimmy.

"That's it. The farmer is silent again. The song finishes, he clicks off the radio, and all we hear are the crickets."

We all give it the thumbs-up.

"If you ever do make that flick," says Tank, "you better pass out plenty of weed."

By 2 A.M. the gang is down to Dave, Jimmy, and me, and

Dave's on his way out. "Great night, gentlemen. I'd stay but I have a midterm in seven hours. Jimmy—what are the chances you can bust out this weekend?"

"None."

"Too bad. Tom, leave Friday night open if you win your bet."

"What's going on?"

"I've got another trim plan." He rubs his hands. "And this one is foolproof. You go home alone, you get your money back."

I laugh. "Just like the last time?"

Every few months Dave comes up with a new plan. His last one had us booking into the Penta Hotel the weekend of a nurses' convention. As Dave pitched it, ". . . four hundred horny girls. Every one of them on birth control, every one of them with a little knowledge of anatomy, every one of them looking for a good time." Well, the best-laid plans . . . A quarter of them turned out to be guys, and most of the rest had thirty years or fifty pounds on us, or both. Once you threw out the married ones and the dogs, we were down to about ten prospects. Worst of all, Dave hooked up with a couple of them and I ended up back at the pad to give him some privacy.

"Just hear me out, Tom. This time it can't miss. Scout's honor."

"Okay," I say, thinking I'd like to see the troop that graduated Dave.

"You know Chippendale's?"

"Sure. The male strippers. I think we're a few situps away from being ready."

"Listen. Every Friday at midnight it turns into a regular bar. Guys can go too."

"So?"

"Boy, you never took critical reasoning, did you? Hundreds of horny women stare at naked guys for hours. They whip themselves into a frenzy—tossing their money, grabbing at loincloths, rushing the stage. Just when they're ready to sneak into the ladies' room and diddle off, in we walk. Straight, handsome, and eligible. What do you say?"

This plan has two things in common with all Dave's others: It's completely outrageous, and going over the logic I can't find any holes.

"We'll be fishing in a stocked tank, Tom. No chance we don't land one."

"I'm there."

"Good." He winks at Jimmy. "We'll tell you all about it."

Dave salutes us and walks out into the night. Jimmy and I are the only customers left in the bar. The lights are down and Marley sings softly from the jukebox. Through my buzz I feel hugely at peace. I put out a hand.

"You know how bad I wanted to win this one tonight, Jimmy. And you were a pistol. Thanks."

He shakes. "My pleasure. Duggan is a prick, isn't he?"

"The biggest."

Jimmy shakes his head and I know he's thinking of Dave. "Jesus, Tom. The single life. It must be something else, huh?"

"It has its rewards."

"You're telling me."

Here it comes. I can always tell when Jimmy's got something on his mind, and it's usually the same something. He got hitched right out of school, like I said, and a year later the bloom is definitely off the rose. Most nights he won't go into it, but get him alone, with enough in him, and he'll come clean. Another drink or two should do the trick.

"Anything you want to tell me?" I ask.

Jimmy pauses.

"Nah. No talk of the front tonight—we're celebrating. Mason, how 'bout some kamikazes, and two more pints."

He sips his beer and seems to be going back and forth in his head. We do our shots and the dam breaks.

"It's just this, Tom. You know, it even pisses her off that I'm here tonight. Not just because I'll roll in at dawn, either. It's the fact I'm out having a good time without her. Christ, I work hard. Is it too much to have a few beers with the fellas once a week?"

He shakes his head. He's quiet a second, but once the water's loose, it's loose.

"I'll tell you another thing I didn't bank on, Tom. Linda hates sports. I mean she hates them. I can't put a game on without her rolling her eyes."

"Maybe she's related to my roommates."

"You should see our weekends. Guess what we did last Friday? Friday night, while you and Dave were out getting loaded. Guess what we did."

"I can't."

"Go ahead. Guess." Jimmy waves his shot glass in the air.

"Rented a movie."

"I wish. We watched the Three Tenors, Tommy. Can you believe it? I'm twenty-three and I spent Friday night on the sofa watching the Three Tenors. Christ."

"Well, at least you had a little action at the end, I hope. Married life ain't all bad."

Jimmy spins his glass on its edge, draws with his finger in the water stain. "Yeah, there's that." He looks up. "Man, I'm drunk. That's why I'm mouthing off like this. Listen, Tommy, can I ask you something? Just between us?"

"Sure."

"I mean really just between us. You tell Dave and I'll play for Duggan next season."

"Hey Jimmy, it's me."

"Okay." He pauses. "When you were with Lisa. Fucking her, I mean. Did you ever pretend she was someone else?"

"What do you mean?"

"You know—someone else. Like a fantasy."

"Hell no. Why?"

Jimmy looks at the ceiling. "Forget it." He looks back at me. "Ah, fuck it. Christ, Tom—it's been a year since I could fuck Linda without pretending she's somebody else."

"Jesus. Like who?"

"Anybody. Some dish on the street that day. Demi Moore in her latest flick. Anybody who gets me hot."

I look at him.

"Hey, you wait. Maybe if you got laid more often . . . Mason, two more here. But it's more than that, Tommy. Before I screw Linda I need a little while to prepare myself. Down a few beers, get something going in my head. And then I'm okay, more or less. Usually it's twice a week and I can gauge the nights, you know, get ready for it. But sometimes she springs it on me. I get home and she's waiting in bed, or she drops the groceries on the table and wants to go at it right there in the kitchen. And Tommy, I'm not kidding, I can't always get the damn thing up."

We take a good draw from our pints.

"And the thing of it is, Tommy, it's not me. Because if I see some knockout on the subway, or my secretary comes in in a mini, man, I'm aching to bust her one right there. It's just . . . where's the thrill, you know? Even if it's lobster, you can't eat lobster every night. You need a burger now and then."

I have Linda slotted closer to a good salmon on my menu, but I don't press the point.

"I'm only twenty-three, Tommy. I don't know how long I can keep this up."

We're silent.

"Well, say something. What do you think?"

I take another swig and spread my hands on the bar.

"I think you're fucked, Jimmy. Bad as it is, you have to figure it'll get worse. She'll want a kid in the pipeline in the next year, right? No doubt a few more after that. Raising them Catholic means church every Sunday, no more beer and football, and with the little monsters running around, no late nights during the week. Hell, I'll be surprised if you're even on the team this time next year."

Jimmy stares at me, then laughs, his mood broken.

"You bastard. Just you wait, Tommy. You won't hold out forever."

We down our pints and walk outside. Only in New York can a guy with no shirt flag down a cab at three in the morning and ride home without explanation. Jimmy ducks into one, but before it starts off he sticks his head out the window.

"Forget all that stuff I said, Tommy. It was the beer talking. We were something else tonight, huh?"

"We were the best."

I watch his face, still out the window as the cab rolls away. I stand on the empty sidewalk a second, then start the walk home. I love the city this time of night. Quiet, but with a hum to it. As I walk along I think of Jimmy. Can you believe it? You should have seen that pair in college. Couldn't pry them off each other. Graduation day they almost missed the ceremony slipping in an extra one in the shower. Now look at him. It's only been a year, and before he can fuck her he's got to get all liquored up and pretend she's someone else.

Jesus. If that's what's waiting at the end of that middle aisle, you can count me out.

I bump into a hydrant and realize for the first time how rocked I am. The next one bites on a head fake and I dance around it. Looking up, in place of the stars I see the few lights still on in the high-rises. Who's still up at this hour, I wonder? I picture a thin beauty, her twenty-second birthday tomorrow, sitting at the window in a lonely sweater. A cup of cocoa in her hands, humming along to the radio as she looks down at me in the street. Just give the sign and I'll come up, honey. We can talk all night about music, if you want, or go at it on the carpet without a word. I'm easy. I walk into a mailbox. Damn.

Between the shots and the beers we must have set a record tonight. I'll pay for it in the morning, but it was worth it. Manhattan champions—what a ring that has. At my building I skip up the stairs and on the third try the key slips into the lock.

"College boy."

I jump. Below me in the street is Duggan. He wears an Irish cap and a coat tied at the waist. He lights a cigarette and shakes out the match.

"Been celebrating, I see."

I look around for the rest of them but he's alone. I should probably feel pretty foolish in just my tie, but not tonight. Let's not forget who the winner is. I look him over. Alone in the street, in that coat and cap, he doesn't look so tough. Hell, he looks like just another down-and-outer. This is the guy who gave me the creeps? I slide down the handrail and land in front of him.

"Let me guess, Duggan—you want to join the team. I'd love to, but there aren't any spots. We could use a chalker, though."

His yellow eyes start to burn, then look down. "What you fellas did tonight was a fluke. It won't happen again."

"I agree with you there. Next time I don't expect you'll get a point."

He tenses, and I think he's coming at me. I'm ready for him, but he looks away, and when he looks back it's with a crooked smile.

"You sure can talk, college boy. Anything behind that mouth of yours?" He takes a long drag, drops his cigarette and grinds it under his heel. He lets the smoke out slowly. "What would you say to a real match, college boy? For money."

I'll be damned.

"Anytime, Duggan. What did you have in mind—five hundred?"

He snickers, blows the rest of the smoke down his chest.

"I'm not talking Girl Scout stakes, college boy. I'm talking real money."

Bastard.

"You name it, we'll play for it."

"Twenty thousand dollars."

"Fine."

"Two weeks from Friday. Our place this time. Same players that played tonight. You don't show, you owe."

"Fine."

"Did you hear me, college boy? I said twenty thousand."

"I heard you. And I said yes."

I turn to head up the stairs but he grabs my tie and pulls me to him. "A word of advice, college boy: Don't run out on this one."

I knock his hand off. "The next time it touches me it better have money in it." I start up the stairs, whip back around. "And no checks, Duggan. And no Irish money. Tell your mick backers I want dollars."

I can feel him burning in the street as I walk up the stairs. At the door I look back and he's gone. I take a big drink of night air. Well, that was easy. Bastard thinks I don't have any balls, does he? I'll show him. Inside, I take the stairs in twos and laugh to myself. The times to be had in this town! Kick Duggan's ass at the dartboard, tell him off in the street and set up a big payday besides. Not a bad night's work.

I soft-shoe into the apartment so as not to wake the girls. Mess with their REM sleep and it throws off their systems for a week. I down two quick pints of ice water, fall into bed in my pants, and grin up at the ceiling.

You the man, Tom.

CHAPTER SIX

NOTHING complements a killer hangover quite like a packed subway car. One more whiff of the guy next to me and I'm going to lose it. At Fourteenth Street it empties out a bit and I lower myself into a seat. That's better. My bleary eyes meet the stare of the guy across from me, who looks to be on his way to church. A Sunday suit on, the Bible open in his lap, a crucifix soft against his neck. My headache worsens and I look away.

Church. Christ. The last time I went to Mass I was home on the base for the summer. I had written from school that I wasn't making service anymore, but moms have a way of forgetting what they don't like to hear. I spent the night before in the bars, showing my old high school buddies I'd learned something useful in college, so when Mom woke me at seven-thirty, my suit over her arm, I was more dead than alive. I might have come out okay pleading sickness, but I was a freshman in college, so I gave her a speech. Told her the way I felt that morning I didn't doubt He was up there, and a mean one He was, too. She slapped me across the mouth, I put my suit on without a word, and we walked to church. Sat next to her in the pew, biting my lip till it bled to keep my stomach down. After the service we walked home in silence and I haven't been back since.

At Delancey Street the train fills up again and I'm thankful for the open window behind me.

Here's my two cents on religion: I don't buy it. Sometimes I wish I did. It's not easy thinking you get one crack at this place. I've looked at it up and down, though, and if you ask me the whole thing is a racket.

Take Joe Catholic across from me. He hasn't lifted his face from the Book since Fourteenth Street. I'll bet the guy is a real all-star. Been doing it by the Church's rules all his life. Never misses a service, digs deep when the plate comes around, steers clear of the books they don't want him to read. The works. All to make sure he's taken care of when the time comes.

Now that's a hell of a reason, sure, but look at the deal from the Church's side a second. Seems to me they milk this guy pretty good. Take him for thousands of bucks, over the years, and when he's not cutting them a check he's out stumping in his free time, bringing in more business. Don't think he sees any commission, either. Then you have his kids. Years of unpaid labor as altar boys and helpers, and when they get a little older the Church has the inside track on signing them up for the distance, too. Hey, if he ever stops to do the math, he'll see the bill is starting to mount. I won't even get into the opportunity cost.

And when does the guy get his payoff? When does the Church have to ante up, to show him all that soul work they were selling him wasn't just a bill of goods? The second he dies. Now that's what I call a smooth scam.

Up he went, they can say, we did our part, and no one can prove them wrong.

That's what gets me about the whole business—they never have to prove anything. They have a little trick called faith to get around all that. The pastors used to spring it on me all the time. Thirteen years I kept asking how can you prove it and thirteen years they gave me the same answer: faith. "How can a man live in a whale, Father?" Faith. "How can a man part the ocean, Father?" Faith.

I didn't want to hear about faith. I wanted to know did the stuff really happen or didn't it? If it did where was the proof? If you can't show the proof, well, that pretty much pulls the rug out from under the whole deal, doesn't it? Faith, Tom. If you have faith you don't ask those questions. Hell, any other salesman tried that line you'd boot him out the door. Put a robe on him and a steeple behind him, though, and I'm supposed to go along.

I'm not trying to pin everything on the Catholics. I'm just sore at them for all the Sundays I wasted in the pew. I'm sure the other religions are about the same.

Look around the subway car. Next to the Bible guy is a Rastafarian. Down from him a Hasidic Jew. You think they chose their faiths after looking hard at all the others and deciding where the truth was? Hell no. The one guy is Catholic and the other Jewish and the other a Rasta because that's who got ahold of them first. By that logic any one of them could have wound up a Nazi.

I look at them. Each sits there with all the answers, knowing he's all set come the big day, and at least two of them are dead wrong. I wouldn't put a dime on the third one, either. Thanks anyway, guys, but I'll take my chances.

At Wall Street I climb the sooty stairs into the August-morning heat. It isn't even 9 A.M. and already my shirt sticks to me. As I walk the short block to work, picking my way through the throng, I fight back my hangover and the nagging feeling that I'm forgetting something. Something important about last night. The match is all pretty clear in my head, especially the big finish, but the rest is a little fuzzy. The victory party comes back in fits and starts. I remember shots, and singing, and taking off our shirts in the bar. I remember walking Stella home. And just how did I get home, anyway? Split a cab with Jimmy, I guess.

Kay smiles as I limp through the oak doors. Someone else's hangover is always a riot.

"What happened to you, Tom?"

"Just something going around."

"Right. The Irish flu." She laughs loudly and I grip the edge of her desk.

"Jesus, Kay, don't do that. You got any aspirin?"

"Take my last two."

Kay is a sweetheart. Our terminally cheerful receptionist, the only one in the firm who knows about my bets. She's always setting me up with her girlfriends, and it's only thanks to a cousin of hers that I'm not zero for '96 in the sleepover department. Kay herself is cute as they come. From the shoulders up, anyway. Start moving downstairs and it's a different story. She got married six months ago and already she's put on twenty pounds. I feel bad for the new hubby. It's probably just dawning on him what he's let himself in for. From what I remember of her mom at the reception, the long-term outlook isn't promising, either. I'm with Dave on this one. Once you fork over the ring, there ought to be a weight clause in there somewhere.

64

"Take one of my doughnuts, Tom. It will settle your stomach."

There's no way I can keep it down but I take it out of respect for her hubby. He always seemed like a nice guy.

At my desk I ditch the doughnut, wash down the aspirin with water, bury my face in a case file and close my eyes. Just let today be an easy one. The phone rings.

"Farrell Hawthorne."

"How's the head, college boy?"

Duggan. Why do I think I've just seen him?

"What do you want, Duggan?"

"Wanted to give you a chance to yellow out."

Duggan. Duggan. It all comes back in a rush. The two of us in the street. Something about a rematch. For money this time. But how much? I stall him.

"I'd love to chat, Duggan, but some of us have real jobs to do."

"Still talking a good game, I see. I assume we're on then, college boy."

Think, Tom, think.

"Sure we're on. Only, aren't you a little embarrassed to play for those stakes?"

"What's that?"

"You want to play for money, Duggan, let's play for money." Silence on the line. What the hell—sometimes you floor it and hope the other guy moves. How much can it be, anyway? "Let's double it."

More silence.

"What's the matter—don't have that kind of dough? Or can't your backers count that high?"

I can feel his hatred through the cord. When he speaks it's through his teeth.

"Double it is, college boy—forty grand. But we see the dough before the match. And listen good. You're not wanking for drinks with the frat boys anymore. If I gotta come get you . . ."

Click.

I walk to the bathroom and splash cold water on my face. Forty grand? Jesus, Tom, what the hell did you do last night? I splash myself again. Forty grand? Add up all the dough I've spent in my life and it doesn't make forty grand. I towel off.

So call him back. Tell him it's no go. I look at myself in the mirror and a strange feeling starts in the pit of my stomach. What a charge if I could raise it, though, huh? All that money riding on a night of darts. And the chance to stick it to Duggan, besides. I look myself over again. One thing I'm not up for, right now, is calling Duggan back to chicken out. No way.

Not that I have the first clue where I'd get the money. Even so. I shake my head. Maybe if I give myself a few days I can come up with something. I'm strictly in survival mode today, anyway, not in any shape to make a big decision. I'll get through the day, sleep on it and see what I think in the morning.

I walk back to my desk and take a seat. I'm wondering if my stomach can handle a soda when the phone rings again. It's Carter.

"Reasons, I need to see you in here."

"Yes, sir."

Carter is in high spirits, pacing the carpet behind his desk like a football coach walking the sidelines. He stops and looks me up and down.

"What's wrong with you? You look awful."

"Stomach flu, sir."

"Yes. Well. I don't want you having any late nights while

66

the Garrett case is on. We need to be in peak form on this one."

Yeah, right.

"Yes, sir."

He starts to pace again. "I thought the depositions went very well. No surprises. I want them summarized by Friday, and this afternoon I need you to sit in on two more. Prego's wife, and Winston Garrett."

"Winston Garrett?"

"He was at the party, too. Not one of the sick ones, luckily. He'll back up Regina on her cooking and catering knowhow. His word will look good."

"Sir, can I ask you something? About Mrs. Garrett?"

"What is it?"

"Well . . . is it just me, or does her story seem pretty shaky?"

Carter frowns. "Her story is her story, Reasons. And as our client her story is gospel. It's not our job to poke holes in it. It's our job to poke holes in the other side. Capisce?"

"Yes, sir. It's just that . . . well, don't you think, given her appearance, and her money, and her—demeanor—that she's not going to cut a very sympathetic figure at trial? That a jury might side with the hardworking immigrant, and jump at the chance to stick it to a rich old broad?"

Carter rubs his hands. "Ah. Now you're thinking, Reasons. That is precisely why this case is not going near a jury."

"Sir?"

"Prego does all right, but he's no moneybags. Once he realizes what this trial is going to cost him, he'll settle."

"But he can't, sir. Settling would kill his business. Nobody would ever hire him again. His only hope is to save his reputation by winning at trial. He's got nothing to lose."

Carter paces again, turning with a bounce at each end of the room.

"Let's just say there are ways of making him settle."

"Like what, sir?"

Carter slows. "Okay, Reasons. Welcome to the law as it's not taught in law school. Think along with me here."

I don't like the sound of this.

"Prego is one of these guys with a lot of ties to the home country. Always shuttling over cousins, nephews to work in his place. You know—the whole immigrant shtick."

"So?"

"So, I don't think we'll have to look real hard to find someone in the pack without a green card. Maybe they're working in his place, maybe for his brother in construction. Either way, we're talking big fines. And if we want to press it—end of business, deportation, the works. Trust me, Reasons. Between us and Immigration, Prego will settle."

My stomach hints at starting up on me and I fight it down.

"Which leads me to today. I've got a friend over at INS who owes me a favor. I want you to meet with him. Ask him to see what he can dig up. Tell him to start with the niece who worked the party. Wouldn't surprise me if little Rosie is missing some papers. Tell him not to act on anything he finds, though. For now it stays just between us."

Back at my desk I stare at the wall. Life sure can be a barrel of shit sometimes. I start in on the depositions, but it's slow going. Reading over Prego's testimony I can't help but think of him back in his shop, mixing his sauces. Full of worry, a crease in his brow, but confident the good lawyers can iron everything out. You don't know what you're in for, Giuseppe. In my year here I've seen a few cases with the truth on one side and the money on the other.

I don't like your chances.

CHAPTER SEVEN

I'VE TOUGHED out a few hangovers in my time, but this one tops the list. Two days and change. As I walk up the East Side Friday after work, an Oil Can in my hand, I'm just starting to feel human again. Nothing like a little hair of the dog. I've yet to have any brainstorms on this Duggan mess, but that will have to wait. First things first—time to pick my game.

I've narrowed it to the Yankees in Chicago or Boston hosting the Angels. Let's see. Cone is on the mound for the Yanks. My favorite ex-Met, and he's riding a three-game winning streak. I don't know, though. Coney's fucked me twice in the last year and I'm not sure I'm ready to trust him again. The last time I bet him he took a 1–0 lead into the ninth and then flipped out on me. Balked in the tying run and wild-pitched in the winner. I lost all my dough and nearly pissed myself besides. Then, too, you have to like the Angels in

Fenway. It's August, so Boston's headed down the tubes, and a good lefty like Langston should give them fits.

At Union Square I lean on a mailbox, close my eyes and wait for a flash from the betting gods. Yanks or Angels? Yanks or Angels? I open them again to see a mother and her little girl eyeing me nervously. I tip my beer at them as they back away.

"Got it."

FOUR HUNDRED on the Angels, Toadie."

He takes my money and I feel the pressure go out of me. Even Duggan, whom I've sensed around every corner the past few days, seems a hundred miles away. Stella greets me with a big hug, still wearing her smile from three nights ago.

"It's good to see you again, Tom. You guys were terrific on Tuesday. Who's our team tonight?"

"The Angels."

Mason puts an Absolut on the rocks in front of me. "Okay, Reasons. Bonus question, seeing as the season's over and there won't be any more dart nights for a while. Ready?"

"Shoot."

He rolls the toothpick in his mouth from right to left, clamps it in the middle. "Every cheap hood strikes a bargain with the world."

I drop my head. "Man, I know that one. Give me a few minutes."

"You got till game time." He walks down the bar.

I'm just dicking him—I could finish the stanza. Go as deep into the album as you want, you won't slip any Clash by me. Just before first pitch he saunters over.

"Let's have it, tough guy."

"Wouldn't be 'Death or Glory,' Clash, *London Calling?*"

"Damn." He pours my drink with a scowl. "You better

pull out your thrash tapes, Reasons. You're starting to piss me off."

I take a deep drink of vodka and feel it spread down my neck and into my arms and chest. How did anybody make it through the week before this stuff? How did they blow off steam? Threw rocks at each other, I guess. No wonder.

Nabholz is the surprise starter for the Red Sox. He's the last pitcher I want to see out there. A big, sloppy lefty, no great shakes, really, but somehow the guy has it in for me personally.

When he was in the National League he couldn't beat anybody but the Mets. He'd get knocked out of the box three starts in a row and then come into Shea and pitch a shutout. Used to kill me. Now banished to the AL, he's trying to fuck me out of four hundred bucks.

"Mason, one more down here. And easy on the ice."

This is it. Three to two Boston in the ninth. Two on, two out. If I told you how the Sox took the lead I'd pop an artery. Edmonds is up there for me with a chance to win it, facing the Boston closer. Come on, Edmonds—I could get a hit off this guy. The count is 2–2. The pitch: Oh, that's hit! I'm up on my chair, waving it on. Get out of there! Get out of there!

Caught at the wall.

I slump in my chair. Toadie walks over, pats my shoulder and slides me a beer.

"Tough one, kid. Hey, how 'bout that Cone? Shut out the White Sox tonight three zip. Son of a bitch went all the way."

I slide off the stool and walk out the door into the night.

The purity of the big bet comes from the gulf between winning and losing. It is absolute. No second place, no moral victories, no nice try. I'm feeling that gulf right now, as I stand in the street. Forty-seven dollars until next Friday. No Irish band tonight and no night on the town with Dave. A

71

week of hot dogs and instant noodles to look forward to. And this whole Duggan business still hanging over me. Christ.

All the introspection I don't have time for when I'm out spending my winnings comes down hard when I lose. What kind of guy gambles away his paycheck, anyway? What kind of guy lives with a couple of clowns, for that matter? Or works a job he doesn't believe in? Or bets forty grand he doesn't have?

I'm too depressed to go straight home, so I make a left and start uptown. At Forty-second Street I cut west. As I pass the big public library the blood in me starts to move a little faster and I pick up the pace. This part of town always gives me a boost.

At Seventh Avenue I see the corner preacher in his usual spot, going strong. Tonight he talks about the Lord Jesus, about the light that came down from the mountain, the fire that awaits the sinner, and the high, the only true high, the all-natural, everlasting high of the believer, for which we need only drop to our knees and accept the Son of God into our hearts. It all sounds pretty easy the way he tells it. Next he drones on about the thousand paths to hell. He mentions a few I haven't covered and I make a note of them for the weekend.

As I come into the heart of Times Square, his voice loses out to singing. I sit for a minute on a low wall in the middle of the square and listen to three bums singing barbershop, one voice starting just as the others fade. Two low, one high, more peaceful than any lullaby I heard as a kid. I start awake a while later and realize I've been sleeping. The singers have pooled their money and bought a six-pack, and sit tapping the cans to the rhythm of the rappers, who dart and glide through traffic. The air tastes sweet, with the barest hint of autumn, and I feel better already. Money or no money, it's still a charge to be young in this town.

Spread out behind me is the grand dame herself, Broadway, lit up like the morning star. She offers her neon hand to me, as she's done before, asks if I won't come dance awhile. Lose myself in her many skirts, breathe in the perfume that is hers alone. Some other night, my lady, when I'm flush. Tonight I'm happy just to sit here and soak it all in.

I sat in classrooms for four years, listening to lectures and theories, and then I moved to the city, came up from the subway into Times Square and forgot everything. At last I wasn't looking at life anymore but living it. Now, anytime I'm all out of gas, a little jaunt to the old quarter picks me up again. Something in the air here stirs my juices. The buzz and hum, the talk of the grifters. People gripe that it's a hard part of town, depressing, but not to me.

To me, Forty-second Street is beyond despair. The lost causes wander in the background, but they're bit players in the performance that starts anew every night. In the spotlight are the stars—pimps and pushers, card jacks, shell men, barkers with silver teeth calling out show times. Rough boys and hookers and pickpockets and men of God who've strayed off the path for a few hours. When evening comes, the curtain lifts on them all. And tonight I have the best seat in the house.

The script changes a little every night, sure, but the grand themes are the same. The bestsellers—sex, drugs, violence, and twisted in there with them something else. Each night, all these people come to Times Square with a little money and with something missing inside, some void that nothing in their life is filling, and for a few hours they try to fill it.

Some fill it with drugs. Crack, speed, heroin. Pot if you

want it, but who smokes that anymore? Big pills and small pills and vials and tin foil and squares. You name it, they got it, and if they don't they'll say they do and give you something close. Smoke it, snort it, and wander the streets dreamlike, giggling at the jugglers and the mimes, touching sweatshirts for the feel on the fingers, spinning from the lights and the rhythms and the candy that is everywhere, in the air even, and just let it last, let this night go on and on and never end.

Or are weapons your game? Duck around the corner, Chief, and check this out. Spring knives, choke strings, Mace. Meet the men in the personal-protection business. It's a rough world, but they'll get you ready. A gun, you say? Well now, that's a little tougher, but I know a guy who knows a guy and twenty bucks gets you a meeting and fifty more gets you a piece. You don't want weapons—hey, no sweat, I got everything else. IDs? Step inside. We take a picture, do a little artwork, and in fifteen minutes your own mother will swear you're twenty-one.

Or maybe sex is what you need. Well, you've come to the right place, because every storefront is selling it. The two-dollar theaters and the dirty bookshops and the porn halls extraordinaire. Slip behind the curtain and you have a choice of thirteen channels. You can watch women and you can watch men and you can watch animals, and if none of that does the trick you can step downstairs and climb into a booth with the real thing, just a plate of glass between you and the girl, who wiggles and poses and does pretty much whatever you tell her to, so long as the coins keep falling. And this is just the minor-league stuff. In the back rooms and the run-down hotels, sometimes in the corner of an alley, the real action goes on. The one-on-one, the personal stuff, where the wallet calls the shots and anything goes.

This performance, like I said, starts again every night. And it's one show that won't be closing anytime soon. Oh, the cops haul a few stars off the stage, sure, but before they even reach the squad car, new players step forward without missing a line. And the critics will rail against it, as always, but she'll keep right on running. Just off Broadway, outlasting all the others. The cops can't kill this show and the critics can't kill it and the mayor himself couldn't kill it, because the people just can't stop coming.

As I step down into the subway to head home, I feel better. Buck up, Tom—things could be worse. Hell, I don't have to work tomorrow, and there's a twelve-pack left at home. Not to mention the place to myself. Mike and Molly are in the Catskills for the weekend for some kind of sensitivity seminar. I can't wait to hear the lowdown on that one.

Back in the pad, I open the fridge to find the beer gone and a note in its place.

> Tom,
>
> We've asked you repeatedly to respect our abstinence and not leave beer on the premises. Perhaps this lesson will encourage understanding.
> Sincerely,
>
> Mike and Molly.
>
> P.S. Be sure to recycle.

In the sink sit the empty cans, in three rows of four.

I'll kill them. I'll wait right here until Molly comes through the door and I'll beat her to death with a copy of *Esquire*. If the shock of seeing that doesn't do Mike in, I'll toss him out the window. Crime of passion. You show me twelve guys in a jury box who wouldn't see my side of it. Acquittal, hell— they'll give me a standing O.

I scout around and come up with a little tequila from the back of the cupboard. Cut it with OJ and there might be enough for two sunrises. I sit at the kitchen table and curse my luck. Right now, at Finn's, Aisling Chara is tuning up for their first set. Right now my waitress is dancing with her drinks, working the crowd with that walk of hers, her thin bra showing hard through her shirt as she starts to sweat.

The phone rings and it's Dave. "Well?" he asks.

"I went down with the Angels. Everything's off."

"Damn."

"Hey, you feel like picking up some beer and coming over here? The Mets are playing on the coast tonight."

"Tell you what. I promised my cousin I'd meet a friend of hers for a drink. I'll come over right after that."

"Yeah, right. See you tomorrow, Dave."

"No, I mean it. This one's strictly pro bono—returning a favor. I've seen a picture of her, Tom. We're talking ten-dollar face. Give me a half hour to give her the slip."

Fifteen minutes later he's back on the line.

"Uh, Tom."

"What's up?"

"I have to pass on the Mets."

"What about the ten-buck face?"

"Turns out it comes with a thousand-dollar ass, Tom. And get this—she lives in the Bronx. I owe it to myself to give this one a shot."

Dave has vowed to land a girl from each of the five boroughs. Only the Bronx has eluded him.

"Tell you what, though. Brunch on me tomorrow. How 'bout the Polo Grounds at noon?"

"Sure."

"Thanks, Tom. Sorry about that. And wish me luck."

Dave's not sorry, and he doesn't need any of my luck. No point getting sore, though. Just because I'm stuck in here tonight is no reason for him to call off the hunt. Still, does the guy have to get laid every weekend? When you're not getting any action it doesn't help knowing guys who are, and right now Dave's giving Wilt Chamberlain a run for his money.

I cut Nabholz's picture out of *The Sporting News*, tape it over the bull's-eye, and start firing away. By 11 P.M. all that's left of him is the bill of his cap. The phone rings again. Don't tell me Dave struck out.

"Hello?"

"Well, I'll be. I figured I'd be talking to a machine. What are you doing home on a Friday night?"

Lisa! Wow.

"I'm broke. Lost my bet and my roommates dumped my beer. So here I am, alone, dreaming of my old girlfriend."

"Ha! Which one, I wonder? Careful, Reasons—you're getting me at a weak time. The date I had tonight makes you look like Mr. Considerate." She pauses. "You want to hear about it?"

Lisa has the best voice of any girl I know. Smooth and light, like water, and always just on the verge of laughter.

"Sure. Say, how about a late-night walk through the Village? It's beautiful tonight. I'll let you buy me an ice cream. Just for an hour, then I'll walk you home."

"You won't try and invite yourself up?"

"Sure I will."

Another pause. "Okay. Let's meet under the arch in Washington Square. In one hour. But no funny stuff, Tom."

I'm in and out of the shower, dressed, and down the stairs in five minutes. Only when I hit the end of the block do I realize I'm almost running. Whoa, there. No sense going round the bend over a little ice cream. I downshift, cruise the street a little slower.

Under the hood, though, the engine is revving.

CHAPTER EIGHT

LISA is my ex.

I broke it off almost a year ago and I'm starting to wonder if I blew it. Not that I'm ready to chuck the single life. Damn, though, hearing her voice was a shot to the gut. Must be all the pressure from this Duggan business. I just need to see a friendly face, I guess. Still . . .

I turn onto First Avenue and start downtown, my hands in my pockets. The night is muggy and hot and I wish I had a cold beer to press to my forehead. Through breaks in the buildings I can see the East River, and the lights of Brooklyn beyond.

The first time I saw Lisa Klein she was at a frat party dancing to "Sugar Magnolia." I stood at the top of the stairs, holding on to the rail after too much Jonestown punch. I spotted her right away. In some girls you can see the sex in their dancing. In Lisa I could see the joy. She lifted her dress as she moved, her thin legs so pretty. Joy and abandon and restraint all at once, as if she were letting herself go but holding back the best part of her. Soon the other dancers receded into a mass of gray, and she alone in the center had color and form. I couldn't look away.

She glanced up, tossed her brown hair and smiled. She couldn't have been looking at me but that's what it seemed like. By the time I made it down the stairs and through the pack, the song was over and she was gone. I woke the next morning with her face still in my head.

Asking around, I learned she was a transfer from Williams. The next semester we ended up in American Lit. together. We'd say hi before class or if we saw each other on the path, but it was a month before I screwed up the nerve to make a move on her. One Saturday night I found her next to me in the beer line at Psi U. She smiled.

"Hey, stranger. I'm Lisa Klein. I'm in your lit. class." She was a little drunk.

"H-hi. Tom Reasons."

She had the sweetest features. Her eyes, most of all. Wide and brown and searching, like they'd trapped a star.

"I guess I'm not much of a flirt, am I?" she said.

"Excuse me?"

She put her hand on my arm and leaned in close to talk over the music. Her mouth turned up a little—skeptical, but ready to smile. "I said I guess I'm not much of a flirt. I've been trying to catch your eye all semester."

She might as well have run a spear through me. I took her beer cup.

"You go ahead out on the porch," I said. "It's quiet out there. I'll get you a refill and join you."

"You don't mind waiting in line?"

"What's a few more minutes? I've waited all year for this."

She met my eyes and her smile as she walked away was

slow but sure, like a lover who knows what she's in for but is ready for it.

Out on the porch we got to talking about music and in five minutes I was gone on her. She looked in my face as I talked as if it were just the two of us on the planet. It's a quality I always loved in her. She might ask what I ate for lunch, and waiting on my answer you'd think she'd asked the key to the universe. Her eyes were so full and innocent. I always wanted to rise to the look in those eyes. To talk better, to think better, to bring her over to my side, if just for a second, just to see her smile and nod.

In no time the frat boys were packing up the speakers and turning us out. Her room was on the far side of campus, near mine, and I walked her home. At her dorm I asked her to dinner the next night and she said yes. As I started away she said quietly, "Aren't you going to try and kiss me?" She stood with her hands behind her back, trying to look casual, but her eyes gave her away. Teasing, but a little scared.

I've kissed Lisa a thousand times since and other girls besides, but that first one is the only kiss in my life I remember. It started soft and ended hard, and she shuddered when I pulled away, like a car engine when you turn it off.

Two weeks later we were at the door of her room. We'd been out twice and both of us knew it was coming. I had borrowed Jimmy's car and driven her to the top of Sunset Hill, where we shared a bottle of wine looking down on the valley. We kissed, but when I went for her shirt she stopped me and said, "Not here." Driving back to campus, it was all I could do to keep the car on the road. I'd been all semester without any one-on-one, and desperate isn't strong enough. If I saw a dog humping a table leg I'd stop to watch.

Lisa backed into her room, her eyes on me. There is a look that comes over a girl's face when she's going to let you in

and it is the sweetest look in the world. I popped the buttons
on her blouse from the bottom up. She was shaking as she
stepped out of her skirt, but her face was game.

I wish I could see a movie of that first fuck. It was something else. Most times in school you're just fumbling in the
dark. Drunk, looking over her shoulder, hell-bent on just
getting it done. Not us. We were face-to-face the whole time,
and if I close my eyes I can hear the catch in her breathing,
see the trust and fear in her face.

Getting it in took a little doing and when I did she gasped
and clenched her teeth, but when I started back out she said
No and grabbed me to her with her thin arms, pulling with
all she had. She didn't know what to do but she did it, setting herself for the thrusts, saying over and over, "Tell me we
can do this again, oh tell me we can do this again." And in
the middle of it, with her cries and her trust and the sweat
on that sweet face as I gave it to her, she said good-bye to
everything and threw in with me.

Good-bye to the backyard in Boston, to the fresh smell of
leaves in the fall and Dad leaning over the rake, tipping his
pipe as he finished up before the game. Good-bye to that,
and to her little brother too, and the cold New England days
running track as a girl. It was all still back there but she
could never have it again in the same way.

When we lay finished, we were a couple. She clung so
tight to my neck and wouldn't let me leave, not even to go to
the bathroom. I felt the tears on her cheek and lifted her
face with my hand.

"What's wrong?"

She bit her lip. "Nothing. It's my first time, that's all."

I rocked her and stroked her hair.

Those first weeks we wouldn't let each other out of bed to
go to class. Everyone should fall in love and get to fuck over

82

and over. We would do it and she'd say, "Tom, we'll do it again in an hour." I'd say okay and lie there thinking of nothing but doing it again and we'd do it and it would be just as good as before and we'd finish and already I'd be thinking about the next one. There weren't enough hours in the day.

And in the moments just after we finished, what peace. For the first time in my life my mind quit working. I'd look at the ceiling, and at Lisa, and I didn't have to say a damn thing.

My mistake was thinking it was just the fucking. I've been with enough girls since to know it wasn't the fucking. It was Lisa.

At Fourteenth Street I cut over and head west. Outside the Palladium I watch a rowdy line of kids liquor up before a concert. They get every last drop out of the wait, tossing their cans away at the final second, just before the bouncer pats them down and waves them inside. I move on.

We had us some times, I tell you. She was a DJ at the college radio station. When she worked the night shift I'd sneak into the control room to neck during the songs. Her voice was a killer anyway, but with my hand on her leg and my mouth in her ear, she drove half the campus nuts just reading a station break.

We came together on music. She had the best taste of any girl I've gone with. We'd argue the merits of the Doors versus Costello, or Marley versus the Cure. She was always wrong, of course, but she stuck to her guns. She knew rock 'n' roll was important. A lot of girls today, even girls in their twenties, couldn't care less. The last one I dated didn't own a single record. Can you believe that?

We were both big R.E.M. fans and they came to campus junior year. Bobby laid in an ounce of pot. I wasn't much of a toker, but with the concert and the whole gang lighting up

I said what the hell. By the time they took the stage in the old gym I was good and gone. Lisa and I were in the front row, swaying, when they broke into "So. Central Rain." She said yes with her eyes and I took her hand and led her down the back stairs and out behind the gym. It was November, cold and clear. Behind us was the football field, above us the stars. We were so high. I remember the joy of breathing in the cold air as I lifted her against the wall of the gym. I remember the music from the open window filling my head, and her face, just above me now, filling my sight. The band sang just for us and we took our time and our pleasure and there isn't a moment in life I was happier. If I ever meet Mr. Stipe, I'll thank him in person.

Sometimes what I liked best was the easy silence between us. Every other girl I've gone with got spooked if I didn't keep up the talk. I'm quiet for thirty seconds, it's time to haul out the relationship and discuss it. Some mornings with Lisa we'd wake, go at it, then dress and walk to brunch, picking up a paper on the way. Twenty minutes later I'd point out something on the sports page and she'd laugh and say, "Reasons, that's the first word you've said to me all day."

I cross Cooper Square, slowing to watch a mime, who stands dead-still till a crowd gathers round, then bends in smooth movements like a robot and whirs like a mechanical toy. I drop change in his cup and he straightens to salute me as I move on.

In some ways we were night and day. I'm not happy unless there's a game on and Lisa can't tell a football from a hockey puck. She comes from a family of Boston democrats, calls her dad every week to talk politics. She could probably name her district treasurer, while I couldn't pick my congressman out of a lineup. You should have seen us trying to rent a movie. I'd always want *Cool Hand Luke* again and she'd reach for some weeper. We'd veto each other for an hour and wind up flipping a coin.

None of that stuff mattered worth a damn. A lot of couples, it's all about control. Force him to give up this, get her to do that. There was none of that with us. We wanted each other happy, and if a case of beer and a Met game did the trick, she'd order the case and lie in my lap during the game. As for me, I must have sat through twenty debates and a dozen poetry readings. Let me sneak in a few beers and sit beside her and I could get through any lecture.

So what happened? Christ if I know. Last semester senior year I started getting jumpy. Jimmy's wedding was in the works and graduation was just round the corner. I felt the world closing in. I should have turned to Lisa, but I turned away. Spent more time with the fellas and less with her. Wasn't so quick to call back when she phoned. All the little things guys do when we're being pricks. Nothing drastic. I sure didn't want to split, and I never told her anything was wrong. She could sense it, though. One day she put her face to mine and said, "Tom, what's wrong? Tell me." I couldn't take the look in her eyes. I said nothing was wrong and held her.

We made it through to graduation and a little after but then the wheels came off. I was twenty-two, just starting at the firm, and spring was in the air. One look at the secretaries spilling into the Seaport that first lunch hour and I knew something had to give.

Listen, I could give you a lot of cock-and-bull, but the truth is this: I couldn't see fucking one girl the rest of my life. I didn't want to break up with Lisa so much as roll things back. Try my luck on the open market awhile. Get while the getting's good, you know.

How the hell do you tell a girl that, though? You can't, of

course. I stammered something about needing space and exploring myself. It was awful.

She took my face in her hands and said, "You tell me, Tom, that you don't love me. You tell me you want to go find someone else."

I tried to look away. "Lisa, it's not that . . ."

She held my face tight. "You tell me. I deserve that. Don't you think I know what you want? You want to comparison shop. And you want me to give the okay. Well, I won't do it. You're a bastard, Tom. From the first I loved you all the way, and everyone knew it. I'm no weekend girl. You want to walk out on me, you walk out all the way."

I couldn't. But I couldn't tell her what she needed, either. We limped along for a few more weeks.

It didn't help that her roommates were determined to sink me. Christ. If you're on the outs with a girl and her friends get ahold of her, you're a goner. They get her on her own and fill her ear with all the ways you don't measure up. He said that? He did what? Don't you let him get away with that! Once the blood is in the water they come full-bore.

The end came one weekend when her roommates were out of town. I was over at her place. We hadn't fucked in weeks. It was one of those miserable nights at the end of a relationship, when neither of you has the heart to talk about the breakup but you can't talk about anything else. We ate in silence, then sat at each end of the couch trying to watch a movie. A love scene came on and Lisa started to cry. On the screen was what we used to have and now we weren't close. We both knew there was no saving us. This was our last night.

I stood to go, our eyes met, and suddenly our misery broke like a fever. I hit the light switch and we tore into each other. We'd done some fucking in our two years but nothing like that. We were murderous and tender at the same time, driving each other crazy but making it hurt. If she said no I said yes and went in, and when it was her turn she damn near took it off. When we finished she wouldn't lie against me. She huddled on her side of the bed, sobbing.

The next morning we sat on the steps of the Natural History museum. The wind was up and it was cold. I started to say something three times, but the one thing she needed to hear I didn't have in me to say. Finally she said, "I don't want you to call me," and walked away.

I must have sat by myself an hour, thinking over and over of the night we met. At last I walked down the stairs and into the first Irish joint I could find. Ordered a pint and a shot of whisky. From the jukebox came the first piano strains and then Paul started in with "Once there was a way, to get back homeward." Christ, a song can break your heart sometimes.

Those first weeks after the split I missed her so damn much I could feel her next to me at night, like they say a sailor can feel the ocean when he first sleeps on land. I called her place a few times but one of the guard dogs would answer and say she wasn't in. She never called back.

On West Fourth Street I pass a trio of kids breaking to Public Enemy on a piece of cardboard, their hands and feet almost faster than the eye. Up the block a guy turns a box on its side and sets up three-card monte. His patter and quick hands form an orbit, and a couple college kids pause on the edge, teeter, and are drawn in. I watch them lose and move on.

It's been almost a year since I threw her over, and like I said I'm starting to wonder if I blew it. Maybe it's some of the dates I've been on. Lisa was my first real girl. Seeing what's out there is sobering me up a little.

Not counting the one-nighters, I've gone with two girls since the split. Well, I shouldn't count Cindy either, since

we knew from the start it wouldn't last. We just needed the
sex. I'd been dry three months at that point and was about in
the market for a blow-up doll. I know just how an alkie feels
when he goes cold turkey. Even he has it a little better,
though, because if he ever wants to jump off the wagon at
least he knows he can get himself a fix.

Anyway, I was dying, and Cindy must have been in the
same boat, because five minutes into the first dinner it was
clear we had nothing in common, but we wound up back at
her place just the same. Somehow we reached an unspoken
understanding that though we had no future and could
barely take each other's company, we both had some making
up to do in the fucking department. And make up we did.

We met twice a week. Before long we dropped the charade
of going to a movie or the ballpark. Just met at her place and
put each other through the paces. By the end we didn't even
bother with dinner. I'd show up at ten thirty, we'd go at it a
few hours, and I'd leave. After two months we'd had our fill,
shook hands and went our separate ways. If I ran into her
tonight, I doubt I'd recognize her.

Debbie was a different case. We lasted a month. I told myself up and down what a sweet girl she was. And she was.
Studying to be a vet. Nice to talk to, and a real looker besides. Liked a Friday night at Shea and a few drinks after-
ward. Not a thing wrong with her. Except she bored me stiff.
And the sex just wasn't the same. Not that she didn't know
her way around a bed. It wasn't that—she'd try anything.

But with Debbie . . . well . . . I wanted her all right, but
the second I'd done my part my mind was out of there, wondering who's on the cover of *Sports Illustrated* or who's starting for the Mets tomorrow. It was all I could do to sweet-talk
her a little after the act. Got to the point I'd put *SportsCenter* on before I jumped her just to have something to tune

into when we finished. A few times I even put my hand over her mouth to hear the scores. I'm a bastard, maybe, but what can you do? The feeling's there or it isn't. You can't make it up. Through it all she bought me sweaters and called twice a day just to say she was thinking of me. I broke it off three months ago and haven't thought of her since.

Since then it's been Kay's cousin and a couple of late-night specials I'd just as soon forget. All of which gets me to thinking about Lisa more and more. Don't get me wrong—I like the thrill of the hunt, and there's nothing quite like landing a long shot. But with most girls you get one thing but not another. She might be great in the sack but you can't talk to her, or maybe she's fine to talk to and okay under the covers but she thinks four times a week is plenty. Or she's got no sense of humor, or can't stand the guys. It's always a trade-off.

With Lisa, though, I had it all. Not just sex but the eyes behind the liner, the soul beneath the blouse.

Now I've got my freedom, but what's it worth? What's the good of being free to go after any girl I want if none of them makes me feel like she did?

A few months back Lisa finally called. She sounded great, too. The laugh was back in her voice, though with a little catch to it. She kept the talk friendly. Just wanted to see how I'd been, let me know her job was going well. We met for cof-fee a month later and I've seen her twice since. Always when she wants to. I'm going real slow. She still has her defenses up, and she gets her digs in if I try to get too casual. That's okay. I hurt her bad, I know, and right now I'm still the en-emy in a lot of ways. Little by little, though, I think she's coming around. Meeting me tonight is a good sign.

At the entrance to the park I turn down three offers of pot. One dealer walks halfway across the grass with me, waving a joint in my eyes, saying I won't find no better stuff, man. Won't take no for an answer. Used to be these guys had manners. They'd wait politely while you sampled their stuff and thank you for your time.

At twenty yards I see Lisa under the arch, crisp as dawn. She watches a folk singer in that intense way she has, and from the way he glances up while he plays it's clear this one's for her. She doesn't see me, so I stop a second to watch her. Damn, she looks good. A cotton dress, a red sweater, my favorite black hair band.

Looking at her face I get the pitchfork in the gut again. In some you can see the weak spot, the place it will fall in with time. Hers will stand every test. I shake my head. Some fisherman you would make, Tom. Throwing back a keeper.

She sees me when I'm almost on her and gives me her cheek. The old look, but turned down a little. She puts a dollar in the guitar case of the singer and he follows us with a mournful stare as we start off east along St. Mark's.

Friday night in the Village—what a scene. Bald women and guys with hair to their asses. Kids with pierced lips and fruits in full flower. Music from a hundred boxes. Reggae to punk to Sinatra in half a block. I wonder what Dad would say about this crowd. As we stop to check out a T-shirt stand Lisa tells me about her night.

"A stockbroker, Tom. I don't know what I was thinking. Maybe I figured the last two were such losers, this one would have to be a nice guy."

The last two?

"At the least I thought I could count on a good meal. Tom, this guy sits across from me in Elaine's and actually tells me how much you-know-what he's getting."

I laugh. "There's an icebreaker. I'll remember that."

She punches my arm. "Then, at the end of the night, he

90

can't believe I won't let him up. Stands there with his foot in the elevator and a stupid grin, saying, 'Do you know how many women are dying to go out with me?' I told him one less than he thinks and ran up the stairs."

We walk on, past the outdoor cafés and jewelry booths. "Well, after a guy like that I must look pretty good, huh?" She gives me her skeptical smile.

"You're okay for a little conversation once in a while. So tell me about the gang. How are Linda and Jimmy?"

"Pretty grim. Extended cease-fires marred by occasional hand-to-hand combat."

"That's terrible." Lisa's eyes show her hurt. "How about Bobby and Tank? And Dave—tell me he's got a girlfriend."

"Several, and working on a new one tonight."

I fill Lisa in on the whole gang, on the darts championship and Stella. On Mike and Molly and the new case at the firm. I leave out Duggan. No sense getting into that. She tells me about her job at the PR company. It's okay except for the glass ceiling, and her scuzzy boss, who's always hugging her at the slightest excuse. She thinks maybe she'll go back to school, if only to kill time till she sorts out in her head what she really wants to do. Her folks are in town from Boston tomorrow and have promised her dinner and a show.

"Your dad must be pretty psyched that I'm not in the picture anymore."

She starts to blush. "Oh, stop. Dad forgot about that a long time ago."

Not likely. Lisa's dad is a great guy but he doesn't have much use for me. One time while I stayed with them over break, he ducked into the garage for a late-night smoke and surprised us on the hood of his Buick. He's hated me ever since, and I can't say I blame him. No man should have to see his daughter getting fucked.

She tosses her hair and half looks at me, dipping her head.
"So," she asks, "you seeing anybody?"
"Nobody."
"Really nobody? Or a lot of nobodies?"
"Nobody."
Who's going to quibble about a score or two?
It's 1:30 A.M. when we end up in front of her building.
We've been walking for two hours. She pats my arm and
gives a weary smile.
"Don't spoil a good night, Reasons."
"We'll do this again soon?"
"We'll see."
At the elevator she turns and waves. Seeing her there
alone, that brave smile on her, I swallow hard. Damn, I miss
her. I want her on my shoulder again, and more. I want to
wake to her in the morning. A year ago we did everything
and now she's off limits. I can't even take her hand when we
walk. Serves me right, I know. Patience, Tom.
It's never been one of my strong suits, but I need it right
now. Because I can see in her face and hear in her voice that
she's starting to forgive me. I just have to sweat it out.
As I walk home my mood comes around. Just seeing Lisa
again did me good. So what if I'm out of money. There's always next week, and maybe next week I'll pick a winner, and
maybe when I do I'll call Lisa and offer to take her some-
place nice. She'll say yes, I'm sure.
I turn onto Second Avenue, stop and stare at myself in a
shop window. Okay, Tom. Time to quit dodging the big one.
Duggan. What the hell do I do about this mess? I set my jaw.
Okay. Strip the problem to its essence and lay it out.
I bet twenty grand on a dart match and doubled it to forty.
I've got to come up with the dough in two weeks or scrap the
match.

Point one. Scrapping the match is not an option. I could never go to Duggan now and chicken out. I wouldn't give the bastard the satisfaction. Then, too, there's the little matter of my ass. You never know who these Irish guys are connected to, especially in Hell's Kitchen. Besides, we can win this match. I know we can. We beat 'em once, we can do it again.

Okay, so we play the match. Now I've reduced it to a fund-raising problem. Point two. How do I raise forty thousand bucks in two weeks? As I walk along Fourteenth Street I pass two banks before stopping cold at the third one. I laugh out loud at the simplicity of it.

I'll get a loan.

Why didn't I think of it before? This is America, after all. Isn't every Tom, Dick, and Harry doing it, every day? Guys with a lot less on the ball than me, hatching schemes and getting money thrown at them. I'm bright, fit, gainfully employed by a top New York firm. What's to stop me from doing the same? That's what banks are here for, right? To invest in human potential? Turn ideas into gold? I can hear the radio ads now—"Our dollars for your dreams."

And I can hear my pitch tomorrow morning. Give him a little Horatio Alger. I can't tell him it's for a bet, of course, but I'll come up with something. Some grand vision, and for a little faith and a little capital I'll let Citibank in on the ground floor. After all, it's not so much the project as myself I'll be selling. And what's forty grand next to a man's character?

That settles it. My branch has Saturday hours. First thing in the morning I'll put on my suit and tie and knock them dead. I look up at the dark windows in the buildings all around me. Sleeping somewhere in this city right now is a loan officer who's in for more than he can handle.

Turning onto my block I run into old man Kretzky and his creaky dachshund, Bullet, who snorts happily and shakes his belly at the sight of me. Kretzky leans on his cane and eyes me gruffly.

"Out carousing again, son?"

"No, sir. Just a good summer walk."

He looks at me suspiciously. "You're not drunk?"

"No, sir."

"*Humpf.* You young people today—that's all you want to do. Stay out late, drink, play your music. Not one of you knows what it means to put in an honest day's work."

"No, sir."

At the steps he gives me Bullet's leash and leans on my arm. "Fifty years I been on this block, son. Watched a hundred kids like you come and go. Seen you coming in drunk, bringing in girls. What kind of girl goes back to a man's place at night? Tell me that, son. What kind of girl goes to a bar, anyway?"

"Times change, sir."

"The hell they do. Church, son. That's where you meet a girl. Church."

"Yes, sir."

Kretzky has outlived everyone he knows so I let him blow off steam once in a while. It does him good. He's been in his fifth-floor walk-up forever. Must pay about a hundred bucks in rent. The landlord can't wait for him to kick off so he can jack it up ten times, but the guy keeps right on going. He's doing better than old Bullet, that's for sure. During the week I walk Bullet a few times to give the old man a break. The dog can make it up one set of stairs but you have to carry him the rest of the way. On the second landing I pick him up and he licks my face.

Kretzky's apartment is down the hall from ours. When the

music's too loud for him he throws a rubber ball against our door. Every so often he'll have me in for a whisky and tell me the problem with us kids. It's always the same lecture. Lazy, no drive, ought to bring back conscription to make men out of us. Tonight he gives me the short version.

"I'll tell you something, son. You kids bitch and moan, but the world is the same pie it's always been. The problem with you is you want somebody to hand you your slice. Get out there and work for it like we did! That's what I say."

"Yes, sir. Good night, sir."

Inside, I brush my teeth and throw a few darts to wind down. I'm still pumped from the night with Lisa and the loan idea. I gather up the empty beer cans and divide them between Molly's and Mike's underwear drawers.

In bed I start to plot my strategy for the bank tomorrow. Remember, Tom—creativity. Initiative. Onward and upward. Drifting off, I think of Lisa and her cotton dress. It must be off her by now. Hanging from a peg on her door, I'll bet. With her sleeping just a few feet away. The window open a crack, as always, Bach turned low on the tape player.

Sweet dreams.

CHAPTER NINE

MR. REASONS, do you know what collateral is?"

"I think so—sure."

Ten minutes into the loan session and things aren't going quite as planned.

"Perhaps I should spell it out for you. Just so there is no misunderstanding."

You should see this guy. A real hat rack. Thin and pale, with a forehead you could land a plane on.

"Collateral serves to guarantee a loan. Typically it is a house or apartment, sometimes a car. Something of value you put up against your loan to ensure repayment. You default on the loan, we gain title to the apartment or car. Is that all clear?"

"Yes, sir."

"Your problem, Mr. Reasons, is one of collateral. To be blunt, your problem is that you have nothing we want."

Just my luck to draw a hard-ass. I come in all nice and po-
lite, in my best suit, and as soon as I mention a loan he starts
in on me. I'm hardly into my pitch before he's playing
Twenty Questions. Wants to know if I've ever applied for a
bank loan before. Like that makes a difference. Wants to
know the last time I had a credit check run on me. Whatever
that is. Wants to know the status of my student loan. Beats
me. I stopped reading their letters six months ago, when
they turned nasty. I start to fidget.

"One thing we look for in an applicant, Mr. Reasons, is
what we call a credit history. Some indication that they have
borrowed before and made good on it. Now we understand
that some applicants will be borrowing for the first time, but
I should warn you that your profile as a borrower is not en-
couraging. Let's call up your account on the screen, shall
we, and see what we have to work with."

Uh-oh. He pushes a few buttons, looks at the screen, then
back at me with a tight smile.

"According to this, Mr. Reasons, your average balance
over the past year has been two hundred twenty-seven dollars. Currently it stands at, ahem, twelve dollars."

I try to explain I like to keep a lot of cash on hand, but I'm
losing him. I try a different tack.

"Okay, sir. I understand you've got to give some weight to
all that technical stuff. But can we set appearances aside for
a second? Forget about money, about apartments or cars.
What you're really investing in here is my character, right?
And the strength of my idea. If you're willing to give me capital it's because you believe in my capacity to make it grow.
And isn't that capacity more a function of my drive, my initiative, my spirit, if you will, than whether or not I own a
house or a car?"

He smiles like you would at the boss's brat climbing over your good furniture. "Just the same, Mr. Reasons, we feel better seeing the house or the car."

"Well, I don't have the house or the car. I'll grant you that. But I do have a solid-gold idea. And I'd hate to see you lose out on it because of a silly formality."

He taps his pen on the back of his hand.

"In a hundred words or less, Mr. Reasons, run this idea by me again. Some kind of hot-dog stand, was it?"

I lean forward.

"Not a hot-dog stand—a life stand. Mobile, like the hot-dog carts, but instead of franks you carry yuppie products. Splits of champagne, designer belts, quiche. Whatever they're buying these days. And here's the kicker—instead of grubby guys in aprons, the stands are worked by babes. Babes in high heels and low-cuts, with a lot to show and none too shy about showing it, if you get my drift. The execs will climb over each other to spend their money there, sir. Put two in the financial district, two in midtown, then just sit back and count the money."

His expression doesn't change.

"I'm underwhelmed," he says.

I can see I'm getting nowhere, and when he starts to stand, I swing for the fences.

"Okay, sir, I'll cut the crap. The yuppie life stand is a crock. I made it up to impress you. It's clear that didn't happen, so let's talk business here." His eyes narrow.

"I really need the money for what you might call a short-term, high-yield speculative venture that's a lock to succeed. Now I don't know if they got you on commission here or what, but you front me the forty thousand today, I'll come back through the door with, say, forty-four thousand in two weeks. That's a nice little profit for the branch—or for you."

I spread my hands. "I'm sure not going to ask where it goes."
I smile. "I make out okay and so do you, and all because you
stepped away from the forms and procedures for a minute
and went with your gut. What do you say?"

He stands. "I say thank you for an amusing morning, Mr.
Reasons. Unfortunately, Citibank is not in the habit of
bankrolling short-term, highly speculative ventures for parties with no credit, no collateral, and twelve dollars in the
bank. Now if you'll excuse me—"

"Just a minute, sir. Forty thousand isn't cut in stone. Let's
knock it down to twenty, and up your cut to five grand.
Surely you can swing that?"

He straightens and talks down his nose. "We are not a
Hong Kong tailor, Mr. Reasons. We don't bargain. Good
day." He marches off.

Back on the street I'm steamed. To think I got up at seven
on a Saturday for that prick. No wonder bankers take so
much shit. Give them a chance to do a little business and
they hide behind procedure. And where does he get off talking to me like that, anyway? He isn't much older than I am.
I should have taken a swing at him. Don't think I don't know
his type. I saw them every day at school. Probably an Alpha
Delta, with a major in BS and a minor in kissing ass. Crois-
sants every morning, reads *The Wall Street Journal* on the
can. Well, screw him. I wouldn't take his money if he chased
me down the street with it.

Man, though, what do I do now? I don't panic easy, but this
is getting serious. Two weeks till game day and not a dollar in
sight. I start down the block. Johnny, the cripple by the subway, shakes his cup at me and I give him my change. I walk
in a long arc, down Second Avenue for five blocks and back
up Third. All right, Tom, think it out. What are my options?

Getting it from the family is out. Dad doesn't have that

kind of dough, and if he did, what the hell could I tell him I need it for? Anyway, I wouldn't go to Dad for this. The gang? Nothing doing. None of them have any real money. I might have been able to bring them in for a grand or so apiece, but the little white lie I told last night scotched any chance of that.

You see, I called everyone on the team and they're all on board for the match. The only thing I fudged on was the stake. They think it's for pizza and beer. I should have fessed up, maybe, but they'd piss themselves if they knew the truth. Even if they agreed to play, the pressure of that kind of money would sink their game, and if we're going to win this one, I need them throwing nice and easy.

Besides, no way Duggan told his team what they're playing for. He'd have to spread some of the dough around and that's not his style. I don't doubt he can raise it, though. He's a bartender, and these Irish bartenders are something else. They all talk like they're worth ten bucks, but when they're up against it they got a stash somewhere, or know someone who does. I've seen it a dozen times. Friday night they hit you up for cab fare and Sunday they open their own place. Just once I'd like to get a look at their tax returns.

An hour of walking up and down and still I'm stumped. Even Johnny stops shaking his cup and wants to know what's on my mind. Same thing as on his, really—raising a little capital. I turn it around and around in my head. I stop in at a bodega for a lottery ticket, pick two numbers, crumple it up and toss it away. I'm licked. I need a second opinion.

I start uptown, for good this time. Only one guy to go to on this one. Only one guy who won't tell me I'm nuts. Hell, he'll like the adventure of it. Dave is that guy, of course, and it just so happens he's buying me lunch today. I go over it all again in my head on the walk up, and by the time I reach the

Upper East Side I'm set to confide. Not over lunch, though. This is one problem that will sound a lot better at night, with a few beers in the both of us.

I walk into the Polo Grounds, where the pretty young grads in shorts and the smell of beer lift my spirits. Any game you'd ever want to see is on one of the ten tubes surrounding the main room. I spot Dave. He's commandeered a table in the middle of the action, with a clear view of the ladies' room. He has a pint in front of him and one ready for me. He looks a little hung over but otherwise his chipper self. I take a seat.

"Why the suit, Tom?"

"I had to pop into the office."

He slides me my pint.

"Cheers," he says. "So, you want the good news first or the bad news?"

"Give me the bad news."

"Two-Hundred-Tenth Street, Inwood Park, is not technically the Bronx. People who live there call it the Bronx, but I checked the zoning laws this morning and it's actually in the borough of Manhattan."

"And the good news?"

"The good news is that state schools are still turning out young women who know how to fuck. I'm telling you, Tom, this girl must have gone on a scholarship. Sorry to blow you off, but you'll be glad to know it was worth it."

I'm tempted to take advantage of Dave's spirits and spill the beans, but I hold off. Instead I lead up to it.

"Dave, I got a problem I need your help with."

"Lay it out."

"I'm in a little deep on something, and I'm not sure how to get out. This isn't the place to talk about it, though. Any chance you could come over tonight? It won't take long."

"You bet. I'll bring some beer. Would you call it a twelve-pack problem or a case?"

"If I didn't live in a walk-up, Dave, I'd say it's more like a kegger."

"Now you got me interested. Don't sweat it. I'll be there at nine." Dave motions to the ladies' room. " You see the one coming out? See the new coat of lipstick? She's seen some-one in here she likes. I don't think it's a stretch to assume it's me."

I shake my head.

"Dave, you just shared the most sacred act two people can share. Surely you won't cheapen that union by starting in on someone else this morning?"

He smiles and tosses back his beer. "You can't get caught up in nostalgia, Tom. Another day, another dolly."

After lunch I leave Dave to make his move and head home for a nap. Most Saturdays I'm just getting up about now. I put the Yanks on the tube and drift off.

TEN P.M. AND I'M still waiting for Dave. I'd kill for a drink but the place is dry. I put *Making Movies* on the stereo and sit in the open window with a soda, one leg out on the fire escape. I love looking out at the city to music. I love the smell of the air, and the sounds of Saturday night. I lived in the suburbs once. Five families on the whole block and you never saw any of them. Here I can look across the way and see into a dozen lives. Tonight I watch the mamacitas lean out their windows in shirtsleeves, shouting to each other or to their kids in the street below. I watch the old guy drop onto the sofa with a beer and play with the ears of his dog, and the girl two floors up come to the window in her nightshirt and pull the shade.

I'll bet two thousand people live on this block. There's always a little of everything in the air. Sadness and laughter and sex. Looking out on it makes me feel a part of things. Tonight, watching the kids play soccer in the street, "Skate-away" coming through the speakers, I feel strangely confident, as if all the answers I need are out there, and it's just up to me to find them. I glance at the clock. Dave's more than an hour late, but I'm not worried. I know Dave. He'll show.

CHAPTER TEN

DAVE CAVANAUGH is the friend I'd call from jail. Chances are, though, one of his schemes would have landed me there.

Dave's never been a big fan of doing things by the book. Where's the thrill in that? No, the fun in life, to him, is seeing what you can get away with. This leads him into some fine scrapes, but it also makes him the guy to turn to when you're up a tree.

He was my roommate freshman year and I'd never met anyone like him. Back on the base, you solved a problem by hitting the other guy harder than he hit you. Dave, though, could figure the angle on anything. The sorority party is invite only? He knew a way in the side door. The big concert is a sellout? He could come up with two on the floor. Out of beer and the stores are closed? Here comes Dave, wheeling a keg.

Dave was born for college. All that free time and no parents around to crumb the deal. Christ, what a spread, too. Bars to close, frats to pick from, a whole new set of fellas for poker and road trips. Pony races a mile up the road and a golf course, can you believe it, right on the grounds. Dave never considered a day official until he'd put in his nine holes. The topper, of course, was the girls. Eight hundred fifty of them, between seventeen and twenty-one, and each handed a primer on birth control, pictures and all, along with her room key, at Orientation.

The only hitch to the whole setup was the damn classes. Dave had nothing against them as a concept, but where was a guy supposed to find the time?

His solution was to compress each semester into three weeks. That way, he could factor classes right out of the equation in the early going. Through Thanksgiving he lived at the pub, the racetrack, and the frats, training his efforts on the one subject he never tired of: getting his end in.

Then as now, Dave sure had a way with the girls. Call it charm or luck or whatever you like, but three weeks into freshman year, while the rest of us still pored through the face book, trying to gauge from their smiles which ones might give it a go, Dave was serving it to the senior who tutored him in French. And nights he wasn't in her room he was kicking me out of ours for some fling after a frat party, all the while, of course, insisting that Julie, from back home, was the only girl he was serious about. Julie was a freshman at Amherst, though, and he could only see her once a month. "I love her and all," he'd say, "but I'm no monk." To Dave, getting a little on the side wasn't cheating. It was a matter of survival.

Weekends when Julie came to visit the fun really started. The whole gang became lookouts, fanning out at frat parties like the Secret Service. If we spotted one of his squeezes in the area we'd give the signal and he'd hustle Julie out of there.

At a state school Dave might have pulled off this arrangement all four years. Ham Tech was just too small, though. You couldn't string too many girls along without one of them getting wind of it. The campus girls all found out about Julie and in the end she found out about them, too, and called things off, leaving Dave high and dry for a time, mumbling about the unfairness of it all. "Fidelity, fidelity," he'd gripe, crossing a few more names out of his book. "That's all anyone wants to talk about."

You'd think Dave would have run out of girls pretty quick in a school our size. That was the kicker, though. Even the ones who caught him dead to rights couldn't stay mad at him, and a few he actually charmed back into the sack. It was the damnedest thing. I'd see him at a dorm party with a girl who dumped him months before, and he's saying, "Tracy, you were right to send me packing. What I did was inexcusable. Lied to you, ran around. You dumped me and I deserved it. That you're even talking to me now is a miracle . . ." and so on, and she's watching him with a wary smile, knowing just what he's up to, but twenty minutes later she's still there, and Dave's saying, "I won't insult you by saying I've cut *all* that stuff out, but I think a guy knows when he's changed, and you still do have the best, and I mean the best eyes since Mom, and if you want to pop up to my room—it's just up the stairs here—I can make us drinks and put on that album you liked and we can dance one last dance, for old times' sake, just to show we came through everything as friends. Or I could walk you home—it's up to you." Damned if she didn't go upstairs, and damned if she came out before the morning.

As you can imagine, though, all those hours chasing the

finer things in life left Dave pretty hard up academically by the time the end of each term rolled around. Boy, could he ever fall behind. I might owe five hundred pages of Poli Sci myself, and start to feel low about it, but then Dave would walk into the room, sigh, say, "I guess it's about that time, Tom," and head off to the bookstore, three months late, to pick up his texts.

Anyone else would have thrown in the towel, but Dave was always at his best when he had to scramble.

He was the king of the late rally, and it was a treat to watch him operate. From Thanksgiving till the end of the term he lived on coffee and uppers, and he pulled out all the stops. Paid nerds from each class ten bucks an hour to tutor him. Combed frat files for exams and papers from the year before. Played audio Cliffs Notes over and over on the stereo, switching to headphones when he began to nod off, convinced of the subliminal payoff.

Then there was his specialty—pleading extensions. Or Cavanaughs, as we renamed them in his honor. No one could plead them quite like Dave. One term he lined up five in five days, two from the same prof. Dave came from a big Catholic family, and toward the finish of each semester they'd start dropping right and left, each good for an extra couple of days on a paper or test. By junior year it got so complicated that he needed a chart to keep track of which relation had died for which prof. His grandfather had it the roughest, kicking off so many times in Dave's four years that when he showed for graduation the whole frat lined up to shake his hand.

Dave wasn't above a little brownnosing, either. Most guys duck the prof when they're bottoming out in class. Not him. One of his theories was that he could let a lot of schoolwork slide if he kept in good with his teachers. He might not have made a lecture in a month, but he'd always stop and chat if he saw a teacher on the path. Knew the books they were working on, their hobbies, their favorite vacation spots. He'd even drop by their offices just to say hi. All to get that break somewhere down the line—the hint about the quiz, the extension on the paper, the benefit of the doubt on the grade.

One time during finals week Tank and I hit the links for a quick round. Who do we see on the first tee but Dave and the Ancient Civ prof, old man Bosworth. Dave's carrying a D in the course, the final is in forty-eight hours, and he's read fifty of a thousand assigned pages. No matter. He puts in nine holes with him and sure enough, maybe with a chuckle after his first birdie in years, or after dropping one a foot from the flag, Bosworth says something like, "Well, I can't be telling you what's on the final, of course, but if I were a student, Mr. Cavanaugh, I would know the Socrates chapter inside out." Bingo.

And when each term was over, when report cards came out and we all met at the pub with long faces to take a body count, Dave would drop his Bs on the table and spring for the first round. Never failed.

HE COMES THROUGH the door tonight with a case of beer on his shoulder and drops it on the kitchen table.

"Sorry I'm late, Tom. Friday night, you know."

"No sweat."

I pour beer into frosted mugs and we move to the living room. Dave drops into a chair.

"Tom, I've been trying to puzzle this one out all day and there's only one thing I can think of."

"Nobody's pregnant."

"Then I'm stumped."

I sit on the arm of the couch and give Dave the lowdown.

From the top, starting with Duggan's challenge, the doubling of the bet, through to the wipeout at the bank today. When I finish he lets out a low whistle.

"Not bad, Tom."

"Thanks."

"Nothing we can't handle, though. How much do you have in the bank?"

"Twelve bucks."

"Hmmm. First off, I don't have a lot more. Dad's laying out for the apartment through B-school, but he's pulled in the reins on the allowance. It barely keeps me in beer."

"Forget it, Dave. I don't want you mixing up your own money in this. I think we should shoot for outside revenue. But one thing—we gotta play this match."

He looks offended. "Of course. Hell, we can beat these guys."

It's good to have Dave aboard.

"Have you told anyone but me?" he asks.

"No."

"Good. You're not thinking of telling the team about the bet, are you?"

"Probably not."

"Definitely not. Even if you fronted all the money, they'd be too spooked to play at those stakes."

"That's what I think."

"Any chance Duggan will tell his troops?"

"None. He's too cheap."

"Okay. What kind of credit do you have, Tom?"

"Zip."

"Well, that's step one. My brother works for MasterCard. Has some say over the applications. I'll give him a call in the morning, get him to get you a card. He can rush it along, maybe get it to you in a few days. And one with a good limit."

"How good?"

"Maybe ten grand."

"That would be a hell of a start."

"Something else, Tom. We have to assume going in that we'll win the match, so we only need the money for a short time, right?"

"Right."

"Okay. A few things are starting to bubble up here." He taps his head. "Give me the weekend to sort it out. You work your end, see what you can dream up."

We settle back with our beers. By three o'clock we've almost killed the case and both of us are good and buzzed. Dave looks at me with a smile.

"There's still a little night left, Tom. I know a place up the block—Gino's. Let's go celebrate the ass-kicking we're going to give Duggan."

"Gotta pass tonight. I'm broke."

"I'll spot you."

I don't need a lot of convincing. As we step into the hallway, I hear Kretzky's door open to the end of the chain. I try to make it around the corner but he sees me. He shakes his gray head.

"Good night, sir," I mumble as we hit the stairs.

THE WAY THESE after-hour joints work is one of life's great mysteries. From the street many of them are just a door. You buzz on the intercom, give the password and they ring you in. Their location can change from month to month, even week to week, and how word of them gets round and people learn the passwords is beyond me. I leave it all up to Dave. On any given night, no matter where we are, he seems to know one around the corner. At the door to Gino's he rings the buzzer.

110

"Password?" comes a voice.

"The end of history," Dave says.

They ring us in.

A long set of stairs leads to another door guarded by a big guy in a suit. He gives us the once-over, then waves us in.

Gino's is a lot classier than our usual late-night haunts. The people at the clubs we tend to wind up in are the ones caught short by last call, drunk but not ready to pack it in. Here it's the tonier set, the ones who ate dinner at midnight and are making their first stop on the early-morning circuit. That explains the ten-buck cover and five-dollar Buds. At these prices we can't afford to stay long.

The place has the look of an old speakeasy. We stand in the main room, which features a pool table, cheap art on the walls, and one-man bars in the corners. A quick scan and it's clear the payoff for the high prices comes in the babes. The room is loaded with them.

"There's some talent here, huh?" Dave says. "Here's a ten, in case you need to buy a lady a drink. I'm off to find Cinderella."

I buy a drink and take another look around. There's nothing like a roomful of beautiful girls late at night, when you have a head full of beer. None gives me an opening, so I wander the room, passing close behind a couple for a whiff of their hair. Walking to the next room I pass Dave, who's explaining to a pert blonde that he needs just a dozen more hours of flight time before his license comes through.

The second room is smaller but less crowded than the first. Tom Waits sings from the stereo, and the music and the jazz lighting and the smoke make me feel I've stepped into a dime novel from the fifties. Without much dinner in me I'm really feeling the beers, riding a peaceful, late-night buzz, content to look at the necks of the girls and laze in the swirl of the music. The Duggan bet drifts right out of the room. With Dave on board I feel much better about it, and I've always had a talent for letting problems out of my mind when they get too much for me. Being loaded helps.

Through my reverie I notice a small crowd in the far corner. They all seem to be gathered around something, but I can't see past them to see what it is. I float over, doing a half-turn to the music, dipping my shoulder, mumbling along, "The bartenders all know my name. And they catch me when I'm pulling up lame." I get a little closer, and when a break in the crowd gives me a view I almost drop my beer. I edge forward. Could it be a joke? I look down at the floor, up at the ceiling, and back in front of me. It's no joke. I'd know it anywhere. The green felt, the betting circles, the dealer pulling from a card shoe. Smack in front of me, in this little rum joint below Third Avenue, is a blackjack table. Regulation, with real-life players.

The sight of it burns off my buzz and I approach warily, like a hunter at a picnic who stumbles on a bear den and wants to make damn sure it's what he thinks it is before going home to fetch his rifle.

I slip into the crowd of watchers. Seated at the table, gambling, are three guys. They play with chips and it's clear from their reactions that there's real money behind them. The rules seem to be standard Atlantic City, plenty fair. All the players' cards face up. Dealer hits 16 or less, stands on 17. One card when you split aces, double down on anything, insurance pays two to one. What really gets me, though, are the cards. Only two decks in the shoe, and no cut card. They deal all the way through to the finish.

Behind the table, just back of the young dealer, a big guy in a suit stands with folded arms. Gino himself, I presume, from his bearing and the way he eyes the whole room. It's not hard to guess who he's hooked in with, either. Come to think of it, all the workers in this place—the bartenders, the bouncer, the dealer—have that Chicago look to them.

My mouth goes dry when I get excited. Right now it's a piece of leather. I sip my beer and watch the action. The players aren't any good and they're not winning either. They keep buying more chips.

I watch a little longer, then slip away. I have enough on me for a final beer, and as I down it my mind is working. Come back with a real stake this time, Tom. Bet in units of twenty-five. A quick hitter—get in, get out. I take a last look at the table. Gino is scanning the place now, and before he can get around to me I duck back into the front room. I find Dave in the corner with his arm around the blonde.

"Tom, meet Grace. Grace, my friend Tom."

"Hi, Tom. Are you a pilot too?"

"No. Bullfighter."

She tilts her head. "In the city?"

"Over in Jersey."

She nods happily. "I didn't think they had any bulls here."

Over her shoulder Dave gives a little shrug, as if to say, "What can you do?"

"Nice to meet you, Grace. Dave, I'm heading out. I'll call you Monday. You'll start in on your part?"

He gives a thumbs-up.

Back up on the street, walking home, the night air tastes clean and sharp. Sometimes when you need it most, a chance drops right in your lap. It's no lock, but Christ, it might work. For the first time since I opened my trap to Duggan I see a real plan taking shape.

And for the first time in a long time I start thinking like a gambler again. Laying everything out step by careful step. Not getting ahead of myself, not even dreaming of the final payoff. There's time for that down the road. Crossing the street to my door, I smile to myself and shake my head. They say deliverance comes in a lot of forms. Who would ever think you could find it at Gino's?

CHAPTER ELEVEN

BLACKJACK and I have a history.

I got my first taste of her at twelve, when we lived on the base in Korea. A buddy led me through the back alleys of Seoul to Ma's, a dusty gaming parlor below a whorehouse. The tiny place was a family operation. Mom and her three boys, with Grandpa on a box in the doorway. Mom ran the betting window in the back. The smallest boy worked the floor, running beers and shots to the gamblers. The other two, neither any older than ten, dealt blackjack.

They stood barefoot on crates behind wooden tables, shuffling so fast I couldn't believe it, calling the American GIs over in a mix of Korean and pidgin English. They didn't use a shoe to deal the cards, but simply stacked six decks one on the other and dealt through, top to bottom. No chips, either. You put your money right up on the table.

From the start I felt the pull of the cards. No more video arcades for me. Every chance I could, I made it back to

Ma's. All I ever had was a little lawn money, but I loved the thrill of betting it. The moment of truth when you had to hit or stick, the jump in my heart when the dealer busted. Best of all, the charge of walking out with more money in my fist than I walked in with. Then, too, there was the danger. If any of the MPs saw me and word got back to Dad, I was up the river.

My gambling was strictly nickel and dime, of course. I never had the money on me for a real session. I'd win a little or—more often—tap out, then stand in the back and watch the GIs.

What a sight they were, rolling into the place in uniform after months along the DMZ. All that pay in their hands. Cocked when they came in, they'd stand at the blackjack table tossing down shots of cloudy Korean liquor, chasing them with beer, shouting and cursing as they bet on the cards.

When a winner left the place, Grandpa would signal the whores from his box in the doorway and they came down the street like crows. The lucky soldier would pluck three, sometimes four from the crowd and whoop upstairs with them, his hands on their asses, winking good-bye to his buddies. To a kid of twelve it was a hell of a sight. I never forgot it.

Junior year in college I taught myself to count cards. I learned the basic strategy and count method out of a book, then sat down at my desk with four decks and set to work. I must have dealt ten thousand hands to myself. I dealt with the music up real loud and with the gang playing poker in the room. I dealt with Lisa coming on to me. I learned to keep the count through anything.

Lisa thought I was nuts, that I'd come to my senses before the year was out, but when I finished my last exam, off I went.

Grandma had put a little money in the bank for me the day I was born. By the time I hit twenty-one it was three thousand bucks, and that summer I took all of it and boarded the bus for Atlantic City. Told Mom and Dad I'd lined up a job waiting tables. Actually, I was off to become a gambler.

I took one suitcase and my tape deck and found a room for sixty dollars a week at the Oceanside, a little dive just off the boardwalk, run on her own by Lottie, a young widow with a weary manner and a good figure. That first day she handed me sheets, said the rent's due each Monday, and showed me to my room. Such as it was. A bed against the wall, a rusty sink, a window that looked onto the gray wall of the next building. No kitchen, the bathroom and shower down the hall. I thought it was perfect.

The other tenants were young Irish who worked in the pub next door or old Irish who pushed the cart rides along the boardwalk. You could always tell the pub workers from the others. They were legal and pulling in real dough. They wore good clothes and nodded to you when they passed. The old cart pushers never said a word. They made okay money, I heard, some had been at it for years, but they didn't have green cards, or insurance, or anyone who gave a damn about them or anywhere to go back to when the summer ended. Late at night I'd see them with their flasks of whisky in the soft chairs in the lobby, watching crime shows.

I opened an account at a little bank on the boardwalk. Any money I kept in the room I slept with in a belt around my waist. The door locks at the Oceanside wouldn't stop a kid, and the block was full of shady characters. If you've ever seen Atlantic City you know that once you step off the board-walk, the place is pretty much a wasteland. Whatever the casinos were supposed to do to that town they hadn't done.

The best thing about the Oceanside was that it stood next door to the Irish Pub. I like to think I know a little about bars, and for my money the Irish Pub was the king of them all. Over its door was a quote from Boswell: "There is nothing contrived by man by which so much happiness is produced as by a good tavern or inn." Nobody who went inside would argue.

Pictures and clippings of famous Irishmen covered the walls. A fine jukebox stood in the corner. Drafts were seventy cents and served in frozen mugs by Irish waitresses so pretty I'd sit in the restaurant section just to order from them. None of that, though, is what made it the best bar in the world.

The real beauty of the Irish Pub was that it never closed. Twenty-four hours a day, three hundred sixty-five days a year she was open. Beat that.

Did they ever do a business, too. Inside, you never knew if it was three in the morning or three in the afternoon. The long, circular wooden bar was always jammed with rowdy drinkers, tourists who came back religiously every year, and locals, mainly cops or casino workers stopping in after their shifts. One mick or another was always climbing onto the stage with a guitar, leading the whole bar in a sing-along.

When I told Jimmy and the guys I lived next to a bar that never closed, they were in awe. One by one they made the pilgrimage, and even after I'd carried them out of there they found it hard to believe. I'd stagger up the stairs of the Oceanside, Bobby over my shoulder, barely conscious, mumbling, "Never closes. Damn place never closes."

I went to the Pub in the early evenings, between gambling sessions. Old Artie would put the Mets on for me if I could hold off till eight. At seven-thirty all his buddies from the retirement home lined the bar to play along to *Wheel of For-*

tune. Funniest thing you ever saw. The clue would be fictional characters, the answer would be "Snow White," Vanna's turned over everything but the S, and these guys are scratching their heads, trying to work it out on a piece of paper. If anyone actually nailed it he'd strut down the bar like the Godfather. I didn't mind missing an inning or two for that show.

I gambled Monday through Friday. Noon to four and again late at night, when the casinos were least crowded. I kept track of every session in my notebook. The casino, the clothes I wore, how much I won or lost. By hitting each place every two weeks, always in a different outfit, I kept the pit bosses from spotting me as a counter. To protect my small stake I played the five-dollar tables and put a two-hundred-dollar cap on my gambling each day. Win or lose, I stopped at two hundred bucks.

I started off like a pistol. Won the maximum each of the first five days. Walking home along the boardwalk that Friday, I couldn't believe how easy it all was. Just like I'd drawn it up. I leaned on the sea railing with a beer, looking out over the dark ocean, thinking I knew just how those old conquerors felt after reaching the town they sailed for and kicking its ass. Back at the Oceanside I called Lisa from the pay phone and told her to come on down and bring the gang with her—this weekend was on me.

I made only two mistakes that summer, but they cost me. The first was living the high life.

Every gambler works off a stake, and my three grand didn't leave a lot of room for error. I should have stuck to a tight budget, guarded my early winnings, and kept a fat reserve for the lean stretch that was bound to hit.

That's not how I played it. Tight budget? Screw that. I was a gambler, and what was the point of being a gambler if you had to squirrel away money like a librarian? I was winning, I expected to keep winning, and I was going to live like a winner.

And I did. Spent my money as fast as I made it. Faster, once the winning slowed down. No kitchen in my digs? No sweat. I ate steak or lobster each night, washed down with Heineken. Weekends I road-tripped to Boston or New York, or put up Lisa or the guys in my room, treating them to shows and fights. I felt like Al Capone, and so long as my luck held out, I lived like him.

Bet the cards long enough and you'll hit a dry spell. When my winnings slowed and I made two hundred in a week instead of a day, or in a bad week even lost a hundred, my stake dwindled pretty fast. By mid-July I was down to two grand, even though I was clearing a good profit at the tables. My winning just wasn't keeping up with my spending. Even then, had I put the brakes on the high life and stuck to my strategy, I could have ridden out the summer and headed back to Ham Tech with a nice chunk of change. I got impatient, though, and that's when I made my second mistake— the one that did me in.

What kills me is that I knew better. Every book on gambling warns against drinking at the tables. It's the one cardinal sin. Nobody knew it better than me, either, because all summer long I'd seen the evidence.

Must have happened a hundred times. Some guy fresh off the bus from Philly would drop into the seat next to me. First thing he does is flag down the cocktail waitress. "Free drinks, huh, buddy?" he says, nudging me with an elbow. "Can't beat that."

He pounds them down as he gambles. Maybe he isn't any good, or maybe it just isn't his night, but he loses the two hundred he brought to play with. Sober, the guy cuts his losses and walks the boardwalk until it's time to catch the bus for home. He's got a few in him, though, so he reaches for his wallet. Fuck it, he's thinking, I can win that back, and before he knows it he's down four hundred. Now he's thinking, Christ, just let me get back to the two hundred I was willing to lose to start with, so he stays, and soon he's out six hundred. He's drinking even faster now, to kill the panic and because he might as well get something out of this night, and between the drinks and the losing he forgets any strategy he knew when he walked in and any discipline too, and he starts making bigger bets to make it all back. He's in for so much, the difference between six and eight hundred doesn't register, or between eight hundred and a thousand, and when finally the dealer rakes in his last chip and he's blown a grand, the only reason he walks out of there, dazed, is because he's hit his limit on the ATM and it won't spit out any more money. Free drinks, huh? The guy just paid a thousand bucks for his.

And he was one of the lucky ones. Lucky because he didn't have any credit. The guy with credit, once he's lost all he came with, signs a marker from the pit boss and loses some more. Even if he mounts a comeback he loses everything in the end, because he won't let himself walk away until he's even, and he's too far under for that. So he keeps drinking and keeps betting and keeps losing until he runs through another marker and another one besides. And every time he signs one he's on the lookout for his grim little wife, who's circling the place while he plays, and when she's round again with her hard eyes on him he lies that he's doing just fine, honey, right on the verge of a big run. Of course he's really on the verge of losing it all, and when at last the pit boss won't sign any more markers for him he's finished, and the only thing sadder than the sight of him limping off from the table is the thought of what's in store for him when he finds his wife.

Like I said, I'd seen these guys all summer. Got to the point I could spot them as soon as they sat down. Then I went and joined the club.

I still get cold all over thinking about that last night. The evening started innocently enough, me sitting at the Irish Pub watching the Mets. Instead of my usual seltzer, though, I went for the beers. What the hell, I figured—just a few wouldn't hurt. I'd been good all summer. Maybe a couple cold ones were just what I needed to turn my luck at the tables, where profits had slowed lately. Well, a few led to a few more, as always, the game went to extra innings, and by the time it ended I had a major-league buzz on. Instead of leaving the tables for the morning, though, and heading back to my room, I had a little talk with myself.

Tom, I said, as I walked along the boardwalk, you've been here almost two months and you've never taken a shot at the big-money tables. What's holding you back? The strategy is the same. Why not go for the big payday, just this once? After all, you didn't come here to tread water and head back to campus with a thousand bucks. You came here to make a killing, to lay in enough beer and pony money to last all senior year.

I stopped at the ATM and punched up my balance. Two grand. Hmm. One good session with the big boys and I could double that. I left two hundred in the account for emergency money and took out the rest. I chose the Golden Nugget because Julia Roberts was shooting a flick there and I hoped to get a look at her. Maybe she'd even see me raking it in and stop to watch.

Once inside I headed straight to the high rollers' table. Fifty-dollar-minimum bet. The alcohol was in me and I felt lucky. Hell, a good run here could make my summer. I took a seat, ordered an Absolut on the rocks, and started in.

I never got that run. Instead I hit a stretch of cards I hope I never see again. The devil himself couldn't have dealt them any meaner. If I took a hit, I busted; if I didn't, I fell short; if I doubled down, I lost. The dealer, meanwhile, turned tiger on me, pulling blackjack after blackjack, going ten hands straight without busting, drawing six cards to a 21 to beat my 20. I lost a thousand bucks in an hour.

The more I lost, the more I drank. Card counting is concentration, and when you drink you start losing the count and making mistakes. More important even than losing the count is losing your self-control, that part of you that knows when to stop.

That night I broke every rule I'd lived by for two months. Gambled drunk, blew through my limits, didn't change casinos or even tables to stop the freefall. Just sat there and took it.

After I dropped the first thousand, the dealer shook his head at me and said, "Go on home, son. This isn't your night." I gave him a wink and pulled out the rest of my money. My luck had to change any minute now. It just had to. The law of averages is a tricky business, though. You think because you've lost nine hands in a row you can't possibly lose the next one, so you put out a fat bet. But of course your chances aren't any better than they were for the hand before. That's why you count cards—to take as much of the luck out of the game as you can and get the odds on your side. By that point, though, I was wasted, and I'd even stopped keeping the count. I was betting blind.

An hour later I'd lost the rest of it. In a fever, I took out the emergency money and bet that, too. Soon I was down to my last chip, feeling in my gut the cold panic of the loser. I stuck on my 18, the dealer turned over his 20, swept my chip into the rack and I was busted. I sat a minute, stunned, then climbed down off the stool and dragged my ass out of there like a million losers before me. How many times had I seen the cycle? Drink, bet, lose; drink more, lose more; drink more, bet everything, lose everything. All summer long I'd shaken my head at the suckers who fell into it. Now I was a sucker too.

The walk home along the boardwalk was the longest of my life. Some home, too. A dive room in a dive hotel. I was down to the fifty-two bucks in my money belt. I didn't have the heart to call Lisa and tell her. I looked out over the ocean wondering what the fuck I was going to do. School didn't start for another six weeks, and telling the folks was not an option.

As I stood there, cursing myself, I looked up to see one of the Irish guys from the Oceanside pushing an old couple along in his cart. I watched till they were out of sight, an idea growing in me. I was bigger than any of those guys. If they could push carts along the boardwalk, so could I. Hell, how tough could it be, wheeling lovers and old folks at ten bucks a pop? A guy could probably bring in $100 a day, maybe more. And it would be honest work. I'd be outside, breathing in the sea air, getting my back into my living, as Townshend would say. Heck, I could work up a little stake again, gamble the right way this time and hang on till the end of the summer. I walked to my room and fell into bed, desperate but determined.

The next morning I shook off my hangover and reported to the cart warehouse, a hollowed-out space under the boardwalk where a grunt of a man charged twenty-five bucks, cash up front, to rent a cart for the day. He also sold the red bow ties and white-collared shirts each cart pusher was required to wear. The carts themselves had wheels on the bottom, cushioned seating for two (three if you packed them in), and a metal bar on the back for the pusher to lean into.

I rolled the thing onto the boardwalk and scouted for my first customer. Within minutes I was flagged down by two businessmen coming out of the Tropicana. They'd made a killing in craps and were heading up to Sands to do it again. The fare was ten bucks and they tipped me five more. Dropping them off, I wondered why I hadn't thought of this earlier. This stuff was a piece of cake.

I didn't get my next ride until after lunch. Two wheezers who wanted to go from the Golden Nugget to the Taj Mahal—one end of the boardwalk to the other. Once there, they haggled about the price. By then the sun was pouring down and I could feel the pounds coming off me.

Turned out there was quite a bit of strategy to this cart-pushing business. The Irish guys had been doing it for years and they knew all the tricks. Knew to be outside the casinos when a big show let out, especially the fading comics and lounge acts that draw the old fogies, the ones who like to ride. Knew when each casino ran its big slot promotions and which exit to wait at when they ended. Knew all the good spots to work, and when any new ones came up, they tipped off the other pushers. Except me, of course. None of them would talk to me. By the time I figured out the prime places there was no getting near them, and it seemed to me they got a special kick watching me wheel my empty cart back and forth. They were quick, too, even the old bastards. I'd spot someone calling for a ride and by the time I got there, one of them would come out of nowhere and beat me to it.

It must have been the hottest day of the summer. I spent three bucks an hour on sodas, and by the time 6 P.M. came around I was a whipped dog. Bone-tired, faint from hunger and the heat, blisters on my hands from the metal bars, I rolled the empty cart back to the warehouse and sat down to count my earnings. After subtracting the cost of the cart, the shirt and tie, and all I spent on liquids, my net take for pushing a cart all day, for chatting up the old grumps, simping for tips, melting in the heat and dodging seagulls was minus twelve bucks. At this rate I'd be broke in a few days. Back at the lodging house, the Irish in the lobby smirked as I dragged myself up the stairs.

I checked out the next morning with just enough for a bus ticket to New York. Dave and his brother had a pad in the city and put me up on the couch the rest of the summer. I got a job waiting tables at a tourist trap near Times Square. Back at the Oceanside, Lottie covered for me, sending letters from my folks on to me at Dave's place, and letting me send my answers back through her to get a Jersey postmark.

I had a lot of time the rest of that summer to think about Atlantic City. No two ways about it, my stint as a gambler had been a failure. But it didn't sour me on the cards. Because it wasn't the cards that let me down. When I stuck to counting, and my betting limits, I won money. Even with the disaster of the last day factored in, I won much more than I lost. My free spending and my drunken collapse at the end were what did me in. In short, it wasn't the system that failed me. I failed the system.

And as the summer wore on, and I made coffee and bussed tables and listened to one tourist after another tell me their New York stories, I took the logic a step further. If the system was sound, and it worked once, it could work again. I filed that away and promised myself that someday I'd get another chance, and when I did I'd be ready for it, and I'd make some dealer somewhere pay for that last night at the Golden Nugget, and for every penny I'd left in that grim town.

That day has come.

CHAPTER TWELVE

BACHELOR parties come in two kinds.

The one is just what the girls think it is. The fellas take the groom out and get him loaded. He gapes at a stripper or two, keeps his hands to himself, gets sick all over from the shots, passes out, and they dump him off at home in the morning. Then there's the other kind. In a half hour I'm due at one of those. Tank's brother gets hitched in two weeks and Tank is sending him out in style. What figures to go on? You won't get it out of me.

First I have to escape from Carter. Ten o'clock Friday night and he's got me in the office putting together this affidavit. You should see it. Testimony to Regina Garrett's culinary skills. Written statements from her friends about what a whiz she is in the kitchen, alongside certificates of cooking classes she took twenty years ago and a few photos of her standing with the top chefs in the city—no doubt snapped at some fashion show. Real Perry Mason stuff. Carter briefs

Mr. Garrett on the case first thing in the morning and all this has to be ready when he does.

My plan is to duck out under the guise of getting some dinner, cab it to the place Tank's rented, go easy on the beers during the show, then pop back and stay as late as I need to. The phone rings.

"Farrell Hawthorne."

"Show starts in ten minutes."

"Damn, Tank. Can you stall them?"

"Hey, we go back, but not that far. They charge by the hour. Just get your ass in a cab and get over here."

"I'm out the door."

I stack everything in a neat pile on the desk as Carter marches in, clearing his throat.

"Um, Tom . . ."

Uh-oh. Whenever Carter calls me "Tom," I can hear the theme to *Deliverance* starting up.

"Change of plans, Tom. I just got off the phone with Mr. Garrett and he wants a midnight meeting on this motion. I need it all together, with exhibits, when he gets here."

"Sir, I'm due uptown in ten minutes."

"Cancel."

"I can't, sir. I can go and come back, but I have to be there."

"What is it?"

I pause.

"A bachelor party. I can get you in, sir."

He laughs. "Sorry, Reasons, but your buddies will have to fill you in on this one."

I dig in. "Sir, I really can't miss it."

"Enough. We're not about to blow off Winston Garrett. What would you rather do, Reasons—win this case, or stare at a bunch of tits?"

"Actually, sir . . ."

"Now get to work."

He bangs out of the room. The phone rings again.

"Farrell Hawthorne."

"What the hell's the matter with you?"

"I'm fucked, Tank. I can't make it."

"Make it. Miss every other one if you have to, but make this one."

"If I leave now it's my ass, Tank. You guys go on without me."

I hang up the phone and sit back down. Christ. Four years of school so I can sit in here on Friday night, dead sober, sifting photos of the Grinch. Twenty minutes later Tank is on the line again. Behind him I can hear music and hollering.

"Sisters, Tom. Centerfolds. What these girls can do with a dozen eggs you wouldn't believe."

I hang up the line to cries of "Batter up" as Carter enters the room with more pictures.

"I've got a good one here, Reasons—Regina with Wolfgang Puck. Notice how he seems to be looking at her. Pretty convincing, don't you think? See that it makes it in."

I take the picture without a word.

WE DON'T FINISH UP until almost midnight. I call the club but the manager tells me the party is over.

"Hell of a one to miss, son. I never seen a man that happy. They shoulda killed him on the spot."

I stare at the wall a few minutes, then walk down the hall to Carter's office and hand him the affidavit.

"Do you need me for anything else, sir?"

"No, that should do it."

I turn to leave.

"Reasons, you're not sore about missing that party, are you?"

"No, sir. I know how important this case is to the firm."

"Good for you. Prioritizing, Reasons—it's part of growing up. Knowing what's important and what isn't. Besides"—he gives a wink—"you seen one bachelor party, you seen 'em all, huh?"

"Yes, sir."

In the elevator I press my head to the cool wall to keep my temper down. If Carter has been to one real bachelor party in his life I'll eat my wallet. He's one of these guys who thinks he had a great time in college, though he put in twenty hours in the library for every beer. A night out to him now is a couple of lite beers, then race to Penn Station for the 8 P.M. train back to the Island.

Like everyone else in this place, he's got it backward. He thinks the work is what we're here for and the rest is filler. If that were the case, I'd never make it through the week. This place is the filler, a way to grind out the bucks for the real life that starts the second I'm through those oak doors. What a shot I had at some real life tonight, too. Fifty years from now, when I'm kicking off, I won't remember this place or anyone in it. But two sister centerfolds in an eggfest. Now just once before my time's up I'd like to see that.

In the street I take a breath of night air and curse my luck. There aren't many things in this world I like more than a bachelor party, and after the week I've had I could use the chance to blow off a little steam. Carter's been riding me into the ground on this Prego case. We're due in court in two weeks, so the pressure is on to force a settlement. I should be hearing from the INS guy any day now. For Prego's sake I can't help hoping Carter whiffs on the green-card angle, though if he does I'll have to bring a cot into the office to keep up with all the work he'll lay on me.

I start to flag down a cab but change my mind. It's a nice night. Why not get myself an Oil Can and walk home. I can use the air.

I can use the beer, too. It feels like twenty years since my last one, though really it's been less than a week. Not only have I been too broke to spring for the suds, I haven't had the time. The few hours I haven't been asleep or at the office I've been at the kitchen table, plugging away at my card-counting. Tomorrow night it's back to Gino's to play for real.

In the deli I pop the top with quiet ceremony for the store-keep, who pulls a flask of his own from under the counter, nods and joins me in a swig. I hold the taste in my mouth—the metal of the can, the rich lager. Man, that's good.

I tell you, I can go a few days without a drink if I have to, but damned if I'll say it's healthy. A guy's body knows what it needs, and you can't tell me that keeping the beer away, when every cell is calling for it, is doing it any favors. I start the long walk uptown.

When I reach the Lower East Side I cross over to Bowery so as to pass CBGB's. I've always loved the look of the place, the magic in that crummy awning. A bunch of kids mill around outside, getting psyched for this week's heroes. I don't recognize any of the names on the marquee. I cross east to First Avenue and keep walking.

A little ways up First I find myself at the window of Prego's deli. Without meaning to I chose a route that took me here. I stop and look in. The place is empty now, quiet, a light still on like they do in the city after closing. I cross myself before I realize what I'm doing. Oh well. Giuseppe needs all the help he can get.

Thinking about the case steams me up all over again. One

of the reasons I'm not long for this legal business is the bad habit I have of stripping each case to the truth at the bottom of it. And the whole truth at the bottom of this one is that a Park Avenue hag mixed the wrong spices and poisoned her friends. Then she made up a story to save her ass. That's it.

From that truth a lot of things are going to happen, though, and none of them to the right people. Look at the two principals here—Giuseppe Prego and Regina Garrett. Prego did it all just the way they tell you to. Started at the bottom, worked hard, built a business, raised a family. And Garrett? She got her hooks in a good businessman thirty years ago, when she still had a face on her, and she's been poisoning the social landscape ever since. Literally, it turns out. But who's going to win? She is. Why? She has all the money.

What a system. The villain rides off into the sunset and the good guy gets screwed. If you tried to make a movie like that, the crowd would boo it off the screen.

Good to know there'll be a happy ending for the firm, though. We'll make a killing. In the short run there's the bucks from this case, and once Garrett starts steering business our way we can get ourselves a whole new floor. Carter will make partner and I'll get a pat on the back, maybe even a little bonus. My reward for tossing Prego's dream in the coffin and nailing down the lid. Sure, if it weren't me, it would just be some other paralegal, but it's still a dirty business.

And the core truth I mentioned? The one at the bottom of the whole case? Oh, we've seen the last of that. It will be buried somewhere under all the affidavits and motions. Once this is all over, Prego's welcome to it. He can take it home with him if it makes him feel any better. None of the other parties will have any use for it, that's for sure. Christ.

The whole mess is enough to set a guy drinking, and starting uptown again I stop in at a bodega for a refill.

When I started at the firm a year ago, I sure didn't think it would come to this. Back then, I was pretty optimistic about the law. I figured I'd get an inside look at it for a year or two, and if I liked what I saw maybe even go that route myself. Just out of college, money in my pocket for the first time, life was a breeze. Come five o'clock, the city was one big happy hour, and who was I to worry about the big picture?

About now, though, it's sinking in hard that I really don't do anything. None of our cases ever goes to court—none of them. Sooner or later we settle. Our lawyers know it and their lawyers know it. Before we do, though, there's the little matter of a hundred hours to bill. A hundred hours and a quarter million dollars to settle some beef we would have hashed out in five minutes in the schoolyard. The last thing on anybody's mind is the truth. Lately, I'm starting to think all we do is see that money changes hands—and for that we keep a lot of it.

And the lawyers. I rag on Carter, but at least he keeps his mind on the job. Watch some of the others awhile and you think you're back in junior high. Sending notes ten feet down the hall because they aren't speaking to one another. Fighting about office size and copying rights. And the same loser who had his hand up all through high school is in at seven-thirty writing efficiency memos, only now nobody hauls him behind the gym and shows him what's what.

I never figured this same petty stuff goes on once you grow up. Maybe after a certain age people don't change. Maybe we get a little smarter—bone up on the law, business, medicine—but no better, because maybe nobody's looking to improve the heart. And why should we? There's no money in it.

Some nights it all seems okay. I'll put in a week of long hours on a good case, one of the partners will pat me on the back on the way out, and walking home I'll get to feeling pretty solid about it all. I'll crack a beer in the pad, sit in the window, and think this isn't so bad. Then something good will come on the stereo, "All Apologies," maybe, and it all bleeds out of me. Any desire for law school, any patience for the tricks at the firm. Looking out the window at the city, the lights, I'll feel the meter in me ticking, feel everything that's any good in me slipping away, and no idea how to stop it.

When those moods hit, and they're coming more and more these days, the only cure is the Friday bet. Only when I hand Toadie the money and settle in at the bar do I feel the life come back in me.

I bitch about the firm, but the truth is it's more than that. It's not just the law firm that isn't for me. I look around at what my friends are doing and I feel the same panic coming on. Insurance, ad man, CPA—I can't work up any enthusiasm for any of it.

The truth is I don't want to go to law school and be a lawyer. And I don't want to go to business school and, well, do whatever the hell you do when you get out. And I don't want to go into advertising, or publishing, or sell insurance.

The truth is I can't think of a thing I want to do, except maybe start up a band, and if you ever heard me in the shower, you'd know the chances of that.

Kretzky would say I don't have any work ethic, but it's not that. In two years I haven't missed a day of work. Sure, I come in a wreck sometimes, but I'm always at my desk by nine. I'm no slacker.

It's not a hardware problem, either. Sit me next to anybody and I'll hold my own. A college prof? How 'bout that

Beowulf? Couldn't put it down. A guy reading *Forbes?* I'll talk economies of scale.

It's just that . . . I don't know. My problem, I think, is that *I don't believe.*

Here's what I mean. Jimmy's dad was a big exec over at Coca-Cola. Spent his whole life in the company, right? Worked his way up from line boss to some kind of chairman. Owns a ton of stock, king of his hometown, the works. A success any way you cut it.

Well, last week they threw him his retirement bash. Here it is, the end of the line for him, and no doubt he's looking back on it all and feeling pretty good about himself. And why not? He made his mark. When he started out, the company was a couple of bottling plants. Now look at them—one of the giants of the world. And he had a hand in all that.

But here's the thing. I put myself in his place and you know what I'm thinking? I'm thinking I'm seventy years old, my time's almost up, and how did I spend my life? Selling a soft drink.

Because you strip away all the BS and that's what you got. Fifty years spent getting millions of people across the globe to buy one carbonated syrup mixture instead of another one that's almost exactly the same. And one that rots your teeth, besides. If I'm Jimmy's dad I'm thinking all that and I'm looking in the mirror and I'm saying to myself, It wasn't exactly walking on the moon, now was it? And I'm reaching for the nearest bottle.

That's my problem. I just don't buy in.

Kretzky's always saying how easy we have it, and I never know how to answer him. Because he's right. Next to what he went through, we do have it easy. I've never bought the line that our generation has it so tough. Kretzky's probably right about the world, too, about it being the same pie it's always been, and it's up to us to get out there and grab our slice. It's just that I don't have any appetite.

Not for the pie I see, anyway.

Kretzky, Dad, Grandpa, their lives were all centered around the wars. Everything else fell into place around them. And it made them different. Spend a few months in the mud with shells landing all around you, I guess a steady job and a house of your own look pretty good. You come home so damn glad to still have your ass on you that you marry and set to work and never waste a minute thinking you might have missed something.

It's not the same for us. There's no war around to keep us in line. We come out of school with a million commercials in our head, a million pictures of how it ought to be. A safe job, a family, our own house? I don't know anybody who dreams about that.

I can hear Kretzky now. "That's the problem with you kids," he would say. "You think your life has to be some kind of quest. Bah. You go to work, you marry, you raise your kids. When you kick off, the neighborhood turns up with flowers. What more do you want?"

Jesus. A lot more, old man. I'm just not sure how to get it.

I'm at Twenty-fifth Street now and it's one o'clock. I'm out of beer and almost home, but I'm not ready to turn in. Too much nervous energy in me, thinking about tomorrow. Also, the roomies might still be up, and sober I don't have the heart to face them. All lines of communication have been down since they found the beer cans in their underwear. Talk about a couple that missed the humor boat.

If I hustle I can still make Aisling Chara's second set at Finn O'Shea's. What the hell. I have the bucks to spare since I got paid today and I'm not betting my usual ball game. I considered it, but I'll need cash on hand for incidentals tomorrow, and anyway I'll get all the excitement I can handle at Gino's.

At Twenty-first Street I turn onto Second Avenue and get a lift from the sound of music coming out the front door of Finn's. Kennedy greets me at the entrance.

"You're late, Tom. How'd the bet go?"

I give him the thumbs-up.

"There's a lad!"

Hell, it's just a white lie, and it'll keep the waitress coming around.

Once inside, I feel better. The band is into their second set and into it big. The four of them have quit the stage and are snaking their way through the packed crowd, playing as they go. The little guy with the big electric cello climbs onto the wooden bar and plays fast and hard as the singer launches into "A Pint for the Lads Back Home." I squeeze through the crowd into a spot near the back, wedging myself between a big balding guy and a woman of about thirty. Before I can look around for the waitress she's there with a pint.

"I was afraid we wouldn't see you tonight," she says.

"No chance of that. I've waited all week to take a pint from you."

Her fingers graze mine as she hands it over with a shy smile. I've only ever seen her in jeans, but tonight she wears a black skirt with white tights underneath. Damn, she is a dish.

"How was the first set?" I ask.

"Oh, good, I guess. I've heard them enough now that it starts to sound the same."

That accent. I'd pay fifty bucks to listen to her read the phone book. She pats my arm.

"I must get on, Tom. A lot of thirsty ones tonight. I'll be round with your pints."

138

She turns to go, then turns back, just in time to see my eyes go to her ass.

"By the way, my name's Samantha. I never got round to telling you last time."

She glides away.

I'll be damned. If she weren't so hot and I weren't aching so bad for it, I'd swear she was flirting with me. I give my head a good shake and turn back to the band. Plenty of time to dream when your head hits the pillow, Tom.

Aisling Chara eases into a slow Irish sing-along and the crowd sways back and forth and raises their voices to join in. Someday I'll have to trace back my family tree. I'd lay a C-note it ends in Ireland somewhere. When that tin whistle starts up, and those pipes, and I have a pint in my hand . . . it's the closest I get to a feeling of home.

Not that the folks here would ever have me. They're a tight crew, these Irish. I've come to know a few of the regulars here. They're friendly, sure, but to a point. That's the thing about the Irish. You may know all the songs, same as they do, and you might really feel them, even, but there's no buying your way into this group. You can only be born into it. If you aren't, they let you go so far but no farther. If you are, though, it doesn't matter if you've been in the country ten years or ten minutes, you find your way to a place like Finn's and you have a home. A set of people who talk to you, and listen, who keep an ear open for work, if you're looking, and slide you a Guinness if you're not. Must be nice.

Tonight I'm happy to drink my pint and hear the music, but the guy next to me wants to talk, and packed in as I am, there's no getting away. "Harv," he says, sticking out a fat hand. Harv is backing into his forties but fancies himself a young man, and his talk is of women and sex. To hear him tell it, he's getting more now than he ever did. He knows why, too.

"Kid," he says, pulling out a fat wallet, "no matter what they tell you, it's the size of this thing that counts. Nobody with any money goes back to Jersey with a hard-on. You hit this town Friday with a couple hundred, maybe score a little something to keep the evening going, put up with a movie, dinner, some talk, I'm telling you, you can't miss. Damn, I wish I was an economist. I'd come up with a formula and make a million."

Not that there's anything wrong with insurance. He's been in it fifteen years and picked up a few things along the way. "Travel. You got to knock around a bit when you're young. Meet enough people and you learn what makes 'em tick, and pretty soon you're wearing 'em on your wrist." Harv's riding a hot streak and thinks I should stick with him ("Always hunt with a buddy"), but soon he's cornered the blonde on the other side of him and starts telling her about the army.

I'm free about thirty seconds before Maggie, on my right, starts in on me, telling me the problem with men these days is that none of us knows how to be chivalrous anymore. Either we're cavemen, or too scared of offending them to hold the door. Now she's all for equality, don't get her wrong, but she wouldn't mind being treated like a lady once in a while.

When I see a break in the crowd I go for it, and I manage to make it across to the other side of the room. No sooner do I stake out a new spot when Samantha's there again with a fresh pint.

"Jesus, you're fast," I tell her.

"Maybe I'm keeping my eye on you."

"Why would you do that?"

She smiles and floats away.

140

The band breaks into an instrumental that sets the whole place in motion. There isn't the room to dance, so we all move at the knees. Kennedy flashes the lights on and off and the floor starts to shake from the weight of us. The sweat's on me now from the heat and the pace of the music, which builds and builds until it's just a question of whether the strings will snap before we do. The cello player is in a fever, playing high, then higher, then higher still, until finally with a last flourish he brings the bow slashing down on the strings and ends it. There's a second of dead silence and then we all go nuts.

They segue smoothly into a cover of the Pogues' "Dirty Old Town" and I stop moving. Christ. Just the song I needed to hear.

They do a good version, though you really need the harp at the start leading you into it. If those first few notes don't get you, there isn't a lick of Irish in your bones.

I look down at the floor. I didn't know what Irish music was until Lisa heard "Dirty Old Town" at the school radio station and brought the album to my room. For a month the Pogues were all we listened to. We got hooked on the writing of the front man, Shane MacGowan. At last a guy who wrote something besides love songs. He wrote tough and funny songs about drinking, about the horses, about politics, drinking, being Irish, drinking, girls, and drinking again. And he sang them all in that great voice, a voice without polish but with grit and accent.

They were our band. Lisa had some clout with the concert committee and lobbied hard to bring them to campus. What a show they could have put on in the little gym. By then, though, Shane was full off round the bend. He had a soft spot for the hard stuff, and toward the end was missing shows, passing out on stage, the works. The concert committee declared them a bad risk, said the budget was too tight to gamble on the likes of MacGowan. So come March we all filed into the gym and sat on our hands through Bonnie Raitt.

Lisa and I weren't to be stopped that easy, though. We hitched down to the city for Saint Patrick's Day and caught the Pogues at the Palladium. Shane was a sight. On his last legs, swaying at the edge of the stage with a bottle of JD, trying to sing "A Pair of Brown Eyes" while a prop man kept him up and held a sheet with the lyrics. I knew the words better than Shane did.

Christ, the band was tight, though. They broke into "Fiesta" and the place exploded, spinning and slamming in a mad Irish dance. Lisa and I were swept up in it, she laughing and twirling and me keeping us from getting killed. Shielding her, bouncing off the other maniacs. And when they broke from that into "Dirty Old Town," the song these guys are doing now, well, you haven't seen a crowd until you've seen one sing "Dirty Old Town" with Shane Mac-Gowan on Saint Paddy's day. Even the folks who weren't Irish thought they were. I thought the roof was going to come down on us, and didn't care if it did.

I don't play the Pogues much these days. I can't listen to them without thinking of Lisa. That's the problem with having a band with your girl—you lose the girl and the band becomes a killer. All their songs start cutting you in two.

Jesus, it would be nice to see Lisa tonight. Sometimes I can almost smell her perfume. She never used much. Just a touch, and she smelled so good anyway, it drove me crazy.

Samantha's back with another pint, even though I'm not half done with the last one. She sure is easy to look at.

"You'll have to slow the pace," I tell her. "I'm not much of a drinker tonight."

"I hope that doesn't mean I'm walking myself home." She leaves the pint by my arm and turns off.

What was that? I turn back to her but she slips into the crowd. I look around to see if anyone else noticed, but everyone's watching the band as they break into a cover of "Sooner or Later." The press of the crowd rocks me back and forth, but I can't keep my eyes off Samantha, back at the bar now, or my mind off what I think she said. A few minutes later she's back with a final pint. She hands it to me and I touch her shoulder as she turns away.

"Say, am I hearing things, or did you ask me to walk you home?"

She raises her eyes to mine. "If you're interested."

"I'm interested."

"Good. I'll be off in thirty minutes. Wait for me up the street a block. Liam would have a fit if he saw us leave."

She smiles and walks off.

I take my time with my last pint. I'm going to need the kick it's giving me. The band wraps up the set and comes down into the crowd for a few drinks with their fans. I finish my pint and walk out of Finn's and up to the corner. Around me, happy drunks pile into cabs or cross into the diner for a late bite. I duck into a deli for some Certs and try to keep down my excitement. I see Samantha come out the door and head up the block toward me. Pretty as she looked in Finn's, she looks even sweeter on the street, shivering a little and rubbing her arms.

All you knee-benders who drone on about abstinence, I got a job for you. Show me a Psalm that can match the kick of this—walking a treat back to her place, six pints in you, a decent shot of getting across. You do that, then we'll talk faith. You folks don't know what you're missing.

Samantha lives just a block away. A small one-bedroom

she shares with another Finn's waitress, Eileen. But Eileen isn't home now, she tells me, and won't be anytime tonight. Would I like to come up and see the place?

I'm through the first line of defense. Most times I get stopped right here. Once past the doorman, the odds swing way over to my side. You don't invite a guy up to your place at two in the morning if he doesn't have a chance to stay. If I'm a Vegas bookie, I'm laying 5–3 on Reasons.

At the elevator Samantha turns her eyes on me. I'd only seen them in the dark bar, and in the light of the hallway the clear blue is stunning.

"I've been in this country a year, Tom. You're the first man to see this apartment."

"Why me?"

"There's something about you I like. And anyway . . ." she bites her lip. "It's time."

I know when to stop talking. In the elevator I put a hand on her and she turns into my kiss. She stiffens and melts in the same motion and comes up onto me as I back her into the wall. Over my shoulder she jabs at the floor button. Feeling me through our clothes, she looks hard at me, her eyes bright, her breathing soft and fast.

"Be sweet, Tom. Go easy. I'm a good Catholic girl."

Not for long.

CHAPTER THIRTEEN

I WAKE to a fight in the kitchen.

Seems Molly sent Mike for low-fat bagels and he came back with regular. "Aw, come on, honey—just this once couldn't hurt." I hear the door close behind him. Must have been a hell of a look.

That's right, I'm at home. Six hours ago I was set to put an end to my longest drought since I first drank from the big well. This morning I'm still bone-dry, and the way it played out makes me either man of the year or the biggest sap in town. You tell me.

At Samantha's floor I was for hitting the emergency button and finishing what we started. She nixed that idea sweetly though, so I let her down, aching the way a guy does when he stops halfway home. She was barely hanging in there herself, her face flushed, her hands unsteady with the keys. At her door she kept smoothing her skirt and looking up at me. I could see she was new to this.

Once inside she kissed me, then turned out of my arms and took me by the hand to the living room. In a hot whisper she said, "I'll be in the second room down the hall, Tom. Wait ten minutes, then come."

You want to talk about a woody—I almost had to ice myself down. It's been six months since I've been laid right and four since I had any at all. I can't watch a girl step out of a cab without breaking into a sweat. And there I was, nine minutes away. I walked to the kitchen. I couldn't find any beer, so I walked to the living room again and stood looking out the window. A boxer in his corner before round one, so mad to get started I could barely wait for the bell.

After a few more minutes I stepped into the hallway. Samantha's blouse lay on the floor, five feet from her door. Her skirt lay two feet from it, her tights a foot away, and her bra hung on the knob. I felt the soft cotton with my fingers. I put my head on the door a second, said a word of thanks, and opened her up.

Convince me heaven looks half that good and I'll come back to the fold. Samantha lay on her quilt wearing just a blindfold, her wrists resting above her head, a white silk scarf tied round each one. Jesus and then some. I've always been pretty straight up and down in the sack, but this I could go for. I walked to the bed and looked down at her pale Irish skin, so beautiful in the dark. I looped the scarves gently around the headboard and pulled them tight, and the sounds she made as I did almost set me off then and there. I sat on the bed and ran a hand down her leg.

"Say something in Gaelic," I said. She murmured a few dreamy words and I knew this first session would be a quick one and would have to start right away. I took everything off and climbed aboard. Putting my lips to her hair, I began the slow route down, breathing easy, sliding myself just over the top of her. Jesus, girls are soft, aren't they? If they knew what they do to us, times like those, we'd have a new order in place in a hurry and not so much as a whimper from us slaves. As I moved down her smooth belly, Samantha started rolling her hips and surging softly against the ties. Ten more seconds of that and it wouldn't matter if I was in or not. Time to close the deal.

And then it happened. Over her breathing I could just hear the radio, and as I moved up to ease into her, "Into the Mystic" came on. "Into the Mystic" is a song Lisa and I first heard on her little radio as we went at it one night on a blanket under the stars, and ever after it is the song one of us would put on when we wanted a go.

Hearing it last night set something off in me. I tried to fight it. I looked at the cool silk across Samantha's eyes and felt her bracing beneath me. I'd waited too damn long for this, and I was too close. I arched back to knock it home, but just as I did my knocker gave out on me. All of a sudden he wasn't up for knocking. Believe me, that's never happened before.

I had to ease off her, while she gasped, "Please, please, right now." I answered by running my hands over her again. She thought I'd pulled back from the brink to tease her, and as I trailed my fingers down her belly and toward the heart of her she gave a moan like I don't ever expect to hear again. Old woody was back now, too, and raring for a second go at it, but I stayed where I was, and even as I slipped my fingers just inside her I had it out with myself.

Samantha was in heat but I could think of Lisa and nothing else. In that strange room, set to pop a girl I hardly knew, it all came back to me. The shine in Lisa's eyes when she looked at me, the calm that would come over us in the middle of it, the way her hands trusted my shoulders. I saw it all

147

again, and with the pictures came the feeling, the one that speared me last Friday when I walked her home—that I need her. For those few seconds last night the past and future collapsed in on me and I saw with total clarity. Saw Lisa and me, not just the way we'd been but the way we could be again. I saw that we could have it all back—all of it. The songs we shared, the way we fit together so perfect.

But it wouldn't be free. I had to earn it, and there was only one way to do that. I had to be true to Lisa now the way I was when we went together. Nothing less.

Christ Almighty, I still don't know how I made it out of there. Guys aren't built for that kind of exit. I rose from the bed and dressed quietly, watching her tremble and buck on the quilt. "Tom," she whispered, breathing fast. "I'm here," I said. Then I walked to the bed and freed one of her hands. "Please," she whispered but I put my fist in my mouth and bit hard into it until I was out the door, down the steps, out her building and into the street. I ran all the way home.

I WALK TO THE KITCHEN and say good morning to Molly. "Good morning," she says coldly from behind a book. What's up with her? I wonder. She's been a witch with a capital *B* for days. My guess is all that Kafka's catching up with her. That stuff works on your mood, and for two weeks now she's gone straight from one book to the next.

In freshman English I had a prof who liked to assign us the depressives. Thirty straight days of rain and nothing on the reading list but Kafka and Hardy. By mid-term break the whole class wanted to do themselves in. In Molly's case, you factor in her naturally grim disposition, and look out.

I drop a few strips of bacon into a frying pan. Most times this sends her into the living room, but this morning she holds her ground.

"Do you know how much fat you are about to ingest?" she asks.

Here we go.

"Not today, Molly—I had a rough night."

She lowers the book to her nose. "How so?"

"You wouldn't understand."

"Grant me the opportunity."

I sigh.

"Okay. I was all set to put the blocks to a girl last night, and it fell through."

She looks at me with no sign of comprehension.

"Put the blocks to a girl, Molly—have sex."

Her mouth is a straight line. "I see. With whom, if I may ask?"

"Some waitress."

"A waitress. Am I correct in presuming you were only casually acquainted with this woman?"

"Yes."

"And you accompanied her to her apartment with the intention of having sex?"

"That's right."

She is quiet a full minute, then lowers the book to her lap. "Tell me, Tom, are there any women in this city whom you don't regard as whores?"

Christ. And all I wanted was to cook myself a little breakfast.

"Whores, Molly?"

"Yes, whores, Tom. Women whose value you see purely in sexual terms." Once Molly gets going, it doesn't take her long to hit full throttle. "Men who regard women in this manner, Tom, comp—"

"Stop," I say, putting up a hand. "I don't want to hear it. Not today. My johnson is still sore at me from last night, and

149

the last thing I need is to sit through your standard recital. I've heard it a dozen times already."

"Judging from your porcine behavior, it's made little impression on you."

I look down at the frying pan and count to ten in my head, very slowly. When I finish she's still there.

"You know, Molly, for all the times I've heard your pitch, you've never once let me give my side of it. Don't you think it'd be good to get a guy's perspective for a change? Even things out a little?"

She eyes me warily.

"Do you intend to make a serious argument, Tom, or will you simply try to provoke me?"

"I'll just tell it like it is."

She folds her arms on her chest.

"Very well. Proceed."

"It's all pretty simple," I say quietly. "I'm the first to admit there isn't a girl I meet I don't size up for the sack. That's news? I'm a guy, and us guys start each day with a little something passed along from our ancestors. Something called a set of balls. So long as we have one, a part of us will always be looking to score. That doesn't mean we can't appreciate a girl's mind, or her drive, or her personality. Sure we can. But we're not about to forget what it was that got us looking her way in the first place. Nature, Molly, that's what it's called, and if it makes me a pig, well, point me to the trough—it's feeding time."

I take a crisp bite of bacon and duck just as the book comes at my ear. Molly turns on her heel and marches out.

Twenty minutes later I'm making my bed when she bursts into the room, waving a copy of *Playboy* I must have left in the can. I'm surprised the smoke alarm doesn't go off.

Boy, does she light into me. Now I'm not just a pig, but part

150

of a worldwide conspiracy to boot. A conspiracy to degrade women, of course. To denigrate their ability to think, exclude them from the workforce, and, if they do slip in, to deny them equal pay or a fair shot at promotion. And that's not all. I'm also part of a . . . cabal, I think she said. A cabal of low-minded brutes who've taken it on themselves to turn the clocks back a hundred years. To roll back every advance women fought so hard for, reinforce the stereotypes blocking them at every turn and, above all, keep all the booty for ourselves and condemn them forever to the status of second-class citizens.

And here I thought I just liked to look at tits.

When she's all done she slams the door on me without waiting for an answer. No chance for me even to give my rebuttal. Not that it would have mattered. All I'm armed with are logic and reason, after all, and when's the last time they won out?

I lie back on the bed. Say what you will, what drives us guys crazy is that every fight with a girl winds up the same way. Past a certain point the best logic in the world gets us nowhere, because past a certain point logic and reason don't apply. In their mind you're wrong and that's that. Case closed. I put my hands behind my head and sigh up at the ceiling. If Kant were here today, he'd back me up on this. I'll bet the guy never won an argument with his wife.

 **SHOW TIME.**

Three in the morning and the apartment is still. I dress quietly, rap the bureau twice for luck and slip out of my room. As I step through the pad I spot a lump on the couch. The lump is Mike, and I tap him awake.

"What's going on?" I ask.

"What? Oh . . . we had an argument."

"An argument?"

"Movie rentals." He rubs his eyes. "She trusted me to pick them out tonight. Both had to be foreign, of course. I rented one French one, but then I went for Bruce Lee—*Enter the Dragon*."

"Great flick."

"Yeah, well, I thought we might like a change of pace. If I see one more French talkie I'll go nuts. So anyway"—he pats the pillow—"here I am."

"Hell, it's your bed, Mike. If she doesn't like it, let her sleep out here."

"I know, I know. But you know how she gets. Where are you headed?"

"Out."

He looks wistful. "To one of those bottle clubs with the fellas, huh? Toss back a few brews?"

"Yeah. Hey, tell you what. If we can get Molly out of here for a few hours in the morning, how about we watch some Bruce Lee?"

"Yeah, maybe. If I can't sleep, though, I might put it on tonight without the sound."

Out in the hall I shake my head. The day I get kicked out of my bed ... forget it. I won't even start. I have bigger things on my mind tonight.

I head out the door and over to Third Avenue. A light rain is falling and feels good on my face. In my wallet, taped to my chest, is more money than I've seen in my life. What a country we live in when a guy can walk into his bank with a plastic card and walk out with ten thousand dollars. Twenty-one percent annual interest, maybe, but what the hell.

I have Dave to thank for the dough. He's been Joe Montana on this one. His brother rushed the card through the pipeline and it came into my hands this morning. What a concept, credit. Good thing I never knew about it in college.

Dave came up aces on more than just the card. He has a little scheme that could net another five grand. Check this out. He and his dad play a father/son golf tournament in Oyster Bay each year. His dad takes it all real serious. Side bets with his cronies, bragging rights around the club, that kind of stuff. Last year the two of them won the thing.

This year's tournament is this weekend, and Dave says if

they defend their title the old man will be a soft touch. Will be in just the mood to help his kid out with five grand. What will Dave tell him he needs it for? How about a little lady he knocked up at school, who's making noises about going the distance if Dave can't come up with the bucks to change her mind. Even I flinched at that one, but Dave said not to sweat it, that he's the only Cavanaugh boy who hasn't gone that route for real.

"I'll sit through a hell of a lecture," he said, "but if the trophy's on the mantel, he'll cut the check."

Between Dave and the cards, I could have a good chunk of what I need by tomorrow. Provided my luck holds out.

Now it's time to do my part. The counting has all come back to me pretty good. I won't know for sure until the cards fly at me with money behind them, but I feel ready. This afternoon I squeezed in one last practice session on a blanket in Central Park. I knocked off at 5 P.M., figuring I was as good as I'm going to get, and walked out of the park and over to the Museum of Natural History.

I love it in there at dusk. I went to the room with the big blue whale and stood for a while in the dark quiet, the peace of the place clearing my head. I went over it all in my mind. I thought of Duggan, and of darts, but mostly I thought about tonight, because if tonight goes bad, everything else is fucked. When I felt a good stillness come over me I went home. I took a long run up the East River, a hot shower, hit the sack for a few hours, and here I am.

I haven't told anyone about my session tonight—not even Dave. No sense jinxing the operation. I'll tell him the good news tomorrow.

Except for a few cabs rolling by, the avenue is quiet. Turning onto Twenty-ninth, I pass a deli and a few brownstones and come up on the plain door that hides the club. It hits me that I don't know the password, but a couple is just heading in and I ride in on them. The suit at the inner door waves us all through.

The rain has kept some people away, but otherwise Gino's looks about the same as last week. The outer room is half full, and again heavy on the dolls. Soft-haired blondes and redheads, standing alone or with their fellows. Eyes front, Tom. Tonight is strictly business. I order a seltzer and head for the back room. Crossing into it, I can see the magic table in the corner, manned by the same young dealer as before. Standing back of him again is Gino, filling out another big suit, and taking in the whole room from behind his shades.

You have to hand it to the guy—this setup of his is a real gem. So simple it's a wonder no one else thought of it.

Here's my take on Gino. If I had to guess, I'd say he's a small-timer who's plugged into the Atlantic City crowd through some cousin or other. All those family reunions have taught him what a killing the casinos make, and how much of it comes from blackjack, and after twenty years of hearing about it, one day it hits him—why not stick a table in his own place? He gets hold of an old one, and a few props, tells a cousin to quit that high school bullshit and start shuffling, and he's good to go.

Gino probably figured he could take in a few hundred a night. After the first few nights, counting out a couple grand each time, he starts to realize what a goldmine he has here.

He doesn't even have to cheat. Hell, why bother? Cheating isn't easy. You have to figure out how to do it, for one, and if Gino had any kind of chimney on him, the family would have him below Canal Street, working the heroin angle, not up here in the twenties, running a clip joint he has to pack up and move every few weeks. No, better to keep it simple. Gino doesn't worry about using a lot of decks, or

155

even a cut card. He just opens the table every night, posts the standard rules, and lets the house edge take care of him.

He's not dealing with real gamblers, after all. The typical guy he gets in here is an easy mark, stumbling onto the game at three in the morning with a lot of liquor in him, fancying himself a shark because he once took twenty bucks off the dorm adviser. Gino's setup is perfect for milking the likes of him. All he has to do is let the odds work their magic. They always will.

Blackjack is a good game but not a friendly one. Play well or you will lose. Maybe not the first time, or the second, but soon, and consistently. That you can count on. The crazy thing, though, is that everyone thinks they're an expert. Maybe because the rules are so simple, or because we all learn to play the game as kids.

Knowing the rules and knowing the right way to play aren't the same thing, though. Most people know just enough to get them in trouble. Believe me, I saw a lot of "experts" in my summer in Atlantic City, and the way most of them played it would have been quicker and a lot less painful if they'd just been mugged on their way into the casino. They knew the rules of the game but not the strategy. And they got creamed.

A few words on the strategy. In blackjack, both the house and the player have certain advantages. The big advantage for the house is that the player can bust first. This advantage is so big it keeps casinos in business around the world. The edge for the player is free will. He can take a hit whenever he wants, or stand, or double down, or split his cards. The dealer has no free will. He hits 16 or lower and stands on 17 or higher. Thus a player can stick on a weak hand and win, while the dealer never can.

A good player takes the advantage away from the house in

two ways. First, he masters the basic strategy. This means he knows what move to make in every situation, no matter what cards he has and what the dealer has showing. Nobody should play blackjack for real money unless they've learned the basic strategy, and this is relatively easy to do.

Back in the seventies, when computers came on the scene, some card sharks hooked up with a couple of math dweebs and cracked the game of blackjack. They fed all the possible card combinations into the computer, played out every conceivable hand millions of times, and figured out once and for all the best move a player can make in every circumstance. The result was a few simple charts, and learning the basic strategy is just a matter of memorizing those charts.

Once you learn it, you have about an even shot of beating the house. The way to really swing the odds away from the casino and over to your side is to count cards. Counting cards means keeping track of the cards that have been played, and, more important, the ones remaining in the deck. The premise behind it is simple. There are times when the deck favors the dealer, and times when it favors the player. By keeping track of the cards remaining, you know when these times are and can bet accordingly. When the deck favors you, you bet a lot of money. When it favors the dealer, you bet a little. A guy playing basic strategy and not counting and a guy counting cards might win the same number of hands, but the card counter comes out way ahead because he has more money on the hands he wins and less on the hands he loses.

The real blackjack ace combines the basic strategy and card-counting. He bets high when the count is favorable, and he considers the count when deciding whether to hit or stick. That's the way I'll be playing tonight.

Legitimate casinos do a lot of things to frustrate card

counters. They deal eight decks at a time, and deal them fast. They use a cut card, to keep you from winning big near the end of the shoe. They crowd a lot of players into a few tables, to stop you from going one on one against the dealer, and hire pit bosses to watch all the action.

Gino's has none of these safeguards. They deal only two decks, and they deal them all the way through. A pro might play his whole life in casinos and never find these conditions. Gino can get away with it because of the players he gets. Like I said, the house edge will take care of his usual fare. But his setup is vulnerable to a card counter.

I'm banking on a couple of things tonight. One is that Gino and his dealer can't spot a counter. Odds are they can't. A good one can sit right in front of a seasoned pit boss in Vegas and not arouse suspicion, and Gino is no pit boss. Wouldn't surprise me if he's never heard of card-counting. One look at the dealer tells me he's no pro, either. He can't shuffle worth a damn, and every time he flips a card it takes him a few seconds to do the math.

I'm banking on luck most of all, though. The best counter in the world can't win if the cards don't let him, and even with two decks dealt all the way through, and the table to myself, in one night of gambling there are no guarantees. So luck, be a lady tonight.

I come up on the table with a grin, pulling out my wallet and slurring my words.

"I'll be damned—blackjack. Whatsa fella gotta do to get in?"

Gino looks me over without looking at me, and from nowhere comes a waitress who wants to freshen my drink. Bingo. I down my seltzer in a gulp and say, "Sure, another vodka—no rocks this time." An old gambler's trick. If they peg me for a drunk, they'll want all the action I can give them.

"Chips you buy from me," says the dealer. "We have 'em in five, ten, and twenty-five. What'll it be?"

"I'll take a thousand. And don't bother with the small stuff—I'll take it all in twenty-fives."

The dealer stops. "Boss?" he says, glancing over his shoulder.

Gino checks me out through his shades. The waitress returns with my vodka and I take a deep drink. I turn up my hands.

"Hey, I don't have all night. If you guys can't handle me, just say so."

Gino is silent another five seconds, then gives the nod.

"What are you waiting for, Vito? Deal the man in."

CHAPTER FIFTEEN

I TAKE the corner seat at the felt table as Vito hands me my chips. Beside me is a guy who looks to be just the kind of gambler Gino likes—a dumb kid with too much booze in him. Even bad players make the right move most of the time, out of common sense, but this guy manages to do the wrong thing every hand. He lasts ten minutes. After he slinks off, two other guys try his seat, but a few big early bets on my part scare them away, and soon I have the table to myself.

Just as I hoped. The ideal play for any counter is to go solo against the dealer. You don't want anyone else around to dilute your luck. Nothing's worse than waiting through a long stretch with the deck about even, seeing the count come over to your side, putting a big bet on the table and then watching the clown next to you, here once a year for the plumber's convention, pull the blackjack.

I settle in. As word of the money I'm laying down gets

round the room, a small crowd starts to gather back of my chair.

I don't impress anyone in the early going. Man, am I cold. Betting in units of twenty-five, as high as a hundred a hand when the count calls for it, I hold even for a shoe or so and then hit the skids. Everything seems to be working backward. I win when my small bets are out there, but any time I put down real money I get slammed. Vito has plain forgotten how to bust, and for every blackjack he spots me he pulls three of his own. After an hour and a half I'm out three grand.

Christ. A nice little hole I've worked myself into. I try not to panic. I've seen losing spells before. If I can just ride this one out I can still turn things around. Time could be a problem, though. It's four-thirty already, and I can't very well stage a comeback if they lock the doors on me. I ask Vito how late he'll keep dealing.

"Seven A.M.—if I got anyone to deal to."

Prick. I take a break from the table to change my luck. In the can I splash cold water on my face and take stock of the situation. I'll have to force the pace if I'm to get what I need out of here tonight, and there's only one way to do that. I decide to jack my base bet to a hundred. That means I'll be laying up to five hundred a hand when the count runs in my favor. I could flame out in a hurry at those stakes, but at this point I don't have much choice. Coming out of here with a few grand won't do me any good. Either I win big, or it doesn't much matter if I win at all.

I have a few things going for me. My early losing streak killed any suspicions Gino might have had. He watched me real close at the start, but the more I lost the more he relaxed, and by the time I cashed in my fourth grand he was bobbing up on his heels like a maître d'.

161

Vito's dealing helps, too. A lot of casinos will sic a speed demon on you, forcing you to tip your hand by hunching over the cards and blocking out the world to keep the count. Vito is so slow I can chat up the waitress and still count away.

As for me, I've done my part. Played the role of the drunk beginner to the hilt. Been taking my time over the cards, as if unsure, and cursing or throwing my hands up when I bust. Been making a show of my drinking, too, by downing the first one real quick and waving my glass around. No question Gino and Vito have bought in. Hell, I have them just where I want them—figuring me for an easy mark. Now all I have to do is prove them wrong.

I ditch the rest of my vodka in the sink and fill the glass with water. On the way back to the table I stop at the jukebox and play all the Creedence and Dead I can find. The next hour could make or break me and I want everything just right. "Fortunate Son" kicks in as I sit back down, and as I slide a hundred bucks into the betting circle I feel cool and focused.

The new shoe opens with a slew of low cards. A few hands into the deck the count is at plus ten. This means a lot of high cards are on their way, which is good news for me. It also means it's time to put up or shut up. I take a good belt of water and start pushing the big bets out there.

The first time I bet five hundred on a hand Vito turns for the okay and Gino waves him on. I let out a breath. If Gino balks at those stakes, I never get a shot at the tear I need. I sneak a look at him. I know just what he's thinking, behind those shades. If the kid can drop three grand at a hundred a hand, what's he gonna leave here at these stakes? Gino's feeling pretty good right now. He has himself a sucker and he figures to milk him. What Gino's not figuring on is the count.

My comeback starts with a hand that seems like a goner. I split twos against a five, five hundred on each, and wind up with a pair of twelves. Vito has a six in the hole for eleven. Looks like I'm out a grand, but he draws an ace to give him twelve and then a face card to bust it. I'm off.

A run of cards is something to see. Most times blackjack is ebb and flow. You win some, you lose some. Over time your luck adds up, good or bad, and you go home up or down. A good run, though, is magic. It comes from out of nowhere, like a twister, and by the time it sets you down again, you're in the money.

My luck turns and turns hard. Bad as it was early, it's twice as good now. I win four hands in a row, lose one, then win four more. Still the deck runs favorable and my bets stay high. Blackjacks, so scarce a little while ago, are pouring out every few hands now, and landing in front of me instead of Vito. All of a sudden the guy can't beat me. If he has 19, I have 20. If he has 20, I have 21. I can't get my bets down fast enough.

One-on-one with the dealer you can win or lose with stunning speed. Five hundred a hand, three or four hands a minute, it all adds up in a hurry. In no time I'm in the black.

Vito shuffles the decks, stacks the cards back in the shoe and starts in on a new deal. My luck holds. Low cards come out early again, so I keep the big bets coming. I play two hands at once. Five hundred, even six hundred a pop. And I keep winning. Every which way you can, too. Splitting cards, doubling down, sticking on low totals. I'm so hot that when the count evens out again I don't lower my bet.

As the roll keeps on, the crowd at the table gets behind

me, like crowds will behind a winner. Guys high-five me after every blackjack, and whoop it up and bang the back of my chair. A few of the ladies take a sudden interest in the handsome guy with the big stack of chips, and rub my brush cut for luck between hands.

Vito is not taking all this well at all. He keeps turning to Gino, saying, "I can't believe it, boss. I never seen nothing like it."

Gino himself stands stone-straight now, his eyes leaving the table only to go to me. The dumb grin on my face says I'm pissing myself at the luck, no idea where it's coming from. When the waitress brings a drink I won't let her leave until I lose a hand, then I give her a five for herself and one for the jukebox and tell her to keep the Creedence coming.

Vito deals out the shoe again and starts in on a third one. I lose a few hands early, but then go right back on my tear. Lady Luck herself, it seems, is handing me the cards. I hit a sixteen and pull a five. I stick on a twelve and Vito busts. I double down my soft eighteen and the three of hearts, the very card I imagined, falls to the felt and nudges me to twenty-one.

As my winnings pile up I start cashing in two grand at a time. I'm not about to risk saving all my chips until the end. Gino doesn't like it, but what can he do? I have a lot more of his money than he has of mine now. If he wants to keep me at the table, he can't afford to piss me off.

The sweetest point of the night comes when Gino rushes to the back for more dough. I say a silent toast for Atlantic City, for all of us who walked the boardwalk with our heads down or stood desperate at the credit machines, taking out money we didn't have to win back money we couldn't afford to lose in the first place. Every gambler dreams of breaking the house, and now I know the feeling.

Gino hurries back with the money, afraid I might leave on him. What a sap. Here he is, desperate to keep me at the table, where I sit three feet away from him, counting my ass off, killing him in his own joint. Taking half the cut from his last hit, probably, while all the while he figures it for a hot streak and waits for me to give it back. No wonder these guys all wind up in the clink.

My run lasts for three shoes and when it finishes I'm loaded. Gino would be on to me if I try to cut out, so I stay put. I'm not about to chance giving back my stash, though. I knock my bets down to ten bucks and relax. Stop counting, even. Just spend the next hour sipping tall vodka tonics and playing basic strategy. I win a little, lose a little, but it hardly matters anymore. I'm like the winning quarterback in the last minutes of a rout, all the big plays behind me and the outcome determined. I'm simply running out the clock.

Only now, once I've buried him, does Gino seem to think something's up. Twice he tells Vito to stop in the middle of the deal and shuffle the cards.

"If you don't mind," he says, glaring at me.

"Not at all."

The second time he does it I go to the can to count my winnings. I count my pile twice before I believe it: $15,225 to the good. I look at the stall door in front of me and let out a breath. Damn near say a prayer of thanks.

Time for me to clear out. When your luck's been as good as mine, you don't give it a chance to turn on you. With Gino ordering shuffles, and the sun almost up, I've gotten all there is to get out of this place. I weave back to the table and say I want to cash in.

The vibes coming off the Italians are not good. Vito counts out my bills in harsh strokes, glaring at me between hundreds. Gino must have given the word while I was in the can, because the bartenders are rounding up glasses and starting to move people toward the door. It's almost 6 A.M.

As I put the money away Gino steps from behind the table and I see for the first time how big he really is. Almost as tall as me and a good fifty pounds heavier.

"What's your name, kid?" he asks.

"Alex."

"Alex what?"

"Kevins."

"That was quite a run you had tonight, Alex."

"I'll say. Can you believe it?"

He steps closer and folds his arms over his chest.

"You ever played blackjack before, Alex?"

"Sure. Just with the fellas, though. Nothing ever like this."

"You seem to know what you're doing."

"He sure did," Vito chips in. "I never seen nothing like it."

I give a humble shrug. "Heck, I'll probably give it all back next week. I just had one of those nights. You saw me— everything I did turned out right."

"Yeah." Gino leans toward me without moving his feet. "You got a business card, Alex?" He takes off his shades. "Sometimes we run specials."

I pat my pockets. "Left all that stuff at home."

Vito edges around the table and takes up a spot between me and the door to the front room. I notice that all of a sudden the place is nearly empty. I turn to go but Gino speaks up again.

"Alex, how about stepping into my office a minute."

It isn't a request, and it hits me that in all my planning I never gave any thought to an exit. One thing I'm not going to do is spend any time in the back with Gino and Vito.

"I would but I'm bushed, guys. Next time, okay?"

I see from Vito's stance that he doesn't figure on letting

me by. I try to gauge the best route past him, but his eyes are on me for any moves.

"Hey, it's the bullfighter!"

Brushing past Vito comes Grace, the blonde Dave cornered here last week. She walks right up to me.

"No fights on Sundays?"

Cindy Crawford never looked so good. I take Grace's hands in my right hand and with my left around her shoulder I say, "Guys, meet my fiancée. Fiancée, the guys." I spin Grace to Vito, then back to Gino. "We have to go now. Fiancée needs her sleep."

Vito stays put. He takes a nod from Gino and pats his coat under his armpit, his eyes still on mine. Grace is working about thirty seconds behind the rest of us. "Fiancée?"

The few customers left in the place have spotted the commotion and are looking over. Now or never, Tom. I step to Gino, drop the grin and slur and speak in a clear voice.

"Here's how it works. I won my money fair and square. Now the girl and I are leaving."

The game is over. Gino knows the truth and I know he knows. But I have him. He'll have to pull a gun to stop me, and he can't do that, not in front of customers. He looks past me and shakes his head ever so slightly at Vito.

I have a tight hold of Grace now. I pull her past Vito, who doesn't step aside but doesn't stop me. Boy, does he look pissed, though. At the front stairs I turn for a last look back at Gino. I wish I hadn't. His big arms are still crossed, his face red, and his eyes tight and hard on me. He looks like a guy with revenge on his made-up mind. Up on the street I let go of Grace and flag a cab.

"Sorry to drag you out of there, but if I were you I wouldn't go back. Those men are gangsters."

"Really?" Her eyes are wide. "So what are you, a cop too?"

"Something like that. I gotta go." I jump into the cab.

"Hey wait, wait."

I roll down the window.

"Tell your friend to call me. He said he'd take me flying."

I tell the cabbie "Brooklyn" and keep my eyes out the back of it until we're over the bridge. Brooklyn always gets painted as a hole, but she looks sweet to me this morning. I have him take Flatbush to Fourth Avenue, cut up through the Slope, head to Grand Army Plaza, circle the block twice, and let me out at the big statue.

In the early morning only a few people are out with their dogs. I walk down into the subway, buy a token and stand close by the booth till the train comes. I choose the middle car and take a seat by the biggest guy in it.

I pick up an old *Post,* and with my heart still going three beats a second and twenty-five grand tucked into my crotch, I nod to the Rastafarian across from me and ride home.

I COME IN THE DOOR to an empty apartment and a note on the fridge from Molly. "Off to the Met and more, will return in the P.M." On the answering machine is a message Dave must have left this morning. He says they're in the finals, that the stiffs they're up against don't know a 7-iron from a hard-on, and that I should consider the money won.

I walk to the bedroom, dump all the cash on the bed and fall on top of it. I toss a few stacks in the air. Man, what a night. I should have been an Old West gambler. Riding from one tombstone town to the next, fleecing the locals in the saloon, and tipping my hat to the madams on the way out. I make a pillow out of five thousand bucks or so, relax and close my eyes.

Dave's phone call wakes me at noon.

"Just starting the back nine, partner."

"What's the story?"

"We're down a little, but nothing we can't handle."

"Down? I thought these guys were pushovers."

"I did, too, but seems Junior's been practicing. And I can't put two good holes together. Lucky for me it's match play."

"Jesus, Dave. Will Dad still give you the money if you don't win?"

He laughs. "If we don't win, Tom, he won't give me a ride to the station."

"How far are you down?"

"Gotta go. I'll call you from the clubhouse."

I hang up and lie awake, looking up at the ceiling. I hate to sound greedy after the night I had, but I could sure use this five grand. At three the phone rings again.

"I hope your bank takes third-party checks, Tom."

"You won?"

"Never in doubt. The one-hole playoff was just for show."

"Christ. And Dad? He came through with the money?"

"But of course."

"Dave, you're a champ. How'd the lecture go?"

"I wish I had a tape of it. It was in the top five."

"You done good, Dave. Speaking of fund-raising, though, I haven't had a bad weekend myself. I paid Gino a little return visit."

"Gino?"

"Yeah. If you weren't so busy bird-dogging young women, you might have noticed he runs a blackjack game in the back. I took a crack at that game last night."

"And?"

"And I took the bastard for fifteen grand."

"You're shitting me."

"Swear to God."

"Jesus, Tom. You took fifteen grand off of Gino? And I thought I was kicking some ass."

"Not bad, huh?"

"I'll say. Goddamn. Tom, he doesn't know where you live, does he?"

"No."

"Keep it that way. You have any idea who he's connected to?"

"I can guess."

"You guessed right. Trust me, you don't want to be on a first-name basis with that crowd. They play for keeps."

"Don't worry—they've seen the last of me."

"Damn, Tom. Fifteen grand . . . So, what's the tally?"

"Well, if my math is right we've got ten grand to go."

"And five days to raise it. Any ideas?"

"Yeah. Actually, I've got one that might put us in the clear."

"Run it by me."

"Tell you what, Dave. Let me see if it's any good first. I'll give you a call tomorrow. If this pans out we'll be all set. If it doesn't, we'll have some brainstorming to do."

"Sounds good. I'm off for some celebrating here. The sister of the guy we beat can't take her eyes off me, and I'm in the mood to do a little consoling."

"Good luck. And thanks, Dave."

"What's a friend for?"

CHAPTER SIXTEEN

I'M BRINGING the team in for a grand apiece.

Only thing is, they don't know the money's on the dart match. They think it's going on a horse.

I've told the story four times now and it sounds so good I half believe it myself. The horse's name is Spirit, and the sure tip comes straight from his trainer. Spirit has been hurt all season and is sure to go off a long shot. Spirit is healthy, though, and running times in his workouts he never came close to before the injury. More than that, Spirit is a mudder. The track is wet already, more rain is on the way, and the other mudder in the field pulled out last week. The clincher? We're only betting him to show. Knocks the profit way down, sure, but at these stakes we need a lock, and you could sleep at the track all season and not get wind of a better one.

The gang trusts me because a few months ago I really did come through on a horse. We got smashed one dart night and I talked everyone into tossing twenty bucks on a French flier I had a hunch on in the Belmont. We bet her to win, she came across at 4–1 and I looked like a genius. So when I called around last night and laid Spirit on real thick, everyone came aboard. Pretty shitty, I know, but I'll make it up to them. We'll win the dart match, I'll cut them in, and no one ever has to know the difference.

So now I'm in a booth at Pete's Tavern Monday night, waiting for Claire. She's due here any minute with her thousand. I order a pitcher and two mugs from the waitress, and when she brings them I fill one and take a long sip.

There's always been a little something between me and Claire. We met sophomore year in math. I was better at it than she was, prepped her for a couple of quizzes, and soon was flirting in the casual way you can with some girls. I was in one of my stretches at the time, I remember. All semester without a whiff.

One night at a frat party I got loaded and came on to her. I was none too subtle, apparently, but instead of slapping me one Claire just held me off in that cool way of hers and struck up a deal. Don't ask me how we got from point A to point B, but the upshot was we'd meet every Wednesday for Scrabble. If she won I had to do her math homework, and if I won she had to fuck me.

English wasn't my strong suit, but with seven weeks left in the term I figured just the luck of the letters should be good for a win, and if I could pull off even one, doing her homework for six weeks would be the bargain of the year.

Beats me why people think college kids get laid all the time. Before Lisa I was lucky to get lucky twice a term, and I might remember one of those. At Ham Tech, like at a lot of schools, the jocks got the lookers—in our case, all ten of them. The rest of us made out the best we could.

For the guys who struck out on the grounds, there wasn't a lot of relief off campus, either. If you weren't up for dipping into the local high school, you could try your luck down the road at Colgate. You had to watch your ass, though. Their guys didn't take kindly to outsiders trying to work their stream, and anyway, nothing you could land there was worth taking one in the teeth for.

So Scrabble it was. What I didn't know was that Claire had been high school Scrabble champ of Long Island. Knew every word in the language that starts with q. When I showed up in her suite for the first match she had another surprise for me—she came to the table in shorts and a T-shirt. For a skinny girl Claire has quite a chest on her, a combo that kills me even today. Back on the Hill, where I was lucky to see a bare arm between October and March, it just wasn't fair. She'd lean over to play her tiles and I'd forget any words I was working on. She beat me by two hundred points.

I knew I had to get serious, so I bought myself a Scrabble dictionary and checked into the library for the first time since they taught us to use the place at Orientation. Nothing like a little incentive to bring out the student in a guy. I put in a couple of hours a night and after a few weeks started closing the gap on her. Lost by a hundred, then fifty, then by just thirty. The last week of the term I thought I had her. She was stuck with five and six vowels most of the way, and I pulled ahead near the end. I could barely hold myself in. I was all set to make her pay up then and there, but on her final turn she played out her letters and beat me by three points. I didn't sleep for a week.

After such a close call I always figured it was a matter of time before Claire and I went the distance. Most times, if you stay friends with a girl long enough, something winds up throwing you together, if just for one night. You both get drunk, maybe, or one of you gets jilted, and what starts as a consolation hug ends up as the whole nine yards.

Never happened with Claire, though. I'm not sure about her sometimes. The rest of my friends I know inside out, but there's something in Claire I can't quite get to. She seems to come on and sidestep in the same motion. As long as I've known her she's never had a steady. She dates guys two, three times, but nothing comes of it. She's very . . . careful. Lately I'm starting to think we may never hook up. Which is fine, too, I guess.

She comes through the door and gives a wave when she spots me. She slides into the booth and leans across for a quick kiss.

"Hi, there."

"Hi."

She's in a tight blue suit with white hose, her legs together, her blond hair framing her smooth face. She looks straight at me with a cool smile.

"So tell me again about this magic horse."

"Best investment you'll ever make. He can't miss."

"If you say so, Tom. So why do I feel so uneasy?"

"Maybe because you don't cultivate the gambling side of your nature, Claire. You really should. I think you'd be a natural."

"Thanks." She pulls an envelope from her purse, holds it to her chest with both hands, and sighs. "Lean forward."

When I do she taps the envelope on my head.

"Sir Tom, I knight thee for luck." She sighs again and hands it over. "My bonus, Tom—please make it grow."

"Consider it done."

I tuck the envelope away and raise my mug.

"To Spirit," I say. We clink.

"To Spirit."

FROM PETE'S I CAB down to First and Tenth and cross the street to the ruined awning of Downtown Beirut. In New York there are dives and there are *dives*. Downtown Beirut is the latter. One forty-watt bulb lights the whole place, which at least keeps you from seeing the art on the walls. Or the beer mugs. I'm a veteran of the East Village but I order from the bottle here, and I'll walk the twenty blocks back to my place before I'll use the can. I've seen homeless guys get a peek in there and head out.

The place smells like a swamp and the regulars look as if they haven't been outside in weeks. The jukebox is as good as you'll find, but through the ten-dollar speakers all the songs sound the same, and you wind up picking punk just so you can hear it. It's always eighty degrees inside, the crowd favors nose rings and green hair, and most nights you can count on at least one good fight. I try to make it here once a week.

I'm on my second beer when Bobby walks in. He tosses me his jean jacket, feints with a right uppercut, and rubs the top of my head.

"Sixteen dollars, Tom."

"What's that?"

"Sixteen dollars. That's what I got left. Till post time, anyway, when this horse of ours blows away the field. Buy me a beer?"

"Sure."

Bobby was the easiest sale on the team. I knew he would be. He likes any plan so long as he's in on it, and he said yes to Spirit before I could even tell him the details. I've known Bobby six years, and I can't remember him ever saying No to anything. Friendliest guy I've ever met. Hates conflict of any kind.

At school, we used to express Bobby's personality in terms

of an equation: it was equal to *x*, where *x* was equal to the last guy to enter the room. You tell Bobby the Democrats are ruining this country and he'll say, "Damn straight they are." He'll really believe it, too—until he runs into someone who says the Republicans are screwing everything up, at which point he'll say, "You got that right," and shout a toast to the Kennedys. Bobby's not a whole lot of good in a debate, but you won't find a better drinking buddy.

If I could have a kid brother I'd make him just like Bobby. Nothing dark or brooding at the bottom of him. Grew up a good Catholic boy and even when he crossed over to the pipe in school he stayed straight and clean inside. He's a little guy, like I said earlier. Five feet three. Keeps a chip on his shoulder about it, but it comes out in all the right ways. A scrappy athlete, second or third one picked when choosing teams. Then there's the way he can hold that piss. Damnedest thing you ever saw.

My only worry about Bobby is his girl Polly. She's perfect for him, and you hate to see that. He'll be the next of us to drop, I figure, though on the bright side Jimmy's sideshow with Linda has probably bought Bobby another year with the gang. I worry if Polly hits him with an ultimatum, though. Shutting off a guy's supply can make him do crazy things, and Bobby never had a girl at school.

He pulls an envelope from his shirt, drops it onto the bar and slides it over to me. I reach for it but he keeps his hand on it.

"Before I give it over, Tom . . ."

"What?"

"Cost of doing business with me—one movie opening."

"Christ, Bobby. You just gave us one the other night."

He starts to pull it back. "If you don't want it . . ."

"All right, you win. Hit me."

He smiles. "Close your eyes."

"Closed."

"Okay. The scene is a park bench in daytime. Two Hasidic Jews sit at either end, hunched over their books. It's dead quiet. Suddenly, a big long-haired teen skates into the picture, Pearl Jam blasting from a boom box on his shoulder. He stops to tie his skates and sets the box on the bench between the two readers. Doesn't even turn it down. He takes his time with his laces, lets a full song play through, then picks up the box and skates off. The Hasidic guys look after him, shaking their heads. Finally the one speaks up:

" 'Doesn't compare to their early stuff.' "

I give Bobby the thumbs-up as Tank comes in, waking a few of the regulars by slamming the door behind him.

"Guys."

He nods at us, wipes the sweat off his face, takes a drink of my beer, and tosses an envelope onto the bar.

"This is a week's pay for me, Reasons. Your horse blows this one, I'll beat him up myself."

Either you love Tank or you hate him. His charm is his lack of charm. At the end of a date he'll ask a girl straight out if she wants to fuck. Doesn't see a thing wrong with that.

"How's work?" I ask.

"On my ass."

Tank sells policies for a big insurance company. A year ago he got ripped on poker night and made us all clients. Our net worth wasn't a thousand bucks for the lot of us but we walked around with policies worth a hundred grand. Till the premiums came due, anyway. Then we all promptly defaulted and the head office called Tank onto the carpet for some explaining.

Tank will never end up on the shrink's couch. He makes it through life by keeping things simple. The great event of the twentieth century, for him, was Namath's guarantee in Super Bowl III. The low point was the day the Mets traded Seaver. Tank puts on his suit to U2 in the morning and takes it off to the Who at night. In between, he'll wash down the Mets, Knicks, or Jets with a six-pack. You don't need a degree to figure out his moods, either. If he's depressed the company is working him too hard, or he hasn't gotten any lately, or the Jets lost on Sunday. Jet losses he takes hardest of all, which makes December a tough month for him.

"Buy me a beer, Reasons. I'll go put on some tunes."

I owe Tank big when it comes to music. If it weren't for him I'd still be a Styx fan. The big rub to growing up on army bases is that you listen to the worst music in the world. Top 40 or bust. I hit college thinking Casey Kasem was the balls. Couldn't name you one Hendrix tune, couldn't tell you who the Clash were, but I could sing everything the Little River Band ever did. Jesus. Even now it's a little hard to admit.

Tank wandered into my room that first day, saw my box of tapes, and made me toss them all out before anyone else spotted them. That first semester he made it his personal mission to bring me up to speed.

What a charge it was to hear real music after the stuff I grew up on. My head about flew off. Rock 'n' roll had always been a couple stanzas of gentle rhymes and a chorus you could sing along to. I never dreamed there were bands out there like X, or Hüsker Dü, who play it all a lot faster, a lot harder, with words you can't always understand, or print if you can.

Tank taught me well. By the end of the term the gang trusted me to put on an album, and by spring I could throw together a pretty fair party tape, or be counted on to deliver at the jukebox. These days I can hold my own with anyone.

Tank returns and takes a swallow of beer.

"Now that you have my dough, Reasons, how about a shot and a head butt to seal this thing right."

I order tequilas all around. Tank really steps into the head butt, and I'm so woozy from the force of it I need the shot to set me straight. After we toss them back we raise our mugs.

"To Spirit," I say, still trying to focus.

"To Spirit," says Bobby.

Tank puts up his hand.

"To fuckin' Spirit."

I HAVE A GOOD BUZZ going as I hop a cab uptown, and once inside I roll down the window to let the rushing air clear my head. My last stop tonight will be Gentleman's, an old man's bar across the street from Jimmy's financial firm. I'm hoping Jimmy leaves his trading buddies at the office. Not just because they're pricks, either. I have one tough sell job ahead of me, and I'll need him one-on-one to pull it off.

Jimmy said last night he's good for a grand, but I hope to bring him in for a lot more. If I can get him to lay out seven thousand I'll be in the clear, all the dough I need for the match in hand. That's a big if, I know, and rattling up First Avenue, past hospital row and the UN, I try to figure an angle I can work.

In the old days Jimmy was an easy touch. If I needed a favor I softened him up with a few jokes and he came across. A year of marriage has pretty much killed his sense of humor, though. Hard to believe, because back in school nobody liked a good joke as much as Jimmy. Hell, one of his best ones came at my expense.

Freshman year I signed on to cover sports for the school paper. My first day on the job they handed me the football team. I was all gung ho until I saw the smiles around the room, and started thumbing the back issues the editor tossed me.

Ham Tech football had been terrible forever. I mean terrible. Only a few fossils on the faculty could remember a winning season, and a recent class made it through all four years to graduation without seeing a victory. Not that anyone would have been there to see it. On a sunny day a game might draw a hundred fans. As for the stories in the paper, only the players themselves bothered to read them. Not exactly a plum beat.

The season I covered them they lived up to their rep and then some. With our soft schedule, all we needed was a couple guys who knew which way to run with the ball. No dice. We lost our first nine games, and heading into our season finale at Williams, we were primed to finish winless again. The week of the game a few players I knew from the dorm promised me a night of beers if I could write a story that made them laugh. Williams was a rival, or what passed for a rival in our parts, because they were a little liberal arts school just like us and about as bad on the field. I figured what the hell, nobody gave a damn, so I sat down with a six-pack and wrote the piece. I played it straight until the end, then slipped in a few paragraphs about Williams's freshman quarterback. I said he was having doubts about his intensity because one of the linemen across the ball was a fag lover from high school, and he wasn't sure he could control himself if they wound up together on the bottom of the pile. I made up a few quotes to add weight to the story and filed it right at the deadline.

My editor was a drunk whose idea of a good piece was one that hit the line count. He was pretty far along when I dropped it on his desk, and after counting out thirty-three lines he signed off on it.

The paper came out Friday morning and all the players loved it, though as word got round to the administration they didn't show quite the same sense of humor. A little chat with the editor would have been the end of it, but Jimmy got it into his head to road-trip to Williams Friday night with a hundred copies and drop them all over campus. He even managed to slip one under the door of their president.

The morning of the game the shit hit the fan. Their president called it a "new low" in college journalism and demanded an apology. I wanted the paper to issue a statement saying we stood by our story, but they canned me instead. Might have been worse, but when the dean called me in I claimed I had a source my conscience didn't allow me to reveal.

That was all she wrote for my sportswriting career, though I did get that night of beers. As for Jimmy, he got off scot-free. Thought the whole thing was a pisser, and to this day I've never paid him back.

I walk into Gentleman's to find him alone at the bar and in high spirits. He slides a beer to me.

"Why the great mood?" I ask.

"Linda okayed the horse money. Not only that—after the tumble I gave her last night, I should be squared away till the weekend."

We raise our mugs. "To Demi Moore," I say.

"Bastard." He pulls an envelope from his suit and hands it over.

"Here you go. Now tell me more about Robo Horse."

"Jimmy, we'll never get a chance this good. This baby is a lock."

"That's what I like to hear."

I look up at the ceiling, real casual.

"You know, Jimmy, there's no reason to stop yourself at a grand. I didn't."

He looks at me. "What do you mean?"

"Well, I did a little borrowing, and I've got seven thou on her myself."

"Seven grand?"

"You could come in for the same."

"Seven thousand dollars on a horse? You're crazy. Linda would kill me."

"Not if she didn't know."

"What?"

I pull my chair closer.

"Hear me out, Jimmy." He eyes me warily but lets me talk. "She'd never have to hear about it until after you won. You slip me the money Thursday without marking it down in the book. Spirit comes in a winner Friday night, you get your fourteen grand, then you sit her down and explain it to her. You know the drill—you lost your head, you don't know what got into you, blah, blah, blah, but the good news, dear, is we're seven grand richer, go buy yourself something nice." I spread out my hands.

"And if he loses?"

"Jimmy, if there were any chance this horse would lose I wouldn't bring you in, not even for a grand. I'm telling you, it's the tip of a lifetime."

He shakes his head but I can see he's mulling it over. I order more pints and close in.

"Jimmy, who pulls down the bucks in your house?"

"Me."

"And who's always telling me how bland his life is? How little excitement he's getting?"

182

"Me."

"Well, here's a shot at some real excitement, Jimmy. Take it."
He takes a long pull off his new pint.

"But seven grand, Tommy. They don't make doghouses
that big."

"Do I have to hit you over the head with it? This horse is
not going to lose, Jimmy. Jesus." I look away down the bar
and mumble under my breath.

"What was that?"

"What?"

"What did you just say? And why are you shaking your
head?"

"Nothing."

"Come on, tell me."

I sigh.

"I was just wondering, Jimmy, if you ever get tired of five-
and-diming it. A few years ago you would have been all over
this. Hell, you'd be trying to talk me into doubling the whole
works. Now a hot tip falls in your lap, I give you a chance to
cash in, and you're not even going to pull the trigger." I
shrug and shake my head. "Hey, it's up to you. Just makes
me sad, is all."

Jimmy looks straight ahead a long time. Out of the corner
of my eye I can see him working the inside of his lip with his
teeth. When he talks he still isn't looking at me.

"It is me bringing home the bacon, isn't it?"

"Last I looked."

"And it's not like I'd be pissing it away, right? I'd just be
taking a little chance with it."

"And not much of a chance, either. The horse is gold,
Jimmy."

Thirty seconds of silence. He takes another sip.

"You believe in reincarnation, Tommy?"

183

"No."

"Me neither. So I guess any chances I'm going to take have to be this time around."

He looks hard at me a second, then throws back the rest of his pint and brings his glass down softly on the wooden bar.

"What the hell, Tommy," he says quietly. "Seven grand it is."

I let out a breath. "You won't regret this, Jimmy."

He wipes his forehead with his hand. "I'm already starting to."

I wave down the bartender and he brings fresh pints. Jimmy reaches for his and shakes his head.

"Tommy, I can't decide if you're good or bad for me." He lifts his glass and smiles weakly. "I guess I'll find out Friday night. Okay, what do we toast?"

I lift mine. "What else? A toast to Spirit, Jimmy."

"To Spirit."

The first rush I felt when he caved in dies down and I take a big swig to kill the lump forming in my throat. I really do hate to lie, though I must admit I'm getting pretty good at it. Oh well. Maybe it's not lying so much as talking around the subject. So long as it comes out right in the end, where's the harm? Sometimes, the way the game is rigged these days, you just have to go out on the ledge a little. Hell, in a week's time we'll be at Adam's Curse, celebrating.

An hour and a few pints later we're in our cups and I feel better about the whole business. If you'd told me last week that I could raise forty grand in eight days, I'd have asked what you were smoking. Here it's the Monday before the match, though, and the kitty is full.

We're about set to leave when a couple of Jimmy's trader pals spot us from down the bar. Before I can beat it they move in.

"Sit, sit," says one, waving us back down and handing us

184

each a pint. "A friend of Jimmy's . . . you know the rest. Firm's paying for it anyway." He jerks a thumb at his buddy. "After what we took in today," he says, "we oughtta have the run of the place."

I sit back down. I'll have to drink the one at least. I don't know what it is about these guys but I've never been able to stomach them. Four years of their kind at school should have been enough. Out here in the workforce they're even worse. The soft handshake, the tight smile. Power ties, handkerchiefs, and talk your ear off about the firm. I've met this pair before but I can never remember their names. Both are blond, with paunches and lots of cream in their hair. You know what they look like. The one starts in.

"Would have cost me two mil today if I didn't have call waiting. I'd say it's worth three bucks a month. So what do you do? Law firm, huh? Great." He runs a hand through his thick hair. "Me, it's a wonder I got any of this left. It's like being a gambler, is what it is, except it's five days a week, and you bet millions instead of chump change." He tosses his keys in the air and catches them as he talks. "Actually, if you think about it, it's more like being at the front. Dodging mines and missiles, and squeezing off rounds when you can. Combat pay, that's what we should get. Damn!" He shakes his head. "It's not for everyone, that's for sure."

I speed up on my beer. You want real excitement, guy, try betting your own money. He asks where I went to school, just as he did the last time we met, and when I tell him his eyes light up. "Yeah? I had a date with a Ham Tech girl last week. Looked to be about your year." Jimmy tries to cut him off but he's too late. "Lisa Klein." He leans in, hand to the side of his mouth. "Best piece I've had all year. Didn't think she'd ever stop coming."

I have enough sense to hit him with my left. Good thing

because I get too much knuckle into it. I go for the chin but come up into his nose, though the way the blood comes out you'd think I hit an artery. All down the front of him and onto the bar, too. He's on his back on the floor, holding his face, saying "My nose! My nose!" His friend gives me a shocked glare but no trouble.

Tally up the suit, the shoes, the nose, I figure the punch was worth a couple grand, easy. "You better pick a few winners tomorrow," I say, stepping over him. I shrug at Jimmy on the way out, and he shrugs back over the guy's shoulder as he helps him sit up.

On the street I look at my hand. The knuckle is swelling up but isn't broken. I grab a beer from a deli and walk home with it. I haven't hit a guy in quite a while. Not that I have any regrets. I feel bad for Jimmy, is all, and there's just enough Catholic left in me to spoil the best moments.

What is it about those guys? Even before he mentioned Lisa I could feel it rising in me. It's not the dough they're born to, or the babes. Well, sure it is. But it's more than that.

Guys like that, there's nothing to them. Take away the suit and the haircut and you're looking at air. Those two in there couldn't run a mile in ten minutes, or give you thirty push-ups, or name one batting champ in the last ten. Twenty bucks says the one I laid out was in the front row last week at Kenny G.

I've met them three or four times now and it's always the same. They know squat about anything but making dough. They might say the Knicks look good this year, sure, but ask them the starting five and you got 'em. They know Patrick, oh and that Starks fellow, but who can keep the rest of them straight? Come game night, though, who's sitting courtside, with girls right off a calendar, while I can't get a ticket? Biff and Todd in there. Courtside seats and they can't tell you what a pick and roll is. Five rows back of home plate at Shea and they don't show up until the third inning. Drives me nuts.

They get the tickets and the dolls and nobody ever holds them to account. Well, let's see him explain that nose this weekend. He can tell her he got slugged by a stock option.

I guess what really burns me about those guys is that they are the standard. They're what we've come to, at the end of the twentieth century. They have the bucks and can dress on the left side and spot the salad fork so they pass as men. Christ. If those clowns are men, if they're what the ladies are looking for, who they want steering the ship, then I'm in trouble, because they're the last men I'll ever be. And with them at the helm, it's not hard to see where we're all headed. Straight to a world without chests, if you ask me. A clean, quiet place where we all tip our hats to the neighbors, and put our bottles on the curb, and nobody's any better than anyone else. Makes you want to give up on the whole mess.

But what do I know? I can't figure the rules anymore. What is it makes a man these days, anyway? It used to be simple. You went into the service at eighteen and you came out a man. End of story. Christ knows I've heard that refrain enough times at home. That's the route Dad went, and Grandpa before him, and on back as far as we know.

Not that I think that's the answer anymore, either. Even though Dad's a lifer I always knew I wouldn't join up. I knew it as a kid, the first time I saw the fresh recruits marched all around the base. Told when to eat, when to sleep, when to go to the can. No, thanks. These days, the only guys I see going that route are the bottom of the pile, where the choice is the service or the clink. You know the ones I mean, the guys in high school who couldn't quite pull that D in shop, who drop out one day and you see them on the street three months later, trying to outrun the cops to the recruiting booth.

You should have seen Dad, though, the day I told him I wasn't joining up. I waited till senior year, and when he said, "What the hell else you gonna do?" I handed him my college acceptance. He tore it in two and handed it back. That's Dad for you. A tough guy, just like his father before him. Grandpa was a Navy man who spent his whole life in the yards and who, no bull, once went thirty-two years between sick days. Dad opted for the Army, but he's cut from the same cloth.

Maybe that's why I want to beat Duggan so bad. Sometimes I think he and my old man would hit it off pretty well. Duggan is a tough guy, too. I don't even need to hear his story—I can guess. Came across the foam with nothing, like all the others. Ten years of schooling, probably, tops, but he looks at us with our college degrees and he's not impressed. The kind of guy who takes what he wants when he wants it and never says sorry to anyone. I'll bet he can't wait to get a crack at me.

There's an old Southern expression that says you aren't a man until your father tells you you are. Not much chance Dad will be sending that letter anytime soon. Still, I get the feeling that if I can pull all this off—beat Duggan on his own terms, with everything riding on it—well maybe, for a little while anyway, I'll stop waiting for it.

188

CHAPTER SEVENTEEN

 *I DON'T KNOW* what got into me.

The guy from Immigration called this morning to hand us the case. Not only is Rosa illegal, but it turns out her cousin is too. Works construction off the books for Prego's brother in Queens. Our man has pay stubs, pictures, everything we need. He'll sit on the info, he said, unless he hears different from us.

"What do you think, Reasons? Ought to let you guys put the squeeze on him, huh?"

I thanked him, said we should be in the clear now. Then I walked into Carter's office and told him Prego had come up clean.

"Goddammit!"

Carter slammed his fist on the desk.

The funny thing is, when I walked in here I didn't mean to lie to him. At the last second I saw the little statue he keeps of the scales of justice. You know the one, where she's blind and just weighs the evidence. I saw that and I thought of Prego and it just came out.

"I don't believe it!" Carter says, squeezing his temples with his hand. "I've seen a hundred guys like Prego, and there's always someone hanging around who's not legit. Just my luck to draw the one family who plays it straight."

This is it—my last chance to come clean. If I don't, and the firm ever finds out, that's the end of me. Their biggest case in years, and one of their own is shooting bullets through the heart of it. Christ, what about Prego, though? The guy did nothing wrong, and if it's left up to the system he'll never even get to tell his side of it. I'm the last guy left who can give him that chance.

"You sure he looked everywhere, Reasons?"

Out the window, past Carter's head I can see the water, and far out on it I can just make out the green hand of the Statue of Liberty. Holding her torch. Fuck it. If it costs me, it costs me.

"He covered every angle, sir. Prego's clean."

Carter swivels his chair and stares out at the river himself. "Okay, Reasons. Then we go to Plan B."

"What's Plan B, sir?"

"You'll like it."

He turns back around and taps his fingers on the desk. "Reasons, I think it's about time we brought you into the circle. We have to sooner or later."

I'm all for later, much later, but he launches in.

"Plan B, Reasons, is the Board of Health springs a surprise visit on our Mr. Prego. The inspector pokes around in the cellar awhile, then comes up saying he saw a rat down there you could put a saddle on. That's just how he writes it up, too. Calls the boys over and they lock Prego's doors on him. Put a sign up in the window, 'Closed by Order of the Board of Health.'

"The closure is just 'temporary,' of course, until he can pass inspection. But our friend the inspector, he's a busy guy. This town has a lot of restaurants, after all, and keeping them safe for Joe Public is a big task. So even though Prego calls and calls, his second inspection keeps getting put off.

"Meantime, we're firing motions at him one after the other. His lawyers have to respond, of course, and with his business down he's not generating any revenue to pay them.

"And when, finally, the inspector does get back there, damned if he doesn't see that rat again. Or maybe the motor on the ice unit isn't up to code, or they find a couple bugs on a bag of rice. Whatever it is, the place is never quite up to snuff. So the sign stays in the window. Until Prego is ready to settle, of course." Carter shoots me a smug smile. "It all comes together pretty nicely, don't you think?"

"I guess it does, sir."

He dismisses me and I head back to my desk. So much for any regrets. I should have known, though, that Carter would have a backup scheme, and that it would take more than my little fib to get Prego his day in court. I chase down citations for an hour but can't keep my head in the job, so I walk out on the landing to get some air. Up here on the thirty-third floor you get quite a view. Far down below I can see the New York Post Building standing low and gray by the water. I stare at her a good two minutes before the neon masthead sparks something in me. Well, well. Take heart, Giuseppe, I say to myself as I turn away. We're not done yet.

Back at my desk the phone rings.

"Hello?"

"Tom, she threw me out."

191

"What?"

"Molly, Tom. She threw me out."

"What do you mean, she threw you out?"

"She met someone else. Some guy named Ben who works at the health club. So she threw me out."

Molly with a health-club stud?

"Mike, it's your place. The lease is in your name. Hell, she's not even working now. You're picking up her share of the rent, too."

"But she said I can't come back."

I pull the phone from my ear and stare at it a few seconds.

"Tom, what can I do?"

"I'd tell you, Mike, but you wouldn't do it."

"I will, I promise. What do I do?"

"Okay, listen. March straight home, drag Molly into the street by her hair and throw her stuff out after her. When she stops rolling, tell her if she comes back she better have a rent check in one hand, dinner in the other, and she better be wearing something nice. Then spit and slam the door."

Silence on the line for three seconds.

"Come on, Tom. Be serious. Tom?"

"I'm here."

"You know violence doesn't solve anything. Maybe if I just give her some space she'll calm down."

I bow my head. "Maybe. Mike, I gotta go. You do what you want, and let me know how it turns out."

A minute later I'm still shaking my head at the receiver. Why am I even surprised, though? It was bound to happen. The only shock, really, is that it took this long.

A guy like Mike, he twists himself into a pretzel to be just what his girl wants, but once he gets there, there isn't anything left of him. Molly has her little fellow, who talks like she does and thinks like she does and signs up for every cause she tells him to. She pats him on the head now and then and tells all her friends what a winner she has. She thinks she's happy, and for a few months I suppose she is. But in the end she cuts him loose. Why? Because she doesn't respect him anymore, and when the lights go out no girl wants to be fucked by a guy she doesn't respect. So what else can she do but dump him for someone with a little something to him? Ben, from the health club.

Right now, Mike's learning the hard way that what girls say they want is not really what they want. I've heard it over and over. They tell you they're looking for a guy who is sensitive, caring, who can understand their feelings. I know a dozen guys like that and not one of them gets laid. If you ask me, I think most girls are looking for the same thing us guys are. A little fun out of life, some adventure. A good time in the sack. If you agree on the big picture besides, it's a bonus.

If Mike just pays attention here and takes all this to heart, it could be the best thing for him. He has to wise up sooner or later, and if losing Molly is all the lesson costs him, I call that a bargain and a half. Somehow I doubt he'll see it that way, though. Mike always had a lot of marshmallow in him, even before she got ahold of him.

I CUT OUT OF THE OFFICE a few ticks early and hurry over to the Supreme Court Building. I'm at the work entrance at five sharp. If I know my clerks, I won't have long to wait. Sure enough, at 5:01 my old friend from the filing room comes out the door. Christ, he's even bigger than I thought. Must be six feet eight, at least, and almost half that across. Just the guy I need watching my back Friday night. I wave him down.

"Do you know who I am?" I ask.

He squints at me, then shrugs. "I don't look at faces, kid. I stamp and file."

"I'm Tom Reasons. I work for Farrell Hawthorne."

"Too late. Court closes at five."

"I'm not here on business. Not court business, anyway. I wondered if you'd be interested in making some extra bucks?"

"Back off, kid. You think they let us freelance for law firms?"

"It's not for the firm. You'd be working for me, personally."

He looks me over. "Doing what?"

I explain.

"Why me?"

"You're the biggest guy I know."

"How much?"

"Five hundred bucks."

"When?"

"Friday night."

"Friday night I got opera tickets, kid. Prokofiev—my favorite by a long shot." He takes a step away, then stops and sighs. "I have seen it four times, though. For five hundred bucks I suppose I could skip it this once. Tell me again what I gotta do."

I spell it out, we shake on it, and he lumbers off to his bus.

BACK AT THE PAD Tuesday night I meet Ben for the first time. I can see right away he does more than pass out towels and guard the sauna. He has the huge arms and slim waist of a gymnast, and a shock of blond hair. When I walk in, he and Molly are on the couch. They have an old Giants play-off tape in the VCR, and Ben's taking her through the game of football step by step. Just now he's going over the

194

difference between a 4–3 defensive set and a 3–4, and
Molly's soaking it up as if she were born on the fifty-yard
line. She tells me they've been at it all day.

"Go on, Tom. Ask me a question about the game. Anything at all."

"Okay. What made Bavaro such a good tight end?"

"Really, Tom. Pretty pedestrian. First and foremost, he
blocked well. And he could get downfield and make the
tough catches in traffic."

I look at Ben and he beams. I shake my head as I walk to
the bedroom to change out of my suit.

What can I say? Guys, girls, it doesn't matter. It all comes
down to who holds the hammer. Molly held it over Mike, so
he checked his balls at the door every night. Now Molly's
found something she needs, Ben's got the hammer on her,
and just like that she's a regular offensive coordinator.

It's no mystery what that something is, either. Late that
night, as I lie in bed with my hands behind my head, it
comes through the wall loud and clear. Turns out Molly has
a little cat in her after all. Only when Kretzky starts throwing the ball against the door do they pipe down.

I sigh. Man, I need to get laid. I'm serious. It's not healthy
for a guy my age to sweat it out alone night after night. I
know, I had my shot and walked out on it. Don't remind me.
If I can't win Lisa back, last Friday's near miss will be tough
to live down. The killer is, I can't even tell her. She'd ask
what I was doing there in the first place, and with no good
answer to that, my grand walkout wouldn't score me any
points at all. Christ.

I'm not going to beat myself up for cutting Lisa loose a
year ago. Like I said, she was the first, and no guy with any
weight to him settles in for the long haul without seeing
what else is out there. Still, looking back on it all now, it

seems to me there were a few nights on the Hill when it might have dawned on me she was the one.

One in particular keeps coming back at me.

I was drinking beer with Jimmy and Tank at a party in the gym. Lisa was late joining us because it was Thursday and Thursdays she taught reading and simple math to adults in Utica who needed their GED. I could see the mouth of the gym from where I stood. When Lisa stepped into it, the light over the door fell on her face and I could see she'd had a rough night. Often her class brought her down because so few of her students saw it through to the end. Lisa would get to know them and it was hard on her to go and see the chairs of those she liked empty, or filled with new students facing the same long odds.

Lisa started toward the back of the gym. I watched her move through the crowd, weary, and then as she spotted me I saw the joy rise in her eyes and some of the day go out of her. The last ten steps she put her hands behind her back and came sexy, slow, her eyes right on mine, and I felt such a charge downstairs I had to shift my stance. I had a few in me, and we'd been some days without a go, but it wasn't that.

As she came up on me, and kissed me in the middle of my chest, it hit me like a right cross that for the first time it wasn't her thin legs or her eyes or even the calm way I knew she'd come back at me when I put it to her that had me so primed. No, I wanted Lisa so much that night because she was the best person I knew. I knew she needed to disappear into sex, and it revved me that I had it in me to drive the rough day right out of her. I knew too that she was clean and clear inside in a way I'd never been, and that in ten minutes, in her bed, I'd get to touch that.

She drank her cup of beer while leaning back on me, and as she drank it I whispered in her ear what I was going to do to her. I felt the last of her sadness slip right out of her, felt her skin come to life. She turned into me, rested her cup on my shoulder and finished her beer in small sips. We waved bye to the guys and made straight for her room, almost running, and once there I took off her clothes and she took off mine and I did just what I said I'd do. It was a top-ten fuck, too, believe me, and you'd think somewhere in the middle of it it might have struck me that I had something I should hang on to.

CHAPTER EIGHTEEN

WEDNESDAY night at seven I stand at the door of Stella's apartment, wondering what's up. She called me at work this morning to ask me to stop by. It's funny—I've probably seen Stella twice a week, at least, for the last two years, but I've never been inside her place. I ring the bell.

I hope whatever it is doesn't take too long. I was counting on a quiet night of dart practice back at the pad. Less than fifty hours and counting, now, until the match, and all my fund-raising this past week has kept me away from the board. I'm just now getting my eye back.

I've made sure the rest of the team gets their throwing in, too. Rang them all up yesterday with a little incentive for Friday night. Told them I had a five-hundred-dollar side bet on the match with Duggan, and that I'd cut everybody in for fifty bucks if we win. Made me feel a little better. It's not the truth, I know, or even close to it, but at least it's in the ball-park.

Stella ushers me in with a smile but her face looks drawn and old. Maybe it's just the light in here. She takes my arm on the way to the living room, where she points me into a big, soft chair from about 1970.

"I've made some tea, Tom. Or would you prefer a beer?"

"On the house?"

She smiles. "On the house."

She goes to get it and I look around the big room. My kind of place. One wall is lined with old Giant pennants and framed pictures of the players. Willie Mays chasing one down in center. Durocher fighting the umps. Another is covered by cork bulletin boards full of photos. I spot the gang in a couple. On the mantel is a picture of Stella, it must be fifty years ago or more, standing with a sharp-looking guy in full Navy dress. She returns with my beer and lowers herself into a chair a few feet away.

"Tom, I know about the match Friday night."

The beer slips from my hand but I catch it between my knees. I look at her.

"My canasta partner, Tom. Remember? Papa O'Shea—the owner of County Hell Pub."

"How does he know about it?"

"Who do you think is fronting Duggan his money?"

"Papa O'Shea?"

She nods.

"Don't think he's not taking a big cut if Duggan wins. Still, it'll leave Duggan enough to start his own place. If he loses, though, he'll be working for O'Shea for the next ten years."

"Well, I'll be damned." I shake my head. The room is quiet awhile. Stella sighs.

"Tom, how many beers have I bought you this last year?"

"One."

She laughs softly. "That's one more than some of my regulars." She looks up. "I've always been cheap, Tom. My husband started the bar and taught me to run it. He used to say once you give the first one away you open the dam."

"Stella, we never minded."

"Maybe not, but you kids deserved better. You were always loyal. I know the deals the other bars were offering. And you stayed with me."

She looks straight in my eyes.

"I don't have much family, Tom. I have a grandson upstate, but between you and me"—she leans in— "he's a bit of a shit."

That's how I remember him. Robert. He lived in New York when we started the team and bartended for Stella some nights. One of those guys who was into the authority of the job. Loved to boss the busboy around and make customers wait on their drinks.

"Why are you telling me this, Stella?"

"Because I don't have a lot of time left, Tom."

"What do you mean?"

"You know what I mean."

I start to say something but she waves it off.

"Don't. I'm not going to go into it, Tom, but the doctor is an old friend of mine and he told me square."

"But Stella . . ."

"Now that's the last I'm going to say on the subject, and I don't want to hear about it from you or anyone else. You understand me?"

"Yes. How much time do you have?"

"A year, maybe longer."

We are quiet again. The sounds from outside are peaceful now. A honk there, some voices. I drink my beer and she sips her tea. When she looks up again her eyes are shining.

"I put a bet on you guys, Tom."

200

"A bet?" I can't help smiling. "How much?"

"Fifty thousand dollars. With Papa O'Shea."

"Jesus Christ." I finish my beer in a gulp. "Excuse me."

"If you guys win, I want you to keep half. Twenty-five grand."

"Stella, I don't want you to do that."

"It's you or my grandson, Tom, and if he gets it it goes right up his nose. Say you'll take it."

I look around the room.

"Okay. I'll take it."

She smiles. "Tom, I have what I need around me. Friends, the bar, all the regulars to talk to. What I don't have is any excitement. I want some, Tom. Something to look forward to. To break up the days." She puts her hand on my leg. "And I like your chances. Do you?"

"Sure. We beat 'em last time."

"And I think you can again. They may have the shooters, but you kids play together. I've seen a lot of darts in my time, Tom, and if there's one thing I've learned it's that the team that stands by each other wins." She smiles. "All this talk aside, I wouldn't put a dime on you if I didn't think you could take them."

I smile. "I believe that. We'll come through for you, Stella."

She puts her hand on my arm. "Watch out for Duggan, Tom. He's in real deep. I don't know what he'll try, but be careful. He's desperate."

"I know the feeling."

She walks me to the door and pats my arm.

"Remember, Tom, none of this to anybody." As I start down the stairs, she says, "One more thing, Tom." I turn back with a smile but her face is serious. "Don't lose."

Alone on the street I look across at Adam's Curse. Through the glass I can see the regulars at the bar, and past them the darters, throwing with their familiar rhythm. One, two, three, walk to the board. As I cross the street, I feel a sadness like I've never known. It's not fair. All the losers in this town and it has to happen to Stella. I shake my head hard to break out of it. Walking home, I tell myself this doctor business could all be a big mistake. You hear cases all the time where they tell people they have a year left, or six months, and they wind up living to a hundred. Sure, Stella doesn't look so good, but they don't make them any tougher. If anyone can beat the odds, she can. And we can do our little part for her by winning this match.

Jesus, how about this match, too. Is it spiraling out of control or what? Ninety grand on her now, that I know of. And an extra $25,000 coming my way if we win. *When* we win. Christ, I've been scrambling so fast to raise the dough, I've never stopped to think what I'll do with it when it's over. With what Stella wants to throw my way we're talking a real stash. Enough. Put all that thinking out of your head, Tom. Start getting ahead of yourself and you stop doing the things it takes to win. All I should be thinking about is taking care of my part, and right now that means back to the board to practice.

I get home to an empty apartment and the message light flashing on the answering machine. I hit the button.

"Hi, Tom, it's Lisa. Big news! I'm being transferred to Chicago. They want me on the Zuma account. Can you believe it—it's the biggest one they have. The transfer won't go through for a couple months, but then I'm free of this place, Tom. No more grabby boss, no more glass ceiling. Call me when you get this. I'll buy you a drink to celebrate."

I open a beer and sit down hard. I finish it, open another, and walk down the stairs into the street. I step in front of a cabbie and he leans on his horn and shakes his fist at me through the window. Back on the sidewalk I start up First Avenue, not thinking where I'm headed. When I find myself at Sixty-third Street I buy another beer and cut over to the walkway along the East River. The water is still and pretty, the lights of Queens falling over it from across the way.

Lisa is leaving. How's that for a kick in the nuts?

All the time we've been broken up it never occurred to me she might leave town. And Chicago, of all places. I wouldn't last a week out there. Ten degrees every day of the year and nothing but Bulls fans. The last time Jordan sank the Knicks in the playoffs I vowed I'd never even change planes at O'Hare.

Quit kidding yourself, Tom—you're not invited. I can't believe it. So long as Lisa's been in New York it's as if she was still in my life somehow, even when I didn't see her. I get into bed at night knowing she's less than a mile away, that I can be there in five minutes if I have to. But Chicago. Don't talk to me about long-distance relationships, either. I know how that game goes. You say "I'll write, I'll call," but it's all bull. You put that much distance between two people, that's it.

I stop and look out over the water. What an ass I've been. Playing it cool, going slow, figuring all along that she would come around. Never telling her I wanted her back. Never telling her I miss her so much sometimes I can't take it. That I pull out old pictures, or letters she wrote in the summers.

For the first time I tell myself what I've known all along: I can't lose her. I say it out loud. It sounds hard and strange. I say it again. Okay, Tom—you mean it? Then what's the plan? Because if you don't come up with one fast, and a good one, she's out of here.

I start walking again. I always think better when I walk, and I think best when I'm up against it. That ought to make me Einstein about now. I walk with my hand along the rail, my eyes closed, and as I walk a plan starts to form in my mind. Like any good plan it's simple, and the more I walk, the simpler I make it. By Eighty-third Street I have it sketched out in my head. I flip a quarter into the dark water, cut over to York and flag down a cab. Flying down the FDR I make the plan even simpler, and by the time I step out of the cab in Chelsea, I have it down.

IN THE ELEVATOR up to Lisa's I feel the sweat break out on me. The one thing I'm not any good at is the one thing I have to do. At her apartment I lean my head on the door a second before ringing the bell. Her roommate opens up.

"Well, well," she says, "look who's back. Didn't think we'd see you again."

"I missed you too, Julie. Is Lisa in?"

"I think she's out with some guy."

"Some guy?"

"Yeah. Oh, wait a minute—that was her lunch date, Phil. She's back from that. Then there was her dinner date, Joe, and she's back from that, too. Let's see, it's ten P.M.? Her late-night date's not due for another hour. Just a second, I'll go get her."

I do love a sense of humor in a girl.

Lisa comes to the door in sweats and a T-shirt. Why girls think they have to dress up is beyond me. A T-shirt kills me every time.

"Tom! Hi. What are you doing here?"

"I thought I'd return your call in person. How 'bout that drink you promised?"

"I'd love to. Just let me get a sweater."

It's a short walk from her place to the heart of the Village. I suggest the Red Lion because it's quiet and lead her to a booth in the back. It's nice and dark, a candle in a bottle on the table. We order beers. She smiles.

"You haven't congratulated me yet," she says.

"What—oh. Congratulations."

"What is it, Tom? You're sweating."

"Give me your hands."

She reaches them across the table slowly, her smile curious now. I take them, look down, and close my eyes a second. Okay, Tom—say it straight and quick.

"Don't go to Chicago, Lisa."

"What?"

"Don't go to Chicago."

"What do you mean, Tom? Are you asking me to turn down a promotion?"

"I'm asking you to quit your job."

She sits back, starts to laugh. "Why should I do that?"

"Because I love you."

There, it's out. Lisa's not laughing now. She looks stunned. As for me, I can feel the blood running in me. It's all on the line again. I lean in.

"Lisa, remember how we used to say one day we'd see the country? Just take off, with no plans except to go? Well, I came into some money and I can support us for a year. Come away with me."

She takes one hand away, brushes at her hair. "How did you get this money?"

"I won a bet."

She laughs softly. Her shock is wearing off.

"Go away with you, Tom?"

"Yes."

She looks down at the table, then back at me.

"If I hadn't left that message, Tom, would you be here?"

She takes her other hand back, gently.

"Would you?"

"Yes. Maybe not right now but soon. I'm not just here because you're leaving, Lisa. I'm here because I want us to be together again. Because breaking up with you was the biggest mistake of my life."

"Was it, Tom? Then why did you do it?" I look away but she takes my cheek in her hand. "Look at me, Tom. You never told me, remember? Even that last night together, you never told me." Her lip starts to go but she holds it firm. "Tom, you tell me the truth now, right here, or I walk out. Why did you leave me?"

"I was afraid I'd miss out."

"Miss out on what?"

"Other girls."

I see the stab in her eyes as she looks away fast and then back. "And what did you find out?"

"That there are no other girls. I know that now. And I know what I did to you, Lisa, and I'm sorry. You were my first real girl. I thought what we had is what everyone has. It took losing you to know I was wrong."

She wipes at her eyes and sits back. "Go on."

"I won't lie. I've gone with girls since, and chased others. What it taught me is that you're the one."

She's crying now and I can't tell what kind of tears they are.

"I think of you all the time, Lisa. I'll be walking down the street, at rush hour, and I'll think of us—of the way we used to be. The easy talk, the way you fit on my shoulder. We were special, Lisa. All the people we knew, all the couples—nobody got on like we did. You and me, we . . . we made each other whole." I stop a second. "If you don't think so, Lisa, tell me and I'll leave."

She is crying and she meets me across the table and puts her head on my chest. To smell her hair again, to smell her.

206

I kiss her forehead. She pulls back, digs in her purse for a napkin, wipes her eyes. When she looks at me again her mouth is set in a way I've never seen before. Her voice is soft.

"I thought you wrecked everything in me, Tom. I thought I'd never feel anything again. And when after a while I started to feel, I didn't want to. Then I wanted you to pay. I wanted you to miss me and to come back and I wanted to turn you away. That's what I told myself, anyway." She looks away a second, then back at me. "But deep down that's not what I wanted at all. Deep down I wanted you back, Tom. I wanted to be like we were that first night, and all those others. And I knew. You'll think I'm crazy, Tom, but I knew this day would come, that I would sit here and you would tell me all this and . . ."

She stops.

"And what?"

She shakes her head.

"Just like that, Tom? Two years we went out, and one day it was all over. And now you're back and you say we'll start it up again. Just like that? How do I know it won't happen again? What guarantees can you give me?"

"Guarantees?"

"Yes."

"I won't lie, Lisa. I can't look down the road and see anything clear. I can't tell you when the money runs out I'll go to law school, or back to work in a firm, or anything. The truth is, I don't know what I want to be. But I know I want to be with you. So I guess that's my guarantee. That I'm through leaving you, Lisa, if you give me this chance."

I take her hand again.

"All these months, it's like I've been waiting for my life to start. Like I'll wake up one morning and it'll be official. I

207

know now it doesn't work that way. Hell, my life's a quarter gone already, and what have I done? What have I seen? Well, I've learned this: The only time I was ever really happy was with you. It's taken a while to get that into my head, but it's in there now, Lisa. And all those times we had? We can have them back. We can be that way again."

"Can we?" She takes back her hand. "I don't know, Tom. Maybe we're built different. Or maybe some things you can't get back. Maybe they're precious, and if you throw them away they're gone for good."

She stands up. She puts her hand, small and hot, to my cheek and presses very hard. Her eyes are the biggest I've ever seen them, and the saddest. "I'll call you, Tom."

She walks out of the pub into the street.

CHAPTER NINETEEN

I'M ON a stool in a bar in Bay Ridge Thursday night, Little Vincent on the left of me and Big Dom on the right. I'm the biggest Braves fan in the world. They put away Florida tonight and I'm in the clear again. They don't and I'm fucked. And that's Fucked with a capital *F*.

Everything was jake until Jimmy got cold feet on the horse. He called me this morning at work.

"I can't risk it, Tommy. If I lost I'd be so screwed with Linda I'd never get out of the doghouse. I'm still in for the thousand I gave you, but not the extra six."

"Jimmy, I told you, it's a sure thing. You'll be a hero."

"It's a damn horse race, Tom—anything can happen. Spirit could pull up lame, or take a fall, or some nag no one heard of could come out of nowhere. Then where would I be?"

"Don't do this to me, Jimmy. You said you were in."

"Forget it. Anyway, what do you care? Your money's on it.

What difference does it make to you if I bet a thousand or seven thousand?"

He had me there.

"I'm just trying to make you some dough, that's all. Jimmy, everyone gets a little spooked near post time. Just ride it out, and I swear you'll be thanking me when it's over."

"Sorry, Tommy. A grand's all I can spare. See you tomorrow night."

I dropped my head to my desk and said all the curse words I know. If I'd had a bottle handy I would have taken a stiff jolt. I should never have given Jimmy a chance to think it over. I should have gotten the money from him straight off, right after I had him hooked. Jesus, now what? Here I was, a midnight meeting lined up with Duggan to show the money, and I'm six grand short. Even if I could bluff my way past him tonight, the match is tomorrow and I need it all in hand by then. Christ.

I reached for the sports page. The only honest way I could think of to scare up six grand in a couple hours was to bet a ball game. Hell, it's what I do best anyway. I'd treat it as my typical Friday wager, just with a little more on the line this time.

I scanned the matchups. Greg Maddux starting for the Braves against Florida jumped out at me. If any game tonight is a lock, that's the one. At 3 P.M. I took a little French leave from the office and headed straight up to Adam's Curse to see Toadie. He told me he doesn't handle that kind of action but for a hundred bucks could put me in touch with someone who does. I worked the bastard down to fifty, forked it over, and popped home to get the money. Ten minutes later I was in a cab for Bay Ridge and twenty minutes after that Vincent greeted me at the door of Madge's Corner Pub.

He wasn't at all what I expected. Short and thin, gray up

top, with glasses and a kind face. A real easy manner to him, fatherly, almost, as if I showed up to date his daughter and he's making me at home while he sizes me up. After a few pleasantries he took me by the elbow and walked me to the bar. I was ready to believe he wasn't a wise guy until he motioned with an open hand at a giant a couple seats down.

"Tom, this is Dom. Dom, say hi to Tom."

"Hey, Tom. Pleasure to meet you."

My hand disappeared into his. Dom is about six feet five and three-fifty, with a big friendly face and a smile like a little kid. He's dressed in sweats and a ball cap. He slapped me on the shoulder with his left hand.

"Here to take the boss's money, huh? Go get him."

Vincent introduced me all around, saying, "Hey, everyone, this is Tom," and the seven or eight guys in the place all looked up from their papers and beers and waved. The Godfather this isn't.

Behind the bar, Madge is a friendly, aging redhead with a smile that says she's seen it all. She poured me a pint. "You let me know when you need another, young man."

"Thanks." I looked at Vincent.

"You gamble with me, you drink on me, kid. House rules."

"Thanks."

"Don't mention it." Vincent settled onto his stool and ran his hand through his gray. "Now. Toadie says your MO is to bet four hundred a week, once a week. He says you're looking to take a big step up from that. How much did you have in mind?"

I said I wanted the Braves for six thousand and he explained how it works. Vincent doesn't make you give away runs when you pick a favorite, like Toadie does. Vincent does it the official way—he lays odds. The Braves are 5–3 favorites to beat Florida tonight. That means to win six thousand I have to bet ten thousand. It sounds harsh, but I'd rather do it this way. If the Braves win, I win. Doesn't matter what the score is. If they don't, hell, it doesn't make a lot of difference to me whether I lose six grand or ten grand. I'm fucked either way.

The big reason I'm willing to lay the odds is because Greg Maddux pitching against the Marlins is as close as you'll ever get to a sure thing. Maddux hasn't lost in two months, and Gary Sheffield, the only real hitter Florida has, is sitting this game out with a groin pull. This should be an easy one.

So here we are, a few minutes to game time. Already I can feel the sweat on me.

"You ever bet this kind of money before, kid?"

"Sure, lots of times."

"Yeah? What line are you in?"

I pause.

"Insurance."

"Me too. Hey, Dom, kid's in insurance."

Dom raises his glass. "Good for you, kid. Great line of work, huh?"

I nod.

Vincent turns back to me. "I ought to get some pointers from you. You must be doing real good to have this kind of dough to throw around."

"Well, it's more a one-time thing. Maddux hasn't lost in two months."

Vincent nods kindly.

"So you're a nickel-and-dimer throwing it all on a hunch, huh? I'll buy that. You understand, I don't like to pry. I just want to make sure the people I work with aren't in any kind of trouble. Don't like to see them with any reason to run scared. You know what I mean?"

"Sure."

"Hey, Dom, kid likes Maddux and the Braves at five to three."

"Kid knows his stuff."

"You know, kid, on the face of it I gotta agree with you. The Braves look to be a safe call. A lock, even. But here's the thing. It's baseball, kid, and with baseball you never know. A gust of wind, a bad hop, and the whole thing turns on you. Me, I never bet baseball, no matter how good the game looks. Seen too many of them get away. My kid comes to me for advice, I tell him, 'Don't bet baseball.' Dom, what is it I always tell you?"

" 'Don't bet baseball.' I don't know, though, boss. Like the kid says, Maddux ain't lost in two months. And Florida can't hit for shit. You got a chance to win six grand on Maddux, maybe you lay what you gotta lay. I think the kid's got you beat."

Vincent holds up his hands.

"I'm not saying he don't. It's up to you, kid. You want the bet, you got the bet. All I'm saying is, with baseball you never know. If it's me, I wait till football comes around to start dropping that kind of dough."

"I'll take the bet."

"Maybe you want to do it for less, get your feet wet a little."

I shake my head.

"Okay. Six grand it is. Good for you, kid. You stuck to your guns. Now, this is just a formality here, but I got to ask to see the money."

I take it out and start to count it for him but he stops me. "Hey, that's good enough. I'm sure it's there."

The players take the field. I should have the shakes right now, but the beer helps and I feel real good about Maddux. During the anthem Dom takes his cap off and Vincent bows

213

his head and mutters the words. The Florida starter takes his warm-ups as Vincent waves down Madge for more drinks.

"A beer for the kid, Madge—and two ice waters." He turns to me. "Ain't this America, kid? Head down to the local pub, watch a ball game with a few friends. You can't beat it."

I take a long drink.

The Braves push across a run in the first and one more in the fourth, and the way Maddux is mowing them down I can't imagine it won't stand up. He's putting everything right on the black and hard, earning nods of appreciation from Dom.

"My money's on the kid. Sorry, boss. That's the way I see it."

Vincent shakes his head. "His man sure looks good today." He turns to me. "Teach me to bet against an insurance guy, huh?"

Every time I finish a pint, Madge slides another in front of me. I relax just a little.

Through eight, Maddux is still shutting them out, but it's only 2–0. Pat Rapp of the Marlins picked tonight to throw the game of his life. Even so, I should be up four or five runs. The Braves keep stranding runners, and they've had a few long ones caught at the wall. In the top of the ninth the Braves load the bases with one out, and with a chance to put the game away they pinch-hit for Maddux. Vincent looks up at me from under his glasses.

"You like the move, kid?"

"Not really. You can't argue with it, they can break the game open, but I'd just as soon see Maddux out there in the ninth."

"I'm with you, kid," Dom pipes up. "If I got ten grand on the line I want to see Maddux out there to finish her off."

The pinch-hitter hits one to third and the Marlins turn a 5-4-3 double play to end the inning. Another wasted chance.

214

"Would you look at that," says Vincent. "Your man hustles at all and he beats the throw. A million bucks a year and he can't break his ass with an insurance run on the line. Next thing you know they'll be on strike."

I signal Madge for another pint to get me through the ninth. Come on, guys. Three more outs and I'm home free.

Wohlers comes on to pitch for the Braves. He strikes out White to start it, then Veras bounces a 1–2 pitch off the mound and out into center field. Conine fouls off six two-strike pitches, draws a walk, and all of a sudden two men are on and out of the dugout to pinch-hit comes Sheffield. Dom nudges my shoulder.

"He's gotta be the last guy you want to see right here, huh, kid?"

I take a big swig of beer and I'm still drinking it when Sheffield hits the first pitch so hard it's over the wall before the camera can turn to follow it. Fans dive to get out of the way. It all happens so fast it takes a second to sink in.

Dom has his hands on his head. "Oh Jesus, kid. Oh man."

Sheffield touches them all and is mobbed at home plate as the final flashes on the screen. Marlins 3, Braves 2. I can't move. Vincent sits quietly for a few minutes, looking glum. Finally he waves Madge over. "Bring the kid a drink, will you? A real drink. Jack Daniel's, or anything he wants. What do you say, kid? A little JD?"

I nod.

"Christ, what can I tell you? You made a good bet, kid. Any gambler worth his salt makes that bet. You'll win it eight times out of ten. Today just wasn't your day. Next time, kid, maybe you get me."

It's a few minutes before I can even think. I look at the clock. Almost ten. In two hours I'm supposed to meet Dug-gan. I feel the same sickness in my stomach I felt that night on the boardwalk in Atlantic City. I'm so close, and it's all going to end here, in a Bay Ridge dive. I reach into my shirt and hand Vincent the money. He takes it apologetically, thumbs through it, puts it away. I throw back the shot, slide off the stool, and with a vacant nod at Vincent and Dom I walk to the door. Only when I'm out on the street and the night air hits my face do I snap out of it.

Jesus, Tom, what the hell are you doing? You can't leave this place without the dough. It's not an option. I turn around, bang my head once on the wooden door to clear it, and walk back inside. I haven't come this far to blow it now. Vincent hasn't moved and I walk straight to him and look him in the eye. I know just what I need to do.

"You lend money, Vincent?"

He nods kindly, his hands up and out to me.

"I thought you'd never ask."

IN THE BACK ROOM he motions to a booth and slides in across from me.

"Let me guess, kid—you need sixteen grand."

I stare at him.

"The ten you lost and the six you didn't win."

I nod. He motions to Dom.

"Hey, Dom, bring Tommy here a beer." Dom walks from the room.

"Here's how it has to work. In my business, Tommy, three things are important: interest, prompt payment, and reputation. Interest is how I make my money. Prompt payment is how I keep my reputation. Without my reputation, I never even get to charge interest. So if I don't get prompt payment, Tommy, I'm forced to take certain steps." Dom returns with my beer and Vincent nods at him. "Dom, here, helps me take those steps."

216

Dom blushes and shrugs, like I'd just found out he was an
A student.

"Now, this business venture you're engaged in, Tommy.
When will it be completed?"

"Late Friday night."

"Late Friday night. So you should have no trouble paying
the interest and the principal early Saturday morning?"

"That's fine."

"Okay, let's go over the terms. I lend you sixteen grand today, I need you coming back with twenty. Are you okay with
that?"

I guess I better be.

"Yes."

"Okay. Just a few formalities and then we'll get you the
dough. When's your birthday, Tommy?"

"July fourteenth."

"What's your home address?"

I give it to him.

"Can I see your license, please?"

I hand it over and he checks the info I gave him.

"Good. Your home and work numbers, please."

I give them.

"And someone to contact in case of emergency."

I stare at him.

He shrugs and smiles. "Procedure, Tommy." After taking it
down he stands up. "I'll be right back," he says as he walks
out. When he's gone Dom slides into the booth.

"You like jokes, kid?"

"I guess."

"Got a good one for you. Guy I worked over yesterday told
me this one. What's the best part about a blow job?"

"I don't know."

"Twelve minutes of peace and quiet."

He slaps his hand on the table and shakes all over. "Good one, huh?"

I force a smile.

"Wait'll you get hitched, kid—you'll die laughing. Hey, what'd you think about my timing on that one? They say half a joke is timing. You like my timing?"

"It was great."

He looks right at me, grinning like a ten-year-old.

"They got this comedy club up the street here, kid. Monday nights they let anyone get up on stage and tell jokes. Guy who gets the most laughs takes home a few bucks. I figure what the hell, I'm a funny guy, I'll give it a shot. So anyway, I collect jokes. Sometimes, if I got to put the screws to some deadbeat, maybe I let him off a little easy if he comes up with a few I ain't heard. Get some real good ones that way."

I work on my beer.

"That's how I got the blow-job joke. Guy saved himself a finger with that one." Dom starts shaking again. "Peace and quiet. I tell ya. How 'bout you, kid? You know any?"

"None that I can think of."

"Well, maybe next time I see you, huh?"

We stare at each other a few seconds, then he lets loose with a belly laugh and slaps the table again. "Just joking, kid. How's that for timing, though, huh?"

Dom slides out of the booth as Vincent returns with a paper bag. He sits down, counts out sixteen stacks of hundreds, and slides them across the table. I count them myself and stuff them in the pouch inside my shirt. When I stand to leave they each shake my hand warmly.

"Best of luck with your business, Tommy," Vincent says. "We'll see you first thing Saturday morning."

Dom waves a hand. "Twelve minutes of peace and quiet,

kid," he says and starts to laugh all over again. "Don't forget, if you hear any."

I walk out the door into the night. At the corner I take the first real breath I've had in hours. Christ, Tom, you sure know how to do things the hard way. I'm climbing into a cab when I hear, "Hey! Hey, you!" in a big voice behind me. At the door to Madge's, on his way into the place, is my old buddy Gino. He starts toward me.

I slam the cab door. "Get out of here. Now!"

He steps on it without a word. There's a New York cabbie for you.

"Hey!"

Gino gets as close as the back of the cab, where he bangs his fist on the trunk as we speed off. Out the back I watch him shake his fist, then I turn back and slide down the seat. Christ. I should have figured these Italian gambling types would move in the same circles. What happens if Gino starts milking Vincent about me? Screw it. I have the money I need, and that's all that matters. We win the match and everything else will fall into place. Still, my heart could use a couple minutes off now and then. It's been some week. I look out at the water with a weak smile as we bump over the Brooklyn Bridge. You wanted kicks, right, Tom?

I STOP IN AT HOME to get the money together. I can hear the shower going and the sound of giggling over the water. Molly sure is making up for lost time. I listen at the door on my way by, then open a beer and sit on my bed a minute. I put all the money in my old college knapsack, finish my beer and head out.

I step out of the cab across the street from the public library. She really is beautiful. So white, and regal. Almost makes me wish I'd paid more attention in school. I cross the street. From the bottom of the wide stairs I can see two figures at the top, silent against the stone of the building. Duggan has brought his goon with him. Seeing him there, thick and dark, it occurs to me I should have some backup myself tonight. Oh well. It's strange, but I'm not worried about them jumping me for the money. Duggan wouldn't do that. Not just because Papa O'Shea is in on the match now. Duggan wants to beat me as bad as he wants the dough. Almost as bad as I want to beat him.

I take the stairs. At the top he comes forward with a grim smile.

"I didn't think you'd show, college boy." He lights a cigarette, shakes out the match and tosses it away. "Another ten minutes and Shakespeare here was going looking for you." He motions at the mass behind him. "You remember him, eh?"

Do I ever. Shakespeare is the dude heaver at County Hell Pub. A real bull, with a neck a foot across and tiny red eyes buried in a fat, red Irish face. I've never heard him talk but I've seen him in action. He stands at the bar door all night, until any trouble breaks out, at which point he grabs the biggest guy involved by the throat and holds him in the air until he turns good and blue. End of trouble. Even the dealers who work that stretch of Tenth Avenue know better than to fuck with Shakespeare, or with any of County Hell's customers when he's around.

"Sure I remember him. What's he doing here—returning a book?"

"He's here to get a good look at you, college boy. If you don't show tomorrow, it's Shakespeare's job to go get you."

"I'd hate to have to outsmart him." I see his big neck tense. A Doberman, waiting for the "kill" command. I slide my knapsack off my shoulder. "Let's do it, Duggan."

220

I follow him behind the big stone lion and we crouch in the darkness. He pops the clips on a briefcase and turns a flashlight on the stacks of bills inside. Twenty hundreds to a stack, twenty stacks. I open my knapsack and dump my piles of money onto the ground. I drop them back into the bag as I count them. He nods when I finish and we stand. He holds out his hand. His shake is cold and hard.

"So Daddy came through, did he? He won't help you to-morrow."

He motions to Shakespeare and they walk away down the stairs. At the bottom, Duggan turns and gives me a salute with the left hand.

"You be there, you hear? And remember, college boy—no substitutes."

His grin and confidence bring the sweat out on me again. I watch them walk to the corner, turn west on Forty-second, and disappear into the night. Is he that good a bluffer or does he have something up his sleeve? But what? Walking slowly down the stairs, I think of a saying I heard in high school, about justice in the Old West.

You'll know it when you see it.

CHAPTER TWENTY

FRIDAY morning dawns clear and hot. I lie still in bed, going over it all once more in my head. I think I have everything set. The money is counted and ready and in a bag in the closet. The gang knows to be at Adam's Curse at eight for warm-ups and a few calming beers. My protection will meet up with us at County Hell. That should be everything.

Well, not everything. I'd hoped to come home last night to a message from Lisa. That didn't happen. I haven't heard word one since she walked out of the pub the other night.

Maybe it was a pipe dream, expecting her to go away with me. Maybe I'm getting what I deserve for my low lie about having the money in hand. That was bad, I know, but it was the only lie I told her. The rest was true, and I only fudged on that because I was up against it. Christ. With all I have riding on this match—and it's pretty much everything, by now—I can't stop thinking about the one thing missing—Lisa. Shake it off, Tom. If you can't keep your mind on darts

tonight, winning back Lisa will be the least of your problems. I roll out of bed to meet the day.

I'M NOT EVEN OUT of the elevator at the office when Kay
jumps up from behind her desk and rushes up to me.

"Tom, what have you done?"

"Whoa. What do you mean?"

She takes a quick look over her shoulder.

"The Pharaoh wants to see you." I stare at her. My first instinct is to bolt, but it's too late for that. "He's in his office
right now. Said you're to see him before you do anything
else. Tom, what's going on?"

"I'm not sure, Kay."

"You're okay though, right?"

"Yeah—I guess."

The Pharaoh is old man Farrell, the oldest senior partner
and son of the founder of the firm. We call him the Pharaoh
because of his clout and because he's something of a mythi-
cal figure around here—nobody ever sees him. All the offices
but one are in the north wing, to the left of reception. The
Pharaoh's sits alone in the south wing. In my year here I've
never been in there. They say no paralegal ever has. I turn
back to Kay as I open the door to the south wing.

"If I don't come out, remember this name—Dr. Silver-
man."

"Why?"

"He has my dental records."

The door opens onto a corridor with plush carpeting that
ends fifty feet later at the door to Farrell's office. I stop in
front of it. Word around the firm is that a meeting with the
Pharaoh means one of two things. Somehow I don't think
he's about to make me partner. I knock.

"Come in."

The office is a beauty. Five hundred square feet, easy. Floor-length windows looking west over the water. Big-time art on the walls, a carpet you could sleep on, and at the other end of the room the biggest desk I've ever seen. Behind it, the Pharaoh is pretty big himself. Tall, I should say, with the straight back you see in old men who've done something with their lives. He has all his own hair, though it's white now. His elbows rest on the desk, his fingers together under a sharp nose, his blue eyes hard and leveled right at mine. He looks like an old-time robber baron.

"Good morning, son."

"Good morning, sir."

"Do you know why I called you in?"

"No, sir."

He's silent, his eyes still on me. I get the feeling he's giving me a chance to change my answer and save us both a lot of time. Finally he speaks.

"Carter McGrath played squash with a friend last night."

"How did he do, sir?"

"I should say he intended to play. They never quite got around to the game. His friend, you see, is Dave Jacobs, from the Immigration and Naturalization Service. I believe you've dealt with him."

I look down at my unshined shoes. I won't have to worry about them again.

"Yes, sir."

Of all the ways to be done in—a damn squash match. Dad always said it doesn't matter what a man has on you—look him in the eye. I do.

"You know where this is going, don't you, son?"

"Yes, sir."

We are silent awhile. I do a quick mental revision to my plan as Farrell stands, looks me over one more time, then walks to the window and looks out on the water. He speaks with his back to me.

"In war, son, do you know what happens to soldiers who take it on themselves to jeopardize the success of a mission?"

"No, sir."

"We march them out back and shoot them in the head." He stands bone-straight, his hands behind him, his eyes seeming to follow a lone sailboat as it makes its slow way up the Hudson. "First, though, we give them a chance to explain themselves."

"Prego didn't do it, sir."

"I don't care."

"Sir?"

"We were retained by Regina Garrett to effect a settlement in her favor. What Mr. Prego did or did not do is irrelevant."

"Not to me, sir."

"That's why I'm senior partner and you're fired. You may go."

He doesn't turn around.

"Sir?"

"You may go."

I take a step forward and a good breath.

"Sir, I have a call in to a Mr. Harry Sellers. Perhaps you've heard of him. Mr. Sellers writes a man-of-the-people column for the *New York Post*. His specialty is the David and Goliath story. He likes to take the side of the workingman against the big corporation. Especially likes to take aim at banks and law firms. I think the old term for him would be a muckraker, sir. He's got a pretty rabid following."

Silence.

"When he calls back, sir, I can tell him I admire his work and I'd love an autographed photo. Or I can tell him about the Prego case. I think it's the kind of thing he would run with, sir. I'd give him the bare outlines—a little background on the principals, maybe thirty seconds on the tactics of the Wall Street firm that wants to deny Mr. Prego a fair trial. It wouldn't take much. Just a few words to get the ball rolling. I'd have to guess it's the kind of story his readership would eat up, sir."

Farrell keeps his back to me, his gaze over the water.

"What is it you want, son?"

"I want Prego to have his day in court, sir. No threats from INS, no Board of Health at his door. A fair trial, our lawyers against his."

"What else?"

"That's it."

More silence. At last Farrell lets out a sigh that seems fifty years in the making.

"Boats."

"Sir?"

"Boats, son. Do you like boats?"

"Yes, sir."

"So do I. That's why I still come into the office. In a morning I might count a hundred boats out there. There's one with single rigging—you don't see that much anymore." He swivels around, his arms folded.

"Son, if you had asked me for money you'd be on your way to jail right now. If you had asked for your job, security would be dragging you outside by the collar." He walks to his desk and sits behind it again. He picks a cigar from a case of fat ones, rolls it in his hands, and looks up.

"My father founded this firm when he returned from World War One. I think it is safe to say that the Prego case is not the kind of case he founded a law firm to try. Nor would some of the tactics recently resorted to have met with his approval. I'm not too happy about them myself." He cuts off the tip with a gold cutter. "Unfortunately, this is not a case we are likely to win in a courtroom."

"Doesn't that tell you something, sir?"

A hint of a smile crosses his face. "How old are you, son?"

"Twenty-three."

"You have a lot to learn." He hits a button on the intercom. "Kay, send Mr. McGrath in, please."

Carter comes through the door looking like he wants a go at me. Farrell waves him into a chair by his desk and Carter sits on the edge of it, ready to spring.

"Son, perhaps you'd like to explain yourself to Mr. McGrath."

"No, thank you, sir."

Carter can't hold himself back. "Well, you're going to." He looks at Farrell, who gives the barest nod, and starts in. "Why did you tell me Prego was clean, Reasons? Are you going to try to say you misunderstood what Jacobs told you?"

"No, sir, I understood him fine."

"Why, then?"

As I look Carter in the eye the old betting feeling comes over me—the release. "Because I thought we were on the wrong side on this one, sir."

I swear Carter is going to come right through his shirt.

"The wrong side?" He tries to laugh but his face won't let him. "The wrong side?"

"Yes, sir."

"Reasons, you want to know what the wrong side is? It's the side that's not paying you. That's the wrong side."

"That's not how I see it, sir."

He's up out of his chair. "You little shit. Do you know how much money is riding on this case? Do you have any idea? I ought to tear you apart."

227

"You could try, sir."

Farrell puts up his hand. "Okay, McGrath, sit down."

Carter does but keeps his eyes on me. Farrell lights the cigar he's been holding and turns his chair to face Carter.

"The Constitution and the laws of this state may be a pain in the ass, McGrath, but you might try keeping them in mind. We are still bound by them."

Carter looks around the room, uncertain.

"What do you mean, sir?"

"I mean that in your zealousness to serve our client you have indulged in a few shortcuts."

"But Mr. Farrell, I only did—"

Farrell stops him with a glance.

"Mr. Reasons takes issue with these shortcuts. He has suggested to me that word of our transgressions might find its way to the press. If that were to happen it would cause Farrell Hawthorne no small embarrassment."

Carter gives me a long look that turns slowly from amazement to contempt. "You'd go that low, Reasons."

"I think we're about on the same level here, sir."

Farrell continues. "Mr. Reasons wants to see this case reach the courtroom, McGrath, and currently he has us in a position of disadvantage. To use an old expression, you might say he has us by the diamonds."

"But, sir, we can't take this case to court."

"Why not?"

"Well, it's . . . well, it's not the kind of case . . ."

"You're an attorney, aren't you, McGrath?"

"Yes, sir."

"An aspiring partner, in fact. Yes?"

Carter tries to loosen his collar.

"Yes, sir."

"And if I remember correctly, and I still do sign the checks around here, you draw a pretty good salary. And it is coming up on six years for you, McGrath. Right about time for the firm to be making a long-term decision. Now surely anyone deserving of partner ought to be able to win a case like this on the merits. Don't you think?"

Carter's face is a lot of fun to see right now. There aren't that many colors in a rainbow.

"Yes, sir."

"Splendid. Now go do so." Carter doesn't move. "McGrath, haven't you a court case to prepare?"

Carter walks out. Farrell gazes at the door, puffs his cigar, then turns his attention back to me.

"Son, you do know the standing this firm has in the legal community?"

"Yes, sir."

"Then you know how difficult we can make your life if you decide to bother us again. Good day, and remember, son, our word carries a lot of weight."

"Not where I'm going, sir."

CLEANING OUT MY DESK is a quick job. I don't keep a lot of personal stuff here. I decide against a farewell lap around the office, but do stop at Kay's desk on the way out. She gives me a hug, looks about to cry.

"Tom, how could they? What did you do?"

I wipe her eyes. "No crying—trust me, it's better this way. Tell you what—next week I'll take you for drinks and tell you the whole story."

She lets me go. "I'm going to miss you, Tom."

"Chin up, Kay. I'll see you soon."

Out on the street I turn and give a last look at the building. One year she took from me. As I walk away, it hits me that I'm probably the first Reasons to be fired from anything. The first I know of, anyway. So why do I feel so steady?

Steady, hell—I'm downright pumped. The truth is, I couldn't have plotted it any better. I didn't figure to be long for that place anyway. Sure, I'd rather have given them the boot instead of the other way around, but I got my shots in, and this way I take care of Prego without having to leak anything to the press. He'll get his chance in court, and once that jury gets a look at Regina Garrett . . . well, let's just say I've got all my money on the Italian. As for Carter, I'd have my résumé squared away if I were him.

I let out a breath as I start uptown. Okay. I did the right thing, and it feels good, but now the Good Samaritan act is over. I turn my mind ahead. All of a sudden my life is pretty simple. All the distractions are out of the way and the task ahead is clear.

I've got me a dart match to win.

CHAPTER TWENTY-ONE

I NEVER SAW a thing.

I'm a pretty big guy—give me a chance to get an arm on someone and he'll be the worse for it. But one second I'm heading into my building and the next I'm coming to in the alley next door, a sack over my face and my right arm, from the elbow up, stretched flat over a milk crate, a big hand on my wrist to keep it still.

"You should know better, kid. Cross the boss and it's hammer time."

With that he brought it down. I felt the big two fingers of my right hand split and I went cold and started to vomit in the bag.

It was a few minutes before I realized no one was sitting on me anymore. I rolled onto my knees, pulled the sack off with my left hand, and looked at my shaking right. What I saw made me sick again.

Getting your fingers broken isn't like you see in the

movies. You don't throw back a shot of whisky, tape 'em together and go on. I want to tell you it hurts. Each one is
swollen half the size of my hand before the blow. And the
doctor says I'm lucky. Says the bones could have shattered
and then I would have been in for it. As it is I got a clean
break, and they'll be good as new in two months. Thanks,
Doc. A lot of good that does me tonight.

I'm sitting on a treatment bench at Saint Vincent's. My
fingers hurt like a bastard and all they'll give me for the pain
is a little codeine. Why not just tell me to blow on them? I'm
waiting for the nurse to come back with it.

Duggan.

All along I figured he'd try something to stack the deck. I
never guessed he'd go this far. Christ, now what? Come on,
nurse. I walk to the door and look down the hallway. No sign
of her. Six of us are on the bench, waiting for medicine, and
every one of the others is ahead of me. I look at the clock.
Five thirty.

Screw it. I have some big-time figuring to do and not
much time to do it in. I blow out the main door, down the
steps and into the street, my fingers throbbing with every
step. As I head for home, I can hear Duggan's last words in
my head.

"No substitutes."

AT THE PAD, a little session at the dart board proves what I
already knew—I can't throw worth a damn. The two fingers
they broke are splinted together and stand straight up. By
trapping the dart against them with my thumb and concen-
trating on my release point, I can get it to the board. That's
about it, though. I can't hit what I aim at, and in terms of the
games we'll be playing tonight—501 and cricket—I couldn't
beat a kid. I'll have no chance in singles, and probably bring

down anyone I partner with in doubles. If we go through with this match, we'll have to beat County Hell five players on six. No sane gambler would take those odds.

The phone rings.

"Hello?"

"So when do we leave, driver?"

Lisa!

"Lisa . . . you . . . you mean it?"

"I mean it, Tom."

I sit down. "Jesus. I don't know what to say."

"Say thank you."

"Thank you."

"You're welcome. Hey, I called your office first. You're not too popular there today."

"Yeah, we had a little falling-out. It's been a bad day, Lisa. Damn . . . I can't believe you called."

"Believe it, Tom."

"Lisa, can you come over? We should talk, and I want to see you."

"No, Tom. Not till the morning we leave. It will be more special that way."

"But that could be weeks. You've got to give notice, and also there's something—"

"Notice? Tom, you know how much notice I gave those creeps? Five minutes."

"What do you mean?"

"I quit today, Tom."

"What?"

"You're not the only one who can act on impulse. You should have heard me tell off my boss, too. You would have been proud."

I put my forehead to the receiver and close my eyes.

"Tom, are you still there?"

"Yeah, I'm here. It's just . . . well . . . man, just like that, huh?"

"Just like that. Oh Tom—you were right. We *can* start all over again. I believe that now. And now that my dance card is clear, Reasons, I'm ready to go anytime."

I need a drink.

"How does Monday sound?" I manage to ask.

"Like a date."

I hang up and walk to the window. Christ on a raft. Now I know what they mean when they tell you to be careful what you wish for.

If I back out now, I can save my ass. I've done all the math. I could pay everyone off and still have a grand in shoe money. For what, though? To hide from Duggan the rest of my life? Never mind that he was behind the hammer job. I can't prove it, and if I don't show tonight he'll claim bad faith and sic Shakespeare on me. I'd rather dodge him than Vincent, but it's not much of a choice. Next time it won't be my fingers. And I'd be crying uncle.

And what about Stella? For all I know she's committed her money already, and maybe if we don't show she doesn't get it back.

Fess up, Tom. I could chuck the money and leave Stella out of this and I'd still have to show tonight. Lisa is the real reason I'm playing this match, and right now Lisa is at home packing. The second I asked her to go away with me I set my course. I'd break the rest of my fingers myself before I told her I blew it on this one.

We play.

Except, Christ, it's not just up to me anymore. Bringing the gang in for the money took care of that. Somehow I have to keep them on board, and after the stunt I pulled with the horse it won't be easy.

234

I sit down on the sill. When I think of the gang, a hurt starts in my chest that makes me forget all about my fingers.

What did I think—that I could shoot through to the end of all this without ever clueing them in? I look down at my splint. A real pal I am.

Jimmy picked me out of the bushes the first time I ever got loaded. Tank sat me down and explained to me why you can't put Hendrix and Roger May in the same sentence. And what has Bobby ever done but give me the go sign and say count me in, Tom? And Claire. The night of my first date with Lisa, who bought me a new shirt and told me straight up the tack I should take, back when I thought my haircut was enough? These are my best friends.

Up at school we always knew who the pricks were. The profs who were just mailing it in, the rich boys wowing our girls with their money, always looking to start something. We knew who to trust and who not to. Out here it's not so easy. Out here, the guy holding the door for you in the morning is the same one looking to stick it to you come bonus time. Out here, they like you on the job if you can feed the bottom line, and the super's got a good word for you if you're making rent, and the drunks along the bar are happy to see you if you're buying. But they're not friends. Friends like you all the time. Friends stick together, and look out for each other. Remember the tontine, Tom? I swallow hard.

A tontine is a pact soldiers make in war. They cut their initials into a bottle of hard stuff, and each time one of them goes down, the others drink to their fallen friend. The last soldier left alive finishes off the bottle. Junior year, we did a tontine to marriage. Bought ourselves a quart of cheap wine, signed it, and locked it in the trophy case at Dave's frat.

We had it sent down to the city the night Jimmy got hitched. Ten minutes before the ceremony, Dave shanghaied the groom and waved the rest of us away from our dates. We piled into the church bathroom, six of us, tuxes and all, and as the organist knocked out Pachelbel's Canon, we drank a last toast to Jimmy.

A lot all that counted for, though. The first chance I get to sell them all up the river I take their trust and a good chunk of their money, put it on a bet they know nothing about, and tell them it's on something else. Jesus.

I shake my head hard. All right—what's done is done. All I can do now is go from here. But no more lies. I keep the gang on board with the truth or I don't keep them on board at all.

Out the window I can see the little Catholic church down Twenty-third Street. I wonder if it's too late to ask for a little favor. No fair, I know. If you don't believe, you can't come calling the first time you land in hot water. Still, if ever I was going to get a sign . . .

I walk to the fridge. It's too early to tank up, but I need something to kill the pain in my fingers, and the pain starting up in my head, too. I reach for a beer and then stop still. The sight of the cans, neatly stacked, sets something off in me. Christ, Tom—it just might work. It isn't exactly according to Hoyle, but after the hammer job anything goes, and it's the one shot I have left at evening things up a little.

Lucky for me, Sean Killigan is in the book. Fifteen minutes later I step out of a cab at Thirty-fifth and Ninth. A real swell block—probably gives the morgue half its business. On the corner, not twenty yards from Killigan's building, is a little liquor store. The guy behind the counter is Irish.

"Wha' kenna get you, sir? A little something for the pain, eh?" He points to my hand.

"Maybe. Tell me, do you know Sean Killigan?"

"The darter? Sure. Lives just up the block. Use ta come in

every day. 'Aven't seen him in months now. Rumor is he's off the stuff."

"That's an old rumor. Sean's one of the boys again."

"Well, that's good news fa' me. Sean was one o' me best customers."

"Tell me, when he used to come in, what did he get?"

"Always Guinness Dark, sir. Sean's a man knows his malts. Even if he had but enough for one or two, he always bought the Dark."

"I'll take a case of it then."

"Comin' up. Hey, and you say hi to Sean for me, will ya? Tell him welcome back to the club."

I carry the case on my shoulder to Killigan's building. I wait a few minutes, sneak in behind an old man and take the three flights of stairs to Killigan's door. I can hear the TV going inside. I put the case on the doormat, pound a few times with my good hand, and hightail it out of there.

CHAPTER TWENTY-TWO

I'M THROUGH lying, but this truth session is going to be a bitch.

The whole gang is here, sitting round the kitchen table. I switched the pep talk from Adam's Curse to my place to keep Stella from seeing my fingers. No sense getting her all worked up. I hand everyone a beer.

"Somebody broke your fingers?" Claire asks. "Who would do that?"

"I didn't see them."

"So what's the debate?" Bobby says. "You can't play with broken fingers. Just put the match off for two months."

"We have to play tonight."

"Why?" comes in a chorus from the table.

I feel I'm back in the confession box, only this time I really have to come clean.

"Everybody take a drink," I say. They do and I close my eyes. Here goes.

"There's no horse, guys. I took all your money and I bet it on a dart match."

"A dart match?" Tank asks.

"*This* dart match. The one tonight. I bet it against Duggan."

Everyone is quiet. They look at each other, then all at me. I'd feel better if someone took a swing at me. Tank drums his fingers on the table and shakes his head. Finally he speaks.

"You really are an asshole, Tom."

Bobby looks at me. "What he said."

Jimmy smiles a little, like when you get wise to someone who's been putting it to you.

"You wanted me to bet six more grand on this," he says. I wince.

"You're really something, Tommy. Where did you end up getting the money?" Jimmy asks.

"I borrowed it from a guy in Bay Ridge."

He shakes his head.

"You've got other money riding on this match, don't you?"

I nod.

"How much?"

"Forty grand, all told."

"What?" Sounds of disbelief from around the table.

"And when were you going to clue us all in?" asks Tank.

"After the match."

"Jesus Christ."

"Great."

"Goddamn."

Tank bangs the table. Only Dave is silent. Claire turns to him. "You knew about this, didn't you?"

He nods sheepishly.

"Dave's just a bit player here," I say. "He knew about the bet, but he didn't know I was hitting you guys up for money. That was all me."

Everybody is shaking their heads now. Bobby speaks up angrily.

"I don't believe you, Tom. You know, a thousand dollars may be shit to you, but it's a lot of money to us. You took it and you bet it just like that, without a second thought?"

"I figured we would win, Bobby. And then I'd cut everybody in."

"And if we lose?"

I look down. "I didn't figure we would lose."

"That's just great."

"Why didn't you tell us what the money was really for when you asked us for it?" asks Jimmy.

"Because I didn't think you'd play the match."

"Well, you're right about that." Jimmy throws up his hands. "Jesus, Tom. Believe it or not, some of us can make it through the day without betting everything we have. Some of us actually need our paychecks. For stupid things like, oh, help me out here, guys, what's that big one?"

"Rent," says Claire.

"That's it. And that other luxury. What is that again?"

"Food," chips in Tank.

"Right, right. And you know what? There's more. Clothes, and Christmas presents, maybe a weekend away now and then. And, God forbid this should get out, Tom, but some of us clowns even stick a little in the bank for down the line."

I put up my hands and talk quietly.

"Look, I'm not trying to get out of anything. What I did to all of you was dead wrong. You're the best friends I have and I stuck it to you. I got this bet in my head and I went after it full steam and I didn't think about anyone else. There's no defending it, and I won't blame any one of you if you walk out on me. I've got all your money, here, in cash, and if you want it back I'll give it to you right now."

Everyone is quiet again. At last Tank speaks up.

"What happens to you if we don't play this match?"

"I'm fucked."

"What happens if we play and lose?"

"I'm fucked."

Tank looks at each of the gang in turn, then at me.

"Reasons, go out in the hall a minute, will you?"

"Sure."

I step into the hall and close the door behind me. I sit on the stairs and stare at my busted fingers, not thinking of anything, really. No backup plans, no sales pitches. I'm past all that. It's all or nothing now, and it's up to them. Five minutes later the door swings open. I stand up and walk back into the apartment. The gang still sits around the table. They look at me in silence. Tank sighs and breaks the quiet.

"Don't just stand there, Reasons—talk strategy. Haven't we got some Irish ass to kick?"

CHAPTER TWENTY-THREE

TALK ABOUT a home-court advantage.

The County Hell Pub squats on the corner of Tenth Avenue and Thirty-third street. There isn't a way to approach her that doesn't take you onto one of the worst blocks in the city. If you do make it inside you get to face the dartboard itself. Stuck in the far corner, past the end of the long wooden bar, it features bad lighting and a big dip in the floor right at the throwing line, so that even though the distance to the board is the same as any other, you feel as if you're shooting uphill. Throw in the cigarette smoke, the suffocating heat, and the rowdy crew of drunks who root on the home team for the free drink it gets them when they win, and you've got one tough little place for the visitors. It's worse than Boston Garden.

We huddle up on the corner just outside. "Okay, guys," I say. "We can expect a real lion's den in there. So keep your focus on the board and tune out the rest. Ready?" They all nod.

One step inside and it's clear that word of this match has gotten out. The place looks like an Irish wake, two hours into it. Mulligans stand three deep at the bar and all along the back wall, too, and from the looks of them their first pint was a while ago. In the middle of the room, holding court between the bar and the jukebox, I spot him. His arms crossed, a pipe in his teeth, it's the bull of the woods himself—Papa O'Shea. Come to see his investment pay off, no doubt.

It wouldn't surprise me if O'Shea is behind the big turnout tonight. My guess is he rounded up all the soaks he could find and opened the taps for them for a few hours, just to put them in the mood. They sure look primed to be one loud cheering section.

Through the smoke I see that the only empty space in the joint is the area around the board, which has been roped off from the rest of the throng. The Hellions are back there now, warming up. All except Joe Duggan, that is, who gives a hearty greeting from behind the bar.

"So the Drinkers have the guts to show, eh? Tell you what—just to start 'er off friendly, how 'bout a round of ales for the visitors?" He ducks down behind the bar and comes up with a case of Guinness Dark. "Some good heart dropped her off at Sean's today." He winks at me. "Nice try, college boy, but I been staying with him." He slides a six-pack down the bar. "Enjoy these, fellas—they're all you're taking from here tonight." From the other end of the bar Sean Killigan salutes us with a seltzer. So much for evening the odds.

Duggan's face goes dark when he sees my fingers.

"What kind of trick is this?"

"Not one of mine, Duggan. Somebody broke 'em today. And somehow I don't think you're surprised."

"It warn't me, college boy. I don't need any help." He looks

243

at them real close, then hard into my eyes. "Sorry for the break, if that's what it is, but a deal's a deal. We play tonight. And no substitutes."

"I'm not here to cancel, Duggan. And I know the rules."

A low murmur runs through the crowd and all of us look to the door. Filling it is my new friend, the court clerk. Right on time. His instructions were to look mean and say nothing, and he's off to a good start. He scowls his way over to me. Duggan starts to shoot a look at Shakespeare but I put up a hand.

"He's with me," I say. "Here to handle our money, and to make sure no one on your side gets out of line."

"Has he got a name?"

I pause.

"Call him Keats."

I introduce Keats to the team and they shake their heads in admiration. Claire knocks on his chest twice with a fist, smiles at him.

"I just wondered if it's real."

I turn back to Duggan. "Let's get the preliminaries out of the way."

"Follow me."

Keats and I trail the two of them into the tiny kitchen, where I say a silent thanks that I've never ordered a burger in this place. On a counter in the back we show the money again. When it's counted, Keats puts the knapsack on his big shoulder and pulls it tight. Shakespeare picks up the suitcase. He's as mute as ever, but from the looks he keeps sliding Keats I can tell he doesn't like what he sees. Been a while since he had to look up at anybody, I bet.

"Okay, Duggan, here's how it works," I say. "These guys stand side-by-side at the front door the whole match. Each

244

keeps one hand on his team's money and one hand on the other team's. The second the match ends, the loser lets go."

"Not the trustin' sort, are you, college boy?"

"It's your place, Duggan. I need a way out when we win."

He nods. "Fair enough. But I'll tell you now, college boy— your man sneaks away and none of the rest of your team will get out that door. I promise you that."

We walk out of the kitchen. As the two strongmen take up their spots by the door, Duggan snaps his fingers at a pale, thin guy at the bar. "Egan. Over here." He presents him to me. "Egan here will be chalking tonight—if you approve."

I look him over. It is important that the chalker be quick and accurate. A slow one can kill the rhythm of the shooters, and a mistake, in a match like this one, could start a riot.

"What's one thirty-nine minus eighty-seven?" I ask.

"Fifty-two."

"Two thirteen minus one twenty-four?"

"Eighty-nine."

"How much do seven nineteens score?"

"One thirty-three."

I nod at Duggan. "He'll do."

The chalker walks to the board. "All clear," he calls out. "Adam's Curse has the board for practice. The match will begin in twenty minutes."

As the team makes its way to the board, Duggan calls me back. "One last thing, college boy. That girl of yours—Lisa, is it? I wonder if you might give me her number." I stare at him. "Fancy I might throw one into her after we win."

I'm half over the bar but Tank gets me under the arms and hauls me back.

"Easy, Tom. Come on. He's just trying to rattle you."

"Tell me," says Duggan, grinning now, "how many dates,

do you suppose, until I get inside?" He walks away down the bar.

Dave has joined Tank between me and the bar but I'm okay now. I take a good swallow of Guinness and curse myself. Strategy, Tom. I should have figured he'd try to steam me.

"I'm all right, guys," I say.

"Let's go," says Tank. "With those fingers you need all the warm-up you can get."

We form a practice line, but after a few turns I can see the throws are wasted on me. I leave the board to the others and slip away to a small table in the corner. Any points I score at the board tonight will be a fluke, but there is a way I can help us. I take a second to close my eyes and clear my mind. I've always said a good captain can steal a few points in a match without ever throwing a dart. Now is my chance to prove it. I set to work on the lineup.

The standard play-off format is in effect tonight. It divides the match into three rounds. The first round is six games of singles 501, worth one point each. The second round is three games of doubles cricket, worth two points each. The last round is three games of doubles 501, again worth two points each. The first team to ten points wins.

Before each round, Duggan and I will fill out our lineups "blind"; that is, without seeing each other's. This is where I can't afford to slip up.

Play in the league long enough and you learn the tendencies of the different captains. Some fill out their lineups from strongest to weakest, others mix their shooters around. Divining your opponent's strategy and countering can mean one or two points in a match. Over the course of the season that might be the difference between first place and second or third. In one match for all the marbles, like tonight, it can mean everything.

Duggan doesn't strike me as a guy with a lot of imagination. During the season he always went strongest to weakest. I'm going to bet he simply flops the order tonight and puts Killigan last. I want to be matched against Killigan because I can't beat anybody. If I can get Duggan to burn his best shooter on me, we'll have a better shot at winning the other games. We really need to win four of these singles matches to have a chance, because the doubles games are two points each and with my fingers we can pretty much count on losing two of them.

I take a swig of my drink and write the lineup. Duggan comes from behind the bar and we turn our sheets over to the chalker, who turns and posts them on the board.

Tank vs. Wilson
Dave vs. Kelly
Bobby vs. O'Brien
Claire vs. Gallagher
Jimmy vs. Duggan
Tom vs. Killigan

Bingo. Killigan will waste himself on me, and I've got Jimmy ready to take out Duggan, their next-best shot. It's all I could ask for. The rest of the matchups are toss-ups. After their big two there's not a lot of difference among their other shooters. They all score well and are tough as nails when it comes to taking their outs. But so are we. Tonight it will come down to who is on their game. And who can take the pressure.

At ten to ten we huddle up as a team. I look around the place. The crowd is raring to go. Smoke and old Irish romps fill the air. I send Bobby to the jukebox to put in our favorites, but no dice. It's backed up—twenty songs in the queue and all of them from the home country, according to the drunk standing guard.

"And when they play through we'll put in twenty more," he slurred. "None of that rock 'n' roll shit tonight." By the door, Keats and Shakespeare are side by side and silent.

Our heads are close together. I can see from their shining eyes that they don't need much of a pep talk.

"All right, guys. We know what we're here for. Before we start, though . . . thanks." I look at each of them. "For playing, I mean. Whatever happens tonight, they don't make friends any better. Now let's do it."

We raise our glasses and break away.

"I'm up first, Captain," says Tank. "Give me a head butt."

I step into it and he grins as he heads to the board.

Tank earns the right to open the game by winning the cork toss. That is, by throwing one dart closer to the bull than his opponent. The chalker bangs the wall and holds up his hands as Tank steps to the line. "Game on," he cries.

And so is Tank. He opens with a ton, dart slang for a 100-point turn. He stays just ahead of Wilson the whole time and doubles out the first chance he gets. One for us.

He comes back to the bar and high-fives the rest of the team. "Might have to take back calling you an asshole, Reasons," he says to me. "This night might be worth a thousand bucks."

Claire taps me on the arm. "I'm playing Peter Gallagher," she says. "Which one is he?" I point him out. "Okay, Reasons—you owe me." She slides off her chair and walks to him. "Peter, right?"

I know Gallagher to be a tough little bastard but in front of Claire he softens in a hurry.

"That's me."

248

"Peter, it's you and me tonight. How about I buy you a drink before the match?"

Gallagher looks like he woke up in a pile of money. All he can do is nod and grow wide-eyed as Claire hooks his arm and walks him to the bar. I'd bet my wallet he hasn't been laid this year. Not for free, anyway.

At the board, Dave plays a gritty game but can't keep up with Kelly, a smooth left-hander who pours them into the triple 20. Kelly takes out a double 4 to finish it off, setting the drunks along the bar to banging their mugs and whooping it up. Duggan claps him on the shoulder. One for them.

Bobby is up next and right away I can see he's off. He opens with consecutive turns of 26 and can't seem to get comfortable at the line. I wave him over.

"Maybe you were right not to tell us, Tom. Every time I step up there, I think forty thousand bucks."

"It's just a game of darts like all the others, Bobby. Relax. Here, this'll help." I hand him a shot of tequila.

He knocks it back, grimaces and shakes his head hard. "Thanks." He starts back to the board.

"Hey, Bobby, how's this for a movie opening?" I say. "Little guy starts off slow and then plays the game of his life. Just when his team needs it most."

He gives a determined nod. "I like that."

Thank the tequila or the words, but something went straight to his arm. The comeback is on. He hits a ton, then another, and an 85 to take the lead. Two turns later he's left himself the perfect out—32. O'Brien has 112 left and as he steps to the line Bobby turns his back to the board. He never watches his opponent shoot when he's near the finish. Me, I can't stand not to. O'Brien nails a triple 20 and a 12 to leave 40. He needs a double 20 to close her out. He throws the dart and raises his fist to the bar, which erupts right down the line. All the Hellions step forward to pound his back. But it isn't in.

Just a trick of the poor lighting. The dart sits on the wrong side of the wire, a millimeter above the double 20, and as O'Brien snatches it from the board the chalker signals Bobby to take his turn. Bobby is low with his first dart, left with his second, and dead sweet perfect with his third. One for us.

Claire's been at the bar with Gallagher this whole time. I start over to say a few words, but back off when I see she has everything in hand.

"Our turn, Peter," she says, giving his shoulder a squeeze. "And don't forget tomorrow night." He steps to the line.

"Tomorrow night?" I mouth at Claire. She glares at me.

"And remember, Peter, dress casual. Nothing you can't get out of in a hurry."

He should get a hundred points for not dropping his darts. It's three turns before he hits his first 20 and probably a half hour before he notices. Claire buries the winning dart and joins the team at the bar. One more for us.

Duggan has Gallagher by the collar as soon as it's over. "I ought to kill ya right here. What the hell ya doin'?"

"Go ahead, Joey," says Gallagher. "Take a swing at me. Then what are ya gonna do? You can't sit us down tonight—it's just the six of us." Duggan lets him go and Gallagher straightens the front of his shirt. "I got a little distracted—so what? This match don't count for nothin', and I'm workin' on a date here." He walks away.

Back at the bar I give Claire a hug. "I guess we're even now for all that math homework, huh?"

She gives me a grim smile. "By the end of the night, Reasons, you'll be way in the red."

Duggan and Jimmy pick up their darts and head for the

line. Jimmy looks cool and ready. Duggan wins the cork toss and starts off with an 85. He's good tonight, but Jimmy is better. The game is clean and fast, Duggan hitting big scores and Jimmy coming back even bigger. Duggan leaves himself 40 but Jimmy never gives him a shot at it. He drills a double 16 the first chance he gets, spins and offers his hand. "Good game."

Duggan doesn't take it. "Lucky darts," he says, slamming his own against his leg as he walks back to the bar. Another one for us.

Only our 4–1 lead takes the sting out of my match with Killigan, who makes short work of me. The few turns I get I aim for the center and take whatever points I fall into. About all you can say is I keep my darts on the board. I have 300 left when Killigan takes out the game. One for them. The chalker steps up on his chair. "Four-two," he calls out, sounding like the PA guy at Wimbledon. "Advantage: Adam's Curse."

Between rounds our team huddles back at the bar with fresh pints. We raise our glasses and I let out a good breath and take a long, celebratory draw off my Guinness. A 4–2 lead is all I could have hoped for. "Keep it comin', guys," I say, and then slip away to set the lineup for cricket.

Cricket is a completely different game than 501. Only the numbers 15 through 20 and the bull's-eye are in play. The idea is to close out a number by hitting it three times. Once you close out a number you can score on it and your opponent cannot. To keep you from scoring on it, he must close it out himself. You win if you are even or ahead in points and have all the numbers and the bull's-eye closed out.

I decide to go for the early knockout. I put Jimmy and Tank in the first game, Dave and Claire in the second, and myself and Bobby in the third. I'm counting on a quick win by us to turn them against each other. If they come apart we might even take two of three. The risk is, if Jimmy and Tank go down in that first one, we could lose them all, and if they take an 8–4 lead into the last round, that's about all she wrote. I swallow hard. That's why they pay us captains the big bucks—to make these decisions.

Duggan and I hand our lineups to the chalker and he posts them on the board.

Jimmy & Tank vs. Kelly & Wilson
Dave & Claire vs. Killigan & O'Brien
Tom & Bobby vs. Duggan & Gallagher

I let a little air out through my teeth. We ought to be able to take that first one.

Jimmy picks up right where he left off in 501, winning the cork toss and putting the pressure on early by opening with four 20s and a 19. Tank is on, too, and the pace is too tough for the Hellions, who shoot well but can never quite make up the early deficit. By the end they're cursing their throws and jawing at each other about which numbers to shoot for. Jimmy finishes them off with a double bull.

"Six–two. Advantage: Adam's Curse."

Duggan walks over to me. "Time out, college boy—five minutes." He looks back at his players. "All of you, into the kitchen." They follow.

I couldn't have scripted it any better. We're four points away from closing them out and Duggan is leading them off to rip into them. That's it, guy. Let them have it. Tell them what losers they are. Get them so pissed at you they don't care what happens at the board. I watch Bobby and Claire take a few extra warm-ups, then lay down their darts and nod at me. "You guys need shots, anything?" I ask.

252

Claire shakes her head.

"All square, Captain," says Bobby.

We can throw the knockout punch here. An 8–2 lead would just about clinch it. The kitchen door opens and I turn to watch the Hellions straggle back.

Except no one is straggling. They come through the door in a tight line, their hands on their darts and their eyes on the board. Only Gallagher, trailing the pack, steals a smile at Claire, but he sets his face quickly again. Whatever Duggan said in there, it's turned them into warriors. I take another sip of Guinness.

Killigan is all business when he steps to the line. He plants one in the center cork to earn honors, then starts the game with a round of 7—four 20s and three 19s. There's no coming back from that. Dave and Claire play well from behind, hammering away at points, but it's too little too late. O'Brien nails the final cork to ice it.

"Six–four. Advantage: Adam's Curse."

It's been a good half hour and a couple pints since the bar drunks had anything to celebrate, and they really let loose, banging their fists on the wood and shouting toasts to every Irish hero they can think of. The Hellions themselves, though, are quiet. A few pats on the shoulder for O'Brien and Killigan and fists of encouragement to Duggan and Gallagher as they step to the line. Even the ones who aren't playing keep their attention on the board. Something isn't right here.

As I step forward for the game it hits me—Duggan is cutting them in. That's what he told them in the kitchen. Duggan might be an asshole but he knows better than to screw himself. He found the one way to make sure they care about this match as much as he does. How much is he throwing them? I wonder. Five hundred each? A grand? You can bet he won't break himself. Not when a hundred bucks is a fortune to these guys. I step to the line. I can only hope he waited too long.

Bobby and I take it on the chin in cricket. Forced to aim at the numbers we need, I'm lucky to hit one a turn. Bobby shoots like a sniper, but between Duggan and Gallagher we're overmatched. Down to one bull to clinch it, Duggan lays his darts in his palm and turns to me.

"Pick one, college boy." I look away, so Gallagher points to the dart in the middle. Duggan hands him the other two, steps to the line and nails a bull to close her out.

"Six–six," calls the chalker. "Match even."

At the bar we huddle up again. The night has come down to this—two out of three. If you'd asked at the start if I would take a tie heading into the final round I'd have said ten times out of ten. Now I'm not so sure. All the momentum is over with the Hellions.

"Okay, guys," I say. "Any advice?"

"Any way you want to play it," says Dave.

"We trust you, Captain," says Bobby.

The others nod. Past their heads I can see the Hellions in their corner, confident and determined. I look at Jimmy. "How do you feel, Ace?"

He pats his throwing arm with his left hand.

"Like William Tell."

"Good. Because I have a hunch. You think you can carry me, if you have to?"

He looks at my fingers. "Sure."

"Okay," I say.

I write out the lineup. Duggan and I walk to the board, hand them over, and as the chalker posts them up, a mean smile spreads over Duggan's face.

"Hell of a time to stop thinking, college boy."

The matchups are the ones I want, but seeing them up

there in hard chalk sends me into a sweat. We'll be working without a net on this one.

Tank & Bobby vs. Kelly & O'Brien
Dave & Claire vs. Gallagher & Wilson
Jimmy & Tom vs. Killigan & Duggan

I gambled that Duggan would count on splitting the first two games and would load up on the last one. That's just what he did. I saved Jimmy for the end because even with my fingers, even against their best, we'll always have a shot with Jimmy. Christ, if it comes to that, though, I'll need a heart transplant. What I'm really banking on is the rest of the team stepping up in the first two games and putting them away.

The game is doubles 501. The difference between this and singles 501 is that you have to double in as well as out. You can't start scoring until you hit a double. Any trouble doing that can put a team in a hole that's tough to get out of. The chalker calls the players to the line.

Game one is the kind of tight back-and-forth battle that makes darts such a kick to watch. Unless your ass is on the line, that is. I go through a pint and a half in the ten-minute game, most of it when Tank, with a chance to end it, wires his shot at the double 8, the rest when Kelly steps to the line and throws the point of his first dart into the double 10 and through my heart. The bar explodes.

"Eight–six. Advantage: County Hell."

If the general panics in battle, his troops will. Same for the captain in darts. I pat Dave and Tank as they leave the board.

"Heads up, guys. You played great." I turn to Bobby and Claire. "Okay, you two—Jimmy and I aren't ready to go home

yet. Go up there and give us a shot to win this thing." I slide
Bobby a short one of tequila. "For luck," I say. He downs it
and they head to the board.

Claire wins the cork toss but can't open with a double.
Gallagher gets the Hellions on straight away. Bobby strikes
out with his double too, then Claire, then Bobby again.
Lucky for us the Hellions aren't scoring well, but even so
they cruise out to a 150-point lead. I'm set to bite through
my glass.

"Excuse me a second," Claire says, making her way to the
bathroom. The Hellions snicker, except for Gallagher, who
clears a path for her, then nods back at Duggan's angry look.
"Don't worry, Joey—we got this one."

They haven't invented the drink I need right now. Nothing
in darts is worse than watching your team fail to double on
in 501. You fall farther and farther back, and as captain
there isn't a thing you can do but drink to cut the pressure.
I order an Absolut straight up and down half of it at a gulp.
The drunks can feel a win coming now and the buzz at the
bar is louder than it's been all night.

I start in on the rest of my drink when the din of a second ago cuts out and all I can hear is the door of the bathroom swinging shut and the twentieth straight Irish folk
song coming from the jukebox. I turn to see what's up and
join the drunks and the Hellions and all the Drinkers, too,
in watching Claire walk from the bathroom without her
blouse. She wears a little chemise thing that comes halfway
down her smooth belly, and she's holding her bra in her
hands. The drunk next to me falls clean off his stool. Claire
walks through the awed crowd to Gallagher, slips the bra
over his neck like an Olympic medal and pats his cheek.
"Hold that, will you, sport? I just can't throw free and easy

with it on." The wall behind Gallagher is all that keeps him standing.

Claire steps to the line, throws a double 16 with her first dart and the game, for us, is on. Five minutes later she closes it out. Cold water in the face brought Gallagher back to this week but his game didn't come with him, and he and Wilson never even got a shot at an out. Bobby was a little shaky himself, but Claire didn't need him. She took out a 76 with just two darts to end it.

At the bar, she puts her blouse back on and a jacket, too. She doesn't have the heart to get her bra back from Gallagher, and anyway it would take an army. She smiles weakly at me.

"You don't have to say it, Claire," I tell her quietly. "I owe you forever."

She takes a sip of her pint. "Just go do your part, Reasons, and we'll call it even."

My part. Christ, it's come to that, hasn't it?

"Let's do it, Tommy," says Jimmy, looking like he can't wait to get started.

"Okay. Give me a second."

I start into the can, but I can hear Duggan and Papa O'Shea inside around the corner and something in their voices stops me.

"For Chrissakes, you shoulda finished them off by now."

"We got 'em, O'Shea. They can't win this last one."

"They won enough so far. Do I gotta do it all for ya?"

"What do you mean?"

"What do I mean. I take out the fuckin' captain and you still can't finish 'em off. Don't forget whose money is on this match. Now go win."

"*You* broke his fingers? You bastard, O'Shea. I didn't need your help tonight. I never have."

"You just win that game, Duggan. You win that game or you won't leave this bar long enough to piss for the rest of your days."

If you hit a guy just right, you don't even feel it. It's like a perfect swing in baseball. I get a good two-step start, say "Hey" when I'm almost on him and he turns right into the punch. I catch him under the chin with a left uppercut and he falls back through the stall door and lands on his seat on the can, out cold. Not a drop of blood. Like something you might see in a Chaplin movie.

Duggan looks at him in shock and then with a low smile and pulls the stall door closed.

"Shame he's too big to flush," he says. He turns to me. "I didn't know about your hand."

"I heard."

"And earlier, about your girl. That was talk."

I nod. "Whatever. Let's finish this thing."

He starts out ahead of me but turns at the door. "I'm still gonna beat you, college boy."

"We'll see."

I join Jimmy at the bar as he finishes his pint and calls for another.

"Okay, Coach," he says. "What's the game plan?"

I take a cooling sip of Absolut. "Pretty simple, really. You win the cork shoot, go first and throw a perfect game. I aim for the middle of the board and pray for luck."

"With your track record you might be better off just hoping."

The chalker steps forward. "Adam's Curse and County Hell are tied eight–eight," he calls to the crowd. "Let the final game begin."

Some of the drunks are up on their stools now but they are quiet, caught up in the spirit of the match. There is only the music from the jukebox and a soft murmur from the crowd as we move to the board.

Killigan starts the cork shoot by hitting a single bull. "Pull it?" he asks.

Jimmy has the right to pull the dart to ensure himself a clear shot at the target.

"Leave it." Jimmy steps up and hits a double bull. We will go first.

I miss the noise. In the quiet I can feel the whole bar watching us, and looking at my busted fingers it hits me that I have no idea how we're going to win this one. Come on, Tom. This is no time to lose your nerve.

As I shake hands with Killigan and Duggan, though, I can feel it going. For the first time all night it sinks in that there isn't a thing I have that isn't riding on this match. My neck included.

If only it weren't so damn quiet in here. The song on the jukebox ends and now it's like a tomb, and so hot I have to press my pint to my forehead.

"You all right, Tommy?" Jimmy asks.

"Yeah."

But I'm not all right. Jimmy starts to bob and weave on me, though he's standing still, and I turn to the wall for a second. I close my eyes to shut out the bar but my own visions start coming fast and hard. I see Stella sitting alone, a mourning veil on her. I see Vincent shaking his head sadly, and Big Dom breathing in on me, his fist drawn back, saying, "Make me laugh, kid. Last chance." Most of all, clear as the sun, I see Lisa. She stands in her cotton dress, her hands in mine, and then I see her take them away and turn and pull her sweater about her and walk off.

From a long way away Jimmy is saying, "Tommy, Tommy, snap out of it," and I feel a hand on my shoulder but I'm still looking after Lisa, who is getting smaller now, and nothing matters but keeping her in sight.

My forehead is on the wall now and I'm shaking off Jimmy and then through it all comes the voice of Duggan, saying, "Looks like we got us a forfeit," and the sneer and the Irish in his voice snap me out of it.

I'm in the bar again, looking at Duggan. I reach up, press sweat from my face with my fingers and come all the way back. For a second I feel a shot of panic again but I steel my knees and instead of keeling over I feel the old rush coming on.

The old rush that starts as fear and passes through into peace and calm. And tonight it's more pure than ever. And as my vision clears and I take in the place again I realize I've waited all my life for this moment. The big score. I glimpsed it as a kid, that day on the sidewalk in Seoul, watching the soldier walk off with the girls. I looked for it through the years in the different schools, always the new kid, getting by because I could stick the jumper, or run a game of dice in the hall before class, but always on the outside. I felt it coming that morning on the lawn with Dad, when I said I wasn't joining up and he said, "what the hell else you gonna do"?

And as Jimmy steps to the line I realize it had to come to this. I had to take all the money I had, and a lot more I didn't, and put it all on this night. And then I had to go one better. I had to risk Lisa, too. She's the best thing I've ever seen, and any hope I have for down the line, but to earn her I had to do this. It doesn't even matter that she won't know. I'll know. Tonight, and a year from now and through the years. I'll know and it will be the difference.

And as the chalker calls, "Game on," I see with perfect clarity and know too that it's more even than Lisa. I had to take that last step. To put my skin on the line. That's why the rush is so pure. Because I bet it all. Bet it all on a lousy game of darts so I could stand here for one shining moment and feel a feeling they don't make anymore.

And as Jimmy pulls his arm back to throw, my head is clear and I'm ready for whatever's to come like I've never been ready for anything. I'm free, guys. Free.

Jimmy doubles on with a 16, like he always does. Then my eyes and all the eyes of us Drinkers lock onto the same spot—the triple 20. He puts his second dart in there straight as you please, and after a perfect two-second pause the third dart thuds in beside it. 152 on. 349 left.

Killigan doubles on with a 20, then hits two single 20s for a score of 80. 421 left. In any other game that would be a great start. I step to the line. For the first time all night I feel I belong there. Screw this throwing at the middle and praying crap. I'm a 20s shooter and I'm not changing now. I stare at the 20 until it's all I see on the board and until the red triple spot in the heart of her looks as big as Jersey. I fire away. Single 20, single 20, and a 1. I score 41. 308 left.

Duggan steps up and fires a ton. 321 left.

He might as well have left his darts in the board. Jimmy matches his ton. 208 left.

Killigan stands at the line so delicately I swear I could blow him over. He has one last push in him and here it comes. Triple 20. He shifts to the left just a fraction and throws again. Triple 20. The bar hushes. Single 20. 140 scored. 181 left.

Me again. Look at the target hard enough and the arm will find a way to get it there. I hit a 20, a 5, and the last dart falls into the triple 18 for a big score. Quite a stroke of luck, if you believe in luck. 79 scored. 129 left.

Duggan paws the line like a bull. He sets his sights downstairs. Triple 19. He sets his sights upstairs. Triple 20. He's throwing faster than I can figure his score. He plants his third dart in the triple 16, pumps his fist, and the drunks explode again. Duggan has just hit three triples, scored 165 points, and left Killigan needing only a double 8 to win the match. Sean Killigan can hit a double 8 left-handed.

"Beat that," says Duggan to Jimmy.

"Nice darts," says Jimmy quietly. He turns to me. "Okay, Tommy. Looks like it's now or never. You do the math, I'll do the shooting."

"Okay."

"Just one thing—send me out on a double bull."

"Right."

There's a light around Jimmy now as he steps to the line. I can see it, anyway.

"Hit a nineteen, Jimmy."

He buries it.

If only his wife could see how beautiful he is right now. He has the glow Jordan gets sometimes at the end of games.

"Triple twenty, Jimmy."

He nails it.

"Take her home."

You'll say it's the drinks, but as the dart leaves his hand I swear I can see everyone in the bar. The drunks, mouths open, up on their stools. Claire with her arms around Bobby and Tank, and Dave just behind them, smiling already. Duggan with his eyes on the board and his fists clenched, and Killigan, so small beside him, his darts flat in his palm. And holding on to the wall like a drunk comes Papa O'Shea, staggering from the bathroom just in time to see the finish.

Jimmy splits the cork right in two.

All us Drinkers let out yells and a few of the drunks join in in their confusion. Tank pours a pint over his head and then the team surges to the board to mob Jimmy and I pull out the barstool from the guy next to me, climb it and give Keats the high sign. He pulls at the briefcase, but Shakespeare hasn't figured it all out yet and keeps his grip on it. And as the whole team turns from the board and heads for me, I see a beautiful thing. Keats, our knapsack on his shoulder, lifting Shakespeare clear of the ground with both hands tight around his neck and shaking him like a child. After ten seconds of this a purple Shakespeare drops the case and Keats drops Shakespeare and I'm leading the whole team now, with Claire in the center, in a flying wedge to the door. I grab the briefcase on the way by, and the drunks are parting and the Pogues are playing and I push the gang out the door into the limo I booked and the last thing I see, as I back out, is a sputtering Papa O'Shea, his big face scarlet, reach for Duggan's collar and Duggan come up with a very quick right uppercut that catches O'Shea right where I caught him and sends him backward back into the can. And then I'm in the limo too, saying, "Adam's Curse" to the driver, and I'm in the back seat with all my friends, the best anyone's ever had, our faces close and flushed, and Keats, too, who's not a bad-looking guy at all when you see him up close, and the money's in the car and we're all in the money and as I pop the cork on a bottle of bubbly I make a vow to myself that I'm pretty sure I'll keep.

I'm through gambling.

MANHATTAN sure is pretty this morning.

The buildings, the water, it all looks new. I sit outside Lisa's in my new used car, waiting for her to come down the steps. Another few minutes and we'll be off.

It's taken me a couple days to recover from the victory bash Friday night. Stella sure can throw a party. She gave us the run of the place, top shelf included, until last call, and then turned all the regulars out and locked the door with the rest of us inside. She led us downstairs to a private room with a couple kegs in it and told us to go to work. I think Keats polished off one by himself. I was all beered out by that point, so after a split or two of Moët I stuck to pints of ice water.

It was down there that I divvied up the dough. Sat everyone around a poker table and cut them in. I split Stella's twenty-five grand evenly among the six of us. Bobby, Tank, Jimmy, and Claire I slipped two thousand each on top of the thousand they put in. Figured that as horses go, we would have been a 2–1 shot, at least. I paid Dave back his five grand and another five besides, doubled Keats's paycheck to a thousand and threw five hundred to the limo driver. None of the gang had ever seen that much cash before and after toasting it and ourselves we turned up the music and danced.

The rest of them were still going strong at 6 A.M. when I cut out and cabbed to Madge's Corner Pub in Bay Ridge. Madge herself let me in. Vincent and Dom were waiting for me, sitting at the bar.

"Aloha," I said.

Vincent was very pleasant, commending me on my promptness and saying we'd have to do business again sometime. "By the way," he said, while counting out the twenty grand, "a cousin of mine was in here asking about you the night you borrowed the money."

"Gino?"

"Yes."

"Yeah, I took some dough off him in blackjack. Should I be worried?"

"Nah. I didn't want him interfering with my investment, so I steered him wrong. Not that it matters. I could have drawn a map to your place for him, kid, and it would have taken him a week to track you down. The guy couldn't find his ass with both hands."

At the door I shook his hand.

"Good luck, kid."

"Thanks."

I looked over his shoulder at Dom.

"Hey, Dom, I got a good one for you. Have you heard the one about the chicken who couldn't get it up?"

"No, kid," he said with a big grin. "How's it go?"

265

I paused. "Actually, Dom," I said, "I'm going to hold on to it. Somebody might need to tell it to you someday. Good-bye, guys."

As I walked away Vincent came to the door and called after me.

"Hey, kid—remember my advice."

"What's that, Vincent?"

"Don't bet baseball."

Over the weekend I settled up at the pad. Ben made it easy on me by moving in. A month's rent is all it cost me. I even got a little hug from Molly, who I must say has been one long ray of sunshine since she hooked up with Tarzan.

As it turned out, I had a chance to say good-bye to Mike, too. He came by with a truck to get his stuff and wound up giving me a lift to the storage center with mine. Wouldn't you know, he's moving back in with his folks. Just till he can get over Molly, he says. What can you do? At least he'll still have someone to boss him around.

First thing this morning I dropped in on Revolution Autos, a big lot over on Eleventh Avenue by the river. An old college buddy still works summers there slinging cars. I called him last week and asked him to pick out the best five-thousand-dollar machine on the lot. There she was, a silver Olds, waiting for me with the keys in her.

From there I swung by the bank to tie up the final loose end. Wrote out a ten-thousand-dollar cashier's check to MasterCard and dropped it into a corner mailbox. That made me square with everyone.

On the way over here I pulled up in front of Adam's Curse to give Stella a last hug. Guess what she told me? Duggan took a powder. Walked out of the bar Friday night and nobody's seen him since. Papa O'Shea sent some men by his place but it's all cleaned out. O'Shea's tearing his hair out, according to Stella. Vowing to kill him.

How about that Duggan? Gets somebody else to front the money for him and then walks out on him when he loses. You have to hand it to the bastard. He may not be much on honor, but he can cover his ass with the best of them.

After a tight hug on the sidewalk Stella looked at me good and said she knew this wasn't good-bye. Said I'd be back. Then she told me to get the hell out of there.

So here I am. Twenty-four grand is what's left of the dough and it's inside my knapsack under my seat.

Don't ask me to add everything up. It's too early in the morning, and anyway I've never been any good at spotting the moral. I'll tell you this, though—I have a real good feeling about this trip. My buddy swears this car has the heart of a lion, and the way I figure the money, it can last us a year, at least. When it runs out? Hell, I've never thought that far ahead and I'm not about to start. But with Lisa beside me, and the whole continent before us . . . well, let's say I like our odds.

Here she comes now. She smiles from the top step and as I smile back I know—deep down, where you know things—that she won't be getting away again. I get out and kiss her and we hold it a long time.

"Oh, Tom—where can we go?"

"Everywhere. Anywhere you want."

"Can we stop in Savannah? I've always loved the name."

"Sure."

"Wrigley Field?"

"Of course."

"Graceland?"

"You're pushing it."

"I'm kidding."

I put her bags in the trunk. I open the door for her, come back around to my side and climb in. I start up the car, then look at her again. She smiles. I keep looking.

"What is it, Tom?"

"Do you still have the key?"

"The key?"

"To your place."

"Yes."

I motion with my eyes at her building. "I thought maybe—before we hit the road."

She laughs.

"Oh no, you don't. You promised me a trip cross-country and that's what I'm going to get. Once in every state, Reasons, those are the ground rules—and we've already done it in this one." She crosses her ankles on the dash, folds her arms, and smiles up at me like an angel.

Hell of a thing, women. I slide the Pogues into the tape player and pull onto the FDR.

"We'll be in Jersey in ten minutes."

FRANK BALDWIN is a graduate of Hamilton College. He attended the Berkeley Novel Writing Workshop. He lives in San Francisco with his wife, Lora. He has recently completed the screenplay for *Balling the Jack* and is currently at work on his second novel.